D1736706

Praise for *The Sower*

"You need to read this book. It's a roller coaster of a potboiler of a page-turner. From the very first page it picks you up by the scruff of the neck and takes you on a wild ride. But that's not why you need to read it. That's just a side benefit. The reason you need to read this book is that there are very important and dangerous ideas in it that need to penetrate deep in the consciousness of the world, and spread like a virus. *The Sower* is the Da Vinci Code as seen through the twisted eyes of John Waters and transcribed by the Marquis de Sade."

David Henry Sterry
author of the bestseller *Chicken*

"With a seat-of-pants plot and whip-smart characters, Kemble Scott deflates the 'values' hypocrisy that cloaks today's political culture and, sadly, looks to shroud tomorrow's too. Dark, subversive, and laugh-out-loud funny."

Raj Patel
author of the international bestseller
Stuffed and Starved

"Kemble Scott takes the author's favorite question, 'what if?' and turns it into totally satisfying novel that entertains, enlightens, and manages to push a whole lot of buttons in the process. *The Sower* is one of those 'can't put it down' books that runs the reader though the full slate of emotions from start to finish, yet lingers on in thought provoking vignettes long after the last page has been turned. I highly recommend this darkly humorous yet edgy look at life, love and politics."

Kate Douglas
author of the bestselling *Wolf Tales* novels

"What is moral behavior? Is it about sex or suffering? In *The Sower*, Kemble Scott creates a brilliant parable that reverses every ethical polarity to illuminate what is truly a moral choice. With a simple and realistic genetic switch in a virus on a bacteria, Scott turns our world upside-down: Pariahs become saints, disease becomes a cure, the cursed become the chosen people, and promiscuous sex a moral duty. In the end, a moral leper shows us what is right, humane, and true. Prepare to have your buttons pushed, your assumptions challenged, and your humanity illuminated."

Joe Quirk
author of the bestseller *It's Not You, It's Biology*

"Scott takes an ingenious premise and drives it full-tilt to the end of the line and way beyond. *The Sower* is a fascinating moral argument embedded in a wonderfully plotted thriller riven with outrageous comedy—or is it comic outrage? I laughed out loud at gems like, 'Mon dieu! You Americans are such puritans!' But you'll have to read the book to understand why that's funny."

Tamim Ansary
author of the bestselling books
West of Kabul, East of New York
and Good Morning America national memoir winner
The Story of My Life

the sower

~

A NOVEL BY

kemble scott

VOX NOVUS
A NUMINA PRESS BOOK
SAN RAFAEL, CALIFORNIA

The Sower

Copyright © 2009 Kemble Scott

All rights reserved. No part of this book may be reproduced in any form or by any electronic or mechanical means, including information storage and retrieval systems without permission in writing from the Publisher, except by a reviewer who may quote brief passages in a review.

The Sower is a work of fiction. Names, places, characters, and incidents are products of the author's imagination or used fictitiously.

First Print Edition
ISBN-13: 978-0-9753615-5-9
ISBN-10: 0-9753615-5-4

A *Vox Novus* Book
Published by NUMINA PRESS
www.numinapress.com

An e-book edition of *The Sower* is available on www.scribd.com

Printed in U.S.A.

For

J

The Parable of The Sower

Behold, there went out a sower to sow.

And it came to pass, as he sowed, some fell by the wayside, and the fowls of the air came and devoured it up.

And some fell on stony ground, where it had not much earth, and immediately it sprang up, because it had no depth of earth. But when the sun was up, it was scorched, and because it had no root, it withered away.

And some fell among thorns, and the thorns grew up, and choked it, and it yielded no fruit.

And other fell on good ground, and did yield fruit that sprang up and increased, and brought forth, some thirty, and some sixty, and some a hundred.

And he said unto them, He that has ears to hear, let him hear.

From The Gospel of Mark

1

Bill Soileau wasn't comfortable. Not with any of it.

Sitting on the bare hardwood floor hurt his butt. He crossed his legs Indian style, but that only tied him up in a knot. He curled down into a fetal position. The planks of sturdy pine felt like ice slabs against the side of his face. He'd never gotten used to the cold of San Francisco. Back home, even water from the cold tap ran warm.

There was no way he'd be able to do this. Why did he ever agree to something so insane? Even for a guy like him, *this* was going too far.

"It isn't gonna work," he shouted up into the air.

Mark Hazodo peeked over the ledge of his bedroom, set in a loft ten feet up, his taut naked body draped with a plush black towel. He'd jumped in the shower after asking Bill to push the furniture up against the walls to clear a large open space in the living room.

"What are you talking about?" Mark said as he shook his thick black hair to give it his signature messy style. "It looks great. Now there's plenty of space."

"It's not that," Bill said. "Gawd knows this place is bigger than my high school gym."

Mark owned the entire floor of an old converted brewery at 11th and Folsom. Three thousand square feet – a place that cost a small fortune in the city. Like so many buildings in the gritty South of Market warehouse district, it had been gutted and outfitted with the best of modern living. Brick walls and twenty-foot high windows overlooked minimalist decor, reminiscent of an art gallery. A grand staircase crept up one wall to the enormous master bedroom. Underneath was the kitchen, with stainless steel countertops and a ten-burner Viking Range that had never been used. Bill had visited dozens of times, but the display of wealth still inspired awe. This is what it's like to be really rich, he thought. To own enough to waste. It was about amassing more, whether or not you needed it.

"The floor is too hard. And it's freezing."

"I got you covered, bro." From the bedroom a shower of large black pillows began to rain down on Bill. "I've got dozens of them. They're cheap. We can just toss 'em in the dumpster when we're done."

"You think of everything," Bill said as he dodged the onslaught. He picked one off the floor. It was soft, and large enough for half a man's body to sprawl across. Two of the cushions could form the equivalent of a small bed. He clutched the pillow to his chest and pressed his nose to the silky fabric and inhaled. It had that new smell. Clean. Pristine. Yes, these would make it easier.

Easier? His mind flashed to the night ahead – Mark's sick plan for his latest twisted thrill. Why had he agreed to be a part of this? He wasn't like Mark. He didn't need to go this far to get his kicks. Not that Bill was delusional about himself – he knew he was hardly an upstanding citizen. He and Mark jokingly referred to themselves as "fellow degenerates." They'd never passed up a good time – that's what they loved about each other. Skip work for an afternoon of day drinking in The Haight? You bet. Check out the new basement club in SoMa that doesn't even have a name yet? Sign me up. Mark claimed their adventures were part of some ancient Asian philosophy he was following where life was about accumulating experiences until reaching "enlightenment."

Yeah, right, Bill thought. There was a graphic video someone posted online of Mark caught in a very embarrassing position of *naked* enlightenment. It had become a public scandal that almost cost Mark his career. So much for some quest for nirvana. To Bill, Mark was the anything-goes frat buddy he'd never had in college, each giving the other an audience and permission for any behavior. He couldn't remember ever uttering the word "no" in front of Mark.

Maybe now would be the first time. Until this moment he'd always been able to justify his actions. The way he saw it, he'd earned the right to be the way he was. But *this?*

"Uh, I can't do it."

"We'll throw in some blankets, too. Okay?" Mark came down the stairs and began arranging the pillows with his foot.

"It's not about blankets." Bill tossed the cushion back onto the pile with the others.

"Bill Soileau, Bill Soileau, Bill Soileau." Mark loved saying Bill's name. It was Louisiana Acadian and pronounced *swallow* – the perfect dig from one gay man to another. "I can't do this without you."

The guilt card. Mark had never played it before – he'd never had to. If Bill drew the line now, would this be the end of their friendship? It certainly wouldn't be the same. He hated the idea that he'd be walking on eggshells with Mark from now on, limits suddenly put on what had been a no-seatbelts relationship. With Mark, Bill existed in a realm of complete freedom, so far removed from his own backwater past. Mark was even a bit exotic. Except for TV, Bill hadn't seen an Asian until he got to college.

Mark lived for extremes, as if he'd built up an immunity to feeling regular sensations. As the reigning boy genius of the videogame world, Mark spent his days constantly bombarded with deafening sounds and pupil-exploding images. Maybe Mark needed to push limits just to feel *anything*. Almost everything was turned into a game or competition. Who could drink the most shots? Game on! In sports, the more dangerous, the better. Skydiving and hang gliding were only half steps back from suicide, but for Mark they were regular outings. Drugs? Mark always knew where to get the best. In business, the risks Mark took had made him rich.

"Bill Soileau, I need you. You're my bro! My fellow degenerate! What do you Southern crackers like to say? *Laissez les bon temps rouler!*" Mark exaggerated Bill's drawl.

"Your French sucks," Bill smirked.

"I know how to say *appetizer, entrée* and *café au lait*."

"I'm serious." Bill looked back down at the pile of black pillows. In a short time, they'd be covered in a bacchanalia of bare flesh. He'd probably be the center of attention, as usual when it came to men. They'd line up for their turns on the Bill Soileau ride, like he was some sort of amusement park. "It's wrong."

"Morally?"

"That, too."

"You're gonna lecture me about morals, Bill Soileau?"

Bill grabbed Mark's bare arm and squeezed. The flesh was still damp from the shower. "You act like this is just another game," Bill said through his teeth, surprised by his sudden burst of anger. "Someone is going to die here tonight!"

Mark gently pushed Bill's hand aside. "That's a bit dramatic, don't you think? When the hell did you get all *Steel Magnolias* on me?"

"You don't think it's death? Then what is it? This whole idea is about death. Tempting fate. It's *murder*. Maybe someone laying right next to you on these fucking pillows." Bill kicked a cushion, making it skid across the floor. "*That's* what's hot to you. That's your turn on, isn't it? You think you'll witness the light dim from someone's eyes. Like it's some sort of snuff film!"

"Whoa, whoa, whoa." Mark's brown eyes burrowed into Bill's. It was a penetrating stare of confidence Bill had seen separate so many men from their inhibitions. How did he do that? To charm with just a look? "No one's going to be murdered. Where do you come up with this stuff? It's just a game. A very, very hot game. The risks are manageable. And let's face it, in this day and age, it's not fatal."

"That's easy for you to say."

"Look, it's just going to be a bunch of guys." Mark used his most soothing voice. He moved behind and started massaging Bill's shoulders. It felt good, relaxing. Mark spoke softly, right up against Bill's ear. He could feel the wisps of Mark's breath brushing his lobe. Bill's ears had always been his soft spot. His knees weakened. "They'll all be hot guys, I promise. I handpicked them myself. Just the types you like. Handsome, young, athletic. Blond, brown, red, shaved. Hairy and smooth. And they'll all be naked, like a picnic laid out on these pillows. A buffet of beautiful men, all willing and hungry – eager to please. A feast."

"An orgy," Bill whispered.

"But more exciting than any other you've ever been to," Mark went on, adding a hint of drama to his voice. "No condoms. No safe sex. Just raw, uninhibited, bareback fucking."

Bill shrugged off Mark's hands. "It's a game of roulette."

"No shit. That's why they call it a Roulette Party. That's the excitement. It's not just about sex. It's about risk."

"Risk? That's sugarcoating it, isn't it? We're talking about an orgy where no safe sex is allowed and one guy has AIDS. The bullet in the gun," Bill said. Sure, he'd had unsafe sex before. Everyone did it. But this wasn't some moment of unbridled passion. This was planned with eerie precision.

"AIDS is pretty harsh, don't you think?" Mark scolded. "HIV-positive is more politically correct."

"It's sick. Just to make sex more thrilling, these guys are willing to risk their lives."

"Bill Soileau, *life* is about risk. Look, if it makes you feel any better, I'll say it again. All the guys coming here tonight know exactly what they're getting themselves into. I had to turn people away when I posted an ad online! This is cutting-edge shit, and everyone here tonight is a consenting adult. They *want* this. You're going to pass judgment?"

Mark was right, of course. Bill knew he was the last guy to criticize others, especially when it came to sex. San Francisco loved what he offered, and he was more than happy to oblige. Just walking down the street, he'd make eye contact with some random passerby and the next thing he knew they'd be fucking. Later his tricks would say it was Bill's smile that hooked them, an easy grin you didn't find much outside of the South. His Louisiana manners helped, comfortable most days in jeans and a baseball cap. It didn't take long after moving to the city for Bill to realize that being masculine and gay was enough to get him just about anyone. Even straight guys who wanted to experiment fell his way.

And he took them. All of them. Indiscriminate and promiscuous. When he graduated from LSU and moved to San Francisco a faucet was opened. It reminded him of working on a site where a crew struck oil, but no one could cap the well and get the gusher under control. On a typical day he'd get a blowjob in the gym sauna before breakfast, have a bathroom rendezvous with a guy in a suit during lunch, then pick up a couple in a bar for a three-way before bed. He was insatiable. A few times he wondered if he had a problem, but attending the local chapter of Sex Addicts Anonymous only provided him with an eager new crop of partners.

Just that morning he was filling his Explorer with gas at 6th and Harrison when a young Latino at the next car over gave him the eye. At first Bill worried it was some gangbanger looking to get into a fight. Then the man gave a single head nod while looking down to Bill's jeans. Two minutes later Bill had the guy over the sink in the station's filthy men's room. Bill came quickly, since he wasn't sure he could hold his breath for very long to keep out the sickening stench of the bathroom. He didn't realize the kid wasn't very clean either until he got to work. While at the urinal he noticed a smudge inside the front of his white briefs. He tossed them in the trash and washed himself in the sink, hoping no one would walk in and catch him flopped into the basin.

Judgments? Who the hell was he to sneer at a roulette party? He'd screwed everything with a pulse since he came to the city. Except Mark. He might have, and those eyes were a constant temptation, but they'd become friends first. They were bros. Fellow degenerates. When it came to sex, Bill had just one rule: he never fucked anyone he knew. He didn't even like learning names, and he'd never had the desire to be with the same trick more than once. Nearly every guy asked for a repeat, even the married ones. They were the worst. So clingy and needy.

Perhaps he had it all wrong. Maybe the roulette party would be hot. God knows he'd done just about everything else.

"Bill Soileau. Let me at least appeal to you as a Southerner. May I remind you that a true gentlemen never goes back on his word..."

"Cut it out, Mark. I'm staying. I'm in."

~

It was one in the morning when Bill left Mark's loft and headed east down Folsom Street. As he walked past, Bill noticed there was still a long line to get into the Cat's Alley Club. Club kids. All ready to drop *E* and dance until five. Stupid tweakers.

Bill rubbed the outside of his jeans' front pocket. They were still there. It was time.

He was the first to leave the orgy. Four times in just three hours was the best he'd done since he was a teenager jerking off in his parents' bathroom. If he'd skipped the Latino that morning he would have gone another round.

Mark was right. As promised, the guys at the orgy were all enthusiastic about the game – and they were remarkably grateful to meet a top.

When the men had started to arrive, Bill still wasn't sure he could go through with it. Then as they took their clothes off, he noticed how thin so many of them were, with pale faces drained of their natural color. Meth heads. Soon their beautiful bodies would wither from the drug, and their teeth begin to rot. He should have known that's who Mark would get to show up. Roulette sex was just their latest game, the next frontier. Crystal had numbed their fear of death, so they pursued extreme risks to up the ante and obtain a new type of high. The drug was notorious for making men flaccid, but the proximity to death that night had all aroused. Bill wondered how many of them were already infected, but refused to get tested so they could play games like this. A convenient delusion – to play as if gambling your life, when you're actually already condemned. Maybe next weekend they'd all fly off on a charter to Cabo to temp fate by screwing Mexicans in the middle of the swine flu outbreak. A virus as the ultimate aphrodisiac.

Bill noted how Mark kept a careful watch on the scene all night long, like a snake hiding in the brush. Mark reveled in the adjacency to danger, but made sure he was never on the receiving end of any man. He was, after all, the master game player. So clearly in ecstasy by the success of his plan, Mark was in a blissful trance when Bill finally got up to dress and leave. Mark didn't even say goodbye. All had been accomplished. It didn't matter anymore if Bill stayed longer.

Down Folsom street Bill could see Ahmed's Market still open. He headed to the back and bought a small bottle of water, some brand he didn't recognize. He twisted it open when he got back outside and reached into his pocket to pull out a small handful of pills. Three different kinds, three different shapes and colors. He shoved them all in his mouth, took a swig from the bottle and swallowed with just one gulp. His choke mechanism had disappeared years ago.

Some cocktail, Bill thought. Pills every twelve hours. Will there ever be a cure?

2

Quif couldn't get the acrid smell out of her nose. She'd been on assignment at the refinery site for a nearly a week, but the fumes still bothered her. It wasn't a good sign.

When she worked in the refugee camps of Rwanda, the stench of the makeshift latrines made her gag on her first day. Yet within hours, somehow she'd become accustomed to it. Why was this time so different? Because it was a chemical? Even back in her pristine hotel room, she couldn't shake it. The stink was in her clothes, on her skin and in her thick black hair. Showering didn't get rid of it. Perhaps it had permeated the hotel towels, too.

She powered up her laptop and studied her schedule.

"*Je n'en peux plus*," she sighed. *Enough*. No matter how long she stared at the screen, there was no escaping what her calendar said. She still had another three days in this wretched place. Three more days of gathering samples from around the refinery and nearby towns.

She thought of the sad, cracked old faces of the farmers and villagers as she drew their blood that morning.

"She wants to know why you want her blood," the young man explained to Quif after speaking to an old woman. Quif didn't speak Armenian, and the villagers didn't speak French, so a student from the Macsedan Private School of Foreign Languages in Yerevan had been hired to work as her translator. But with that one old woman there was more involved than a language divide. She raised her hands in front of her face as she spoke, her trembling fingers cradling the air. Her mumbling voice was soft, but Quif could hear pain and disgust.

"She says she doesn't like you. She doesn't like foreigners. She says foreigners have never done anything good for Armenia."

"Melikian," Quif said.

The old woman looked puzzled.

Quif patted her own chest and said her last name again, this time slowly pronouncing each syllable. "Meh-lee-key-an."

The old woman grinned wide, revealing surprisingly healthy white teeth. She leaned over and whispered to the young man.

"She says she knew it all along. She was just testing you," the translator said.

Quif smiled. Her boss at the Institut Pasteur insisted Quif take this assignment, knowing the Armenians would be much more likely to cooperate with someone who shared their heritage. It was much more than just ethnic pride. After the Turkish holocaust nearly wiped out the entire population, followed by decades of brutal Soviet occupation, the Armenians who remained had every reason to be suspicious of outsiders.

Even growing up safe in Paris, Quif knew the stories. Some of her earliest memories were the tragic tales her grandmother shared with her about their ancestral homeland. While her schoolmates heard bedtime stories from books featuring fairies and talking elephants, Quif and her sister were lulled to sleep with harrowing true tales. Like great-uncle Arshag's death-defying escape when he was put on a ship with hundreds of others, only to be deliberately capsized in the Black Sea so all would drown. Arshag was the only one to make it ashore. Then there was the Dilsizian family's awful fate, which Quif thought might be a myth, where the Turks cut off the parents' tongues when they were caught speaking Armenian in their own home. As many as two million died in the genocide aimed at removing the Christian minority from Asia Minor. Quif wondered why she didn't suffer nightmares after listening to the endless accounts of brutality and suffering. Instead she was instilled with a fierce pride and determination. The message was clear from birth. Never forget. Do anything you can to make sure it never happens again.

The old woman grasped an ornate silver crucifix that hung around her neck and held it closer for Quif to see. The tiny face of Christ, eyes shut, his mouth ajar in agony to constantly remind the faithful of his suffering for them. "*Heesoos Kreesdos mér Purgee'chuh,*" she said.

"Holy Savior, Jesus Christ," the young man translated.

"It is beautiful. So, I can have your blood?" Quif asked the old woman. The young man translated.

The woman now beamed, her voice strong and rich in happiness. She took Quif's hand and held it between her own.

"She says, *You are my blood,*" the translator explained.

After Quif filled the test tube, the woman barked to others and soon there was a line of willing patients. The old woman stayed with Quif the entire time, assuring each person with just one word.

"Melikian!"

"Ah, Melikian," they would each respond and happily nod.

The old woman told Quif that the refinery had cast a shadow on their lives ever since it was built by the Soviets. People from the village who went there sometimes never came home. Then when the empire fell, it was abandoned and left to become a decrepit, stinking relic. The younger generation of Armenians also fled the region after liberation, figuring any place on earth would be better than this.

Quif stared at the towering plant in the distance. According to her research, it wasn't even *supposed* to be here. The refinery didn't exist on any map. Officially, Armenia has no refineries – it's completely dependent on the outside world for fuel. Yet here it was in this remote outpost in a desolate southern part of the country, a dirty little secret the Soviets kept from the outside world – until now. The plan to get the refinery running again meant it was suddenly an international concern. That was her specialty these days: investigating man-made health catastrophes.

As she sat in her hotel room staring at her laptop screen, Quif wanted to e-mail the technicians back at the Institut Pasteur and tell them not to bother analyzing the samples she'd collected. What was the point? She already knew what they'd find. Elevated levels of benzene in the water and air. Arsenic and lead polluting the villagers' blood. The refinery had been shut down since 1991, but the fact that it still smelled so bad meant the desecration of the environment had never gone away. It was simply too much for the earth to absorb and heal itself. Death had found a home here and it wasn't leaving just because of a regime change.

She pulled back the curtain from the floor-length window and looked out over the bleak landscape. Everything appeared gray. The sky. The muddy, cracked land. Then she looked down, four stories below, to a shocking burst of color. The bright blue of a swimming pool surrounded by dozens of white lounge chairs – like something found at a resort in seaside Cannes. Except here no one swam in the pool or dared to sunbathe. The odor was too overpowering to be outside.

The hotel was finished only a few weeks earlier, the brainchild of the wealthy oligarch who planned to revive the refinery and tap its riches with a pipeline from Azerbaijan, if and when the two nations stopped feuding. The oligarch knew his plans would never get very far unless he gave government leaders, investors and skilled workers an oasis. When she first arrived, Quif was stunned to find gourmet meals, a full service spa and live jazz at night. Here in the middle of nowhere? It was a cruel contrast to the poverty, contamination, and misery just beyond the plush compound.

God, she missed Paris. And her sister Natara. The delicious paté at lunch only made her longing for home more painful. She picked up the hotel phone and dialed.

"*Allô.*"

"Natara!"

"Quif? Where are you?" Natara mumbled as if half asleep. "Are you coming home for dinner?"

"No, no. Not yet. I am still away." Quif feared this would happen. Natara became so easily confused these days. It was typical of someone in the late stages.

"Where are you?"

"On a trip for work. Remember I told you? I am in Armenia."

"Armenia? There's no such place."

"Well, maybe not the way it was. It is just a little country now. All that is left is a sliver that used to be part of the Soviet Union. You remember that, right?"

"Aren't we Armenian?"

"*Oui*! See – you remember." Quif felt suddenly choked up. The phone call was a bad idea. She took this assignment, in part, because she'd finally be able to visit her roots after being smothered in family stories her whole life. No one she knew had been to the new Armenia. She wanted to share the adventure with Natara, but Quif had no idea the real Armenia would be so dismal and colorless. Now it sounded like Natara was having another one of her bad spells. How much was getting through?

"Quif?"

"Yes, Natara."

"I'm tired. Very tired."

"I know, my love. But you have good days, too, *oui*?"

"I'm so tired."

"Has Dominique been over to see to things? To clean and make you something to eat?"

"I don't want to eat. I'm too tired."

"But you *must* eat. I will be home in a few days. Promise me you will eat. You will make me very worried if you do not eat."

"I promise," Natara said, her voice filled with resignation.

"Natara, I love you."

There was a pause for several moments. Quif didn't know what to say. She wanted to end the call before she started to cry, but a sudden irrational dread overwhelmed her – if she hung up the phone it might be the last time she'd ever hear her sister's voice. Quif struggled to get ahold of her emotions. She was a doctor – she knew better. AIDS didn't kill overnight.

"Quif?"

"Yes."

"Why are you in Armenia?"

A question. At least for the moment, Natara was engaged. Quif took it as a blessing, albeit a small one. Maybe this was just another deep depression, and not the beginning of HIV dementia or cerebral toxoplasmosis. Those were Quif's worst fears.

"I am at an old oil refinery. Before it starts up again, we need to make sure it is safe and no one gets hurt. The EU asked the Institute to do some tests to see if there is any pollution."

"Is there?"

"I will not know for sure until I get the samples back to the lab."

"Oh." Natara's voice revealed her interest in the conversation was quickly fading.

"And tomorrow a crew from America arrives. From San Francisco! Remember when we went there? You loved walking along the Embarcadero, and eating the big, ugly crab with your fingers. And Chinatown. Do you remember?"

"No."

"Well, when I get home I will find the snapshots we took. Maybe those will help bring it all back." Quif's eyes began to fill. The trip to California was their happiest vacation together, a cherished jaunt during those carefree days before the rigors of university, and the dark arrival of disease. Soon she would be the only survivor to remember that time. She shook off the thought and tried to compose herself. "In any case, the Americans will be inspecting the buildings and equipment here to see what is needed to get it working again."

"Sounds exhausting."

Quif knew it was too much to keep her sister on the phone any longer. "Natara, I am going to hang up the phone now. I want you to get some rest, okay?"

"I'm so tired, Quif."

"I know. I love you."

"I love you, too, Quif."

The line went dead. Quif clutched the receiver, as if holding it somehow allowed her to maintain contact with Natara and home.

She looked back out the window. The sun was beginning to set. Even that light was somehow tainted by gray. She thought of Natara and the vigil that would soon begin for her death. It was probably only a year away. Or less. The latest antiviral drugs had failed. At Pasteur she had access to medications in the pipeline that other patients wouldn't see for years, and yet those too had been effective for only a very short time. Little by little Natara's immune army was losing its soldiers. The truth was the drugs simply didn't work for everyone. Quif knew she'd done all she could, and yet she had still failed her sister. She thought of how Natara was named in honor of a kind-hearted Turkish woman who hid and saved a dozen Armenian children from the holocaust. A peasant Muslim stranger had done more for her bloodline than she could.

Quif saw a small farmhouse in the distance, smoke billowing from its chimney. Life hadn't changed here much in hundreds of years, at least not for the better. These poor Armenian souls never got a break.

And now they would suffer again, at the hands of a new tyranny. More pollution and disease, disguised as economic development. She'd seen it far too many times before, traveling the world for Pasteur visiting the cesspools of illness and death left behind by greed. The Armenians, of course, would be persuaded this was being done to *help* them – a source of jobs, money and national pride.

Quif recalled the story her grandmother told of handsome, young Armenian men who volunteered to fight in World War I. They were so proud to be able to do their part to help defend their country, even though the Turks had occupied the Armenians' ancestral lands for hundreds of years. By the thousands they stepped forward to be trained to fight side by side with the Turks against a common foe. The Armenian soldiers were given their own divisions and special uniforms. Their families stood and wept as their fresh-faced heroes marched off to defend them from the enemy. But when they got to the battlefield, the Turks disarmed the Armenian battalions. The brave Armenian volunteer soldiers were lined up and shot, execution style. The seed for the next generation destroyed. That was the plan all along.

Quif looked at the hideous refinery. Perhaps that historic genocide happened right here on this same land.

Now it was happening again. Instead of bullets, this time they'd be wiped out by pollution and petrochemicals.

Unless she stopped them.

3

Bill Soileau hated long plane rides. There was almost never a chance to get laid.

He figured it must be just as terrible for smokers. Airplanes were smoke free these days, leaving passengers crazy and nicotine-starved by the time their flights finally landed. Flying was pretty much sex-free, too, especially since the new post-9/11 security crackdown. He used to be a frequent flier in the Mile High Club. Now he was forced to sit and fight his urges.

That would be tough on such an excruciatingly long trip. He'd be in transit for more than twenty-four hours. He'd already gone from San Francisco to New York. Now he was on the thirteen-hour non-stop to Istanbul. From there he'd take a regional flight to Yerevan. Armavia Airlines? Working as a petroleum engineer for nearly a decade, he'd been all over the Middle East, but he'd never heard of that carrier. Must be Armenian, he figured. Yerevan was where the relative luxury of flying ended. Then the trip would really suck. He'd be dumped into a van for a cross-country drive on rugged roads through the mountains down to the desolate south. They told him the closest town was Kapan. He could barely find it on the map.

He usually loved traveling. Leaving San Francisco, even if just for a week, was like getting a clean start. There were whole nations of men out there who he hadn't fucked! It was always a thrill to figure out how to cruise and bed men in other countries. He only spoke English and a little bit of Louisiana-style French, so there was no way he could talk his way into a foreign guy's pants. It was mostly done with eye contact, subtle gestures, and a carefully placed touch. It never mattered if he spoke the local dialect. He was fluent in men.

He thought back to his first time in Istanbul several years ago. He was stunned to see men walking hand in hand through the streets. I must be in heaven, Bill thought. But here? A Muslim country? He soon learned that handholding between men had nothing to do with sex. It was just the local custom, a sign of platonic friendship.

Bill accepted that explanation, but as he roamed the maze of stone streets off Taksim Square he picked up a vibe, a feeling he'd known ever since he was twelve. It was a sensation that happened whenever he came in contact with those who wanted him. He believed he could literally smell sexual attraction – pheromones. His friends told him it was scientifically impossible, but with each dusty step through the ancient alleys he felt overwhelmed by the scent.

"What are you looking for?" The voice came from somewhere behind. The words were in English with a heavy accent.

"Who, me?" Bill said as he turned. Before him was a ruggedly handsome, beefy Turk. The man was no older than thirty, with a full head of black thick hair and a hearty crop of matching razor stubble. He wore jeans and a striped polo shirt that fit tight around oversized arms. Despite the dark features, the man's eyes were the brightest shade of blue Bill had ever seen.

"You look like you search for something," the man smiled. "You are lost?"

"No," Bill paused for a moment – the man's eyes were so distracting. "I'm just wandering and enjoying the sights. I thought I'd head down to the river to see Dolmabahce Palace."

"It is beautiful," said the man. "But you do not want to go there today."

"Why not?"

"Because you will come with me to my house instead."

It wasn't Bill's imagination – the game was on. It never entered his mind that something sinister was at play, that it might be some attempt to prey on him as an American. He instinctively knew it was only about hooking up. His nose confirmed it.

"And where is your house?" Bill flashed his most charming grin.

"You are standing in front of it."

Later the man told Bill that sex between men was quite common in Turkey, but it had nothing to do with being gay. *Gay* was a western concept. The word didn't even exist in Turkish. Neither did *straight*. Sex was simply not defined the same way here. For one thing, laws prevented men and women from having sex before marriage – couples were still sent to jail for it. And since most men never got married until after they served their compulsory military service, that meant they weren't legally allowed to have sex until they were well into their twenties. That just wasn't practical, so they often turned to each other. Even after marriage, some would continue to have sex with men. Women were fine, but why choose? The man was incredulous when Bill admitted that he only had sex with men.

"Since I got here, I swear the men have been checking me out," Bill said.

"That's because you are an infidel. The fundamentalists say that makes you something less than human." The man shrugged. "No offense."

"Uh," Bill instinctively replied with the disfluency he'd had since his rural childhood, one he'd struggled to banish from his conversation. Despite his best efforts to be more San Francisco urbane, "uh" still crept in whenever faced with an awkward moment.

"I explain. You are foreigner – not Muslim. Our laws do not apply to you. We can have sex with you and it is not forbidden. That is why everyone looks at you on the streets."

"So I'm like a free ride for horny Turks?" Bill laughed.

"Free ride? This I am not following." the man looked confused.

Bill liked the thought of being an infidel – the mysterious outsider. He made a mental note to come back to Turkey more often.

But making more memories would have to wait. On this latest trip, Istanbul was a mere two-hour layover. He wouldn't be allowed to leave the airport. He'd only have enough time to hit customs and then be shoved onto the next leg of the flight.

The prospects didn't look good for men in Armenia. From what he understood, the facility he needed to inspect was out in the middle of nowhere. "Actually," his boss chuckled, "you go to the middle of nowhere, take a left, then keep going another two hundred miles – and there it is!" Bill didn't laugh.

He would need to be on site for four days. Four days without men! It was unfathomable. He thought he might be forced to try to satisfy himself *by himself*, but he hadn't done that in years and it seemed like a major step in the wrong direction. Messing around with fellow employees was out of the question since he'd likely see them again. Four days without sex! It was a test of endurance more than any man should have to bear. Even prison had rape.

Bill flipped through the airline magazine. It was the same one he'd read cover to cover on his last trip. At least he was in First Class. He had so many miles from all of his travel that he was easily able to upgrade. He loved the perk of being in the front of the plane, even ahead of his fellow working stiffs in Business Class. Here everything was served French style, your meal was placed onto fine china at a table wheeled up next to your seat. The flight attendants wore white gloves as they meticulously served each course. The only item that resembled what the rest of the passengers received were the mixed nuts, but instead of a plastic bag to tear open with your teeth, they were warmed and presented as small mountains to nibble on from little white porcelain bowls.

Bill squirmed in his seat. His nuts were warm enough already. He thought they might explode if he didn't figure out a way to hook up pretty soon. He scanned the cabin. There were only ten seats in this part of the plane, and only half were occupied. It afforded the type of privacy that would be perfect for fun, but as it always was in First Class International, the other passengers were all old.

For most people the best thing about First Class International was how the chairs folded down into flat, cushy, real beds about the width of a generous twin – the height of decadence at 40,000 feet. Bill never used the bed. There was no point. No matter what he tried, he couldn't sleep on planes. His body wouldn't allow it.

It didn't make sense. At home he was a great sleeper, once he got back to his own bed. He never slept at a trick's place, even if they'd been at it all night. When they were done, he'd keep one eye on the bedstand clock and give a guy exactly five minutes of post-fucking spooning, just to be polite, and then he was out of there. Hell, if a man needed so much cuddling, he should stick with his wife or boyfriend. Once Bill got back to his own sheets, even if it was just his own hotel room, he'd doze off in minutes.

Not on planes. He wondered if the same powerful engine that drove his sex drive was somehow set to the same frequency of the jet turbines. As long as they were in the air, he'd be wide awake. He'd turn on the most boring movies, the types he'd never get through without nodding off if he watched on his own TV. No effect. He thought that maybe reading the driest periodical on the plane would dull his senses enough to slumber. Instead, he found himself oddly intrigued by a piece on soybean futures in the dreary pink and grey pages of the *Financial Times*. Flight attendants did their best to help by fluffing his pillows and nearly drowning him in after-dinner port. All that couldn't even get his lids to droop. He'd tried melatonin and prescription sleeping bills, but they ended up giving him splitting headaches.

Most of the time it didn't matter. Cross country he'd just tough it out. But long-haul international flights like this were the worst. As all the other passengers turned off their lights, he'd be left gazing into oblivion, alone with his thoughts. Inevitably, something would trigger the memory he tried to avoid – that awful day when everything changed. Most times he could distract himself and fight the thoughts from surfacing, but trapped in like this, his mind had nowhere to run.

The silence of the cabin was suddenly interrupted by a loud snore across the aisle. As Bill looked over, he grinned. The blaring snort had come from a tiny elderly man in a bright white suit jacket who'd fallen asleep with pink newspaper pages littering his lap. Works for some, Bill sighed.

~

"Hate Ivy," she said.

Bill stared at the woman. What did that mean? *Hate Ivy?* Her accent was so dense it was hard to understand anything she said. That's what he got for coming to the campus clinic. They must let the foreign med students practice here to get some experience. He wondered what

Third World country this one was from. Definitely Asian. Chinese from the look of her face and the name on the tag. You'd think they'd at least require a command of English before allowing them to interact with real patients. This was Louisiana State University in Baton Rouge – not exactly the United Nations. He wondered how much shit the doctor had to take from frat boys and rednecks.

He sat in a cocoon of white, a cubicle of bleached curtains hung from steel tracks bolted into the ceiling – not walls, just thin pieces of cloth that separated him from everyone else, an illusion of privacy.

"Hate Ivy," Dr. Mei Lee said again, crunching her face. Bill could tell the woman was searching his eyes and face, looking for some sort of reaction. It was his second visit to the clinic. The first was a few weeks earlier when he came in complaining of stomach pains. He thought the stress of that semester's heavy course load might be causing him to develop an ulcer. They were common in his family, so he went in for tests. They made him swallow a pink barium milkshake that tasted like chalk, and then he posed for a series of x-rays. A lab technician drew a few vials of blood and he was told to come back for the results. All he wanted was a prescription for an antacid like the one his brother took – that stuff would do the trick.

"Hate Eye Veeeee," Dr. Lee said, now stretching out the syllables, as if speaking very slowly would somehow make her poor English understood.

A numb feeling hit the pit of Bill's stomach. He hadn't felt this sensation since he fell out of the backyard tree when he was a kid and landed flat on his back. He was unable to speak, the wind knocked out of him. Time stopped.

"Huh?" he managed to push out as he caught his breath. What was happening to him? Why couldn't he breathe?

Dr. Lee shook her head and picked up a piece of paper from a manila folder she cradled in her arm. She pointed to numbers circled on a page of lab test results. "Seedy four. Seedy hate," she pointed with her pen. "You see? Not right. It's Hate Eye Vee." She said each word slowly and loudly. Exasperated, she pushed her black rimmed glasses up the bridge of her small, flat nose and sighed.

Bill's body understood the diagnosis before it made sense to his mind. *Fuck, just breathe! What's wrong with me?* He looked around at the white sheets again. Through a three-foot opening he could see across to the other side of the clinic where a young woman sat on an exam table with an ice pack on her shoulder. A girl stood next to her, both of them dressed in tennis outfits. The women leaned forward to peer into Bill's cubicle for a closer look, their faces aghast.

Bill closed his eyes. *Inhale.* Even as he tried to shut everyone out, he could still feel the presence of all the others in the clinic. It was filled with doctors, nurses and other students all waiting their turn. Were they all now listening to the words here in his little white cubicle?

Not *hate ivy.* She said H-I-V. HIV.

"AIDS?" Bill whispered to the doctor. It couldn't be. This wasn't happening.

"Seedy four too low," the doctor said. He followed her pen as she pointed to the blood tests again. Somehow he focused for a moment to see that out of the dozens of unfamiliar numbers on the page, she had circled one section in plain blue ink. It said, "CD4 = 403. Below normal."

HIV. It's not possible, he thought. Yeah, he had sex. Lots of sex. Sometimes dirty, sleazy, anonymous sex, especially on his many weekends down in New Orleans. He'd venture away from the crowds on Bourbon Street, up into the darker side alleys that led to Burgundy. But it was always safe sex. He'd never fucked without a condom. *No glove, no love.* For such a bad boy, he'd been good, at least as far as that was concerned. How could this happen? Was it that one night at the Rawhide bar? He remembered how the evening started, but then he could only recall bits and pieces. Too much beer. Needing to use the bathroom. All those guys checking him out. Somehow his mind had put a block on playing back anything more than scattered images.

"I don't understand," he wheezed out.

"Want to do more tests," Dr. Lee said as she scribbled something into the folder. "Need more blood work to confirm diagnosis. We do it today."

More blood tests? HIV? Confirm?

He came in with a stomachache and now had a death sentence. And here of all places. The campus clinic was where students came for scraped knees from bike falls, or maybe an occasional broken bone or birth control pills – not a serious illness. It didn't make any sense. The burning sensation in his stomach was now replaced by the feeling that someone had just booted him in the belly.

"You must be wrong," Bill stammered. "I had tests done for an ulcer. Don't you remember? An ul-cer. I didn't have an HIV test done. There must be a mistake."

"No mistake. I order it."

"Why? I never asked to be tested."

"I need it for paper I am working on. I use clinic to do survey. I make study of young American men for medical journal."

Paper? Study? He couldn't remember agreeing to that. He wouldn't. He'd thought about getting an HIV test, but he'd been avoiding it. Maybe in the back of his mind he feared it would be bad news. He'd been trying to work up the courage to go and get tested, but it wasn't something he could get his head around. *He'd never fucked anyone without a condom in his life!* He'd acted honorably. Now none of that mattered. The tables had been turned and he'd been violated. Didn't he have rights to his own body? With the flick of a pen on some lab slip she'd taken his whole future away. And she was so goddamn casual about it. A medical journal? This was all for some magazine article?

"Don't you need permission? I never said you could test me. What about my life? My privacy!" With each word, the anger grew in Bill's voice.

"Stop yelling," Dr. Lee said. She looked annoyed.

"You didn't have permission!"

"Stop it!"

"You did this without my permission. That's illegal!"

"Keep you voice down!"

Bill stared at the doctor. Strands of long black hair had come free from her tightly bound bun. His eyes stayed on her. Who was this woman to do this to him? Neither spoke for an uncomfortably long time. There were no tears or welled up emotions for Bill to fight back. At that moment he felt only one thing: hate.

"We do more tests now," the doctor finally spoke as she tried to take Bill by the arm.

"Keep your hands off me!" He slapped her hand away.

"You need more test. I confirm diagnosis so I report to health department."

"What?"

"I re-test. Then send name to state. It the law. People who Hate Ivy positive must be reported."

"You gotta be fucking kidding?" Report him to the state health department? "You test me without my permission, and now you want to tell everyone!" Would they also tell his mother? Maybe they'd publish his name in the newspaper too. He'd be banished from everyone and everything he'd ever known. He was only months away from graduating with his degree in petrochemical engineering. Would they kick him out?

Bill clutched his hands into fists. He wanted to strike back, to backhand the doctor across the face. He spied neatly packaged sterilized exam instruments on a tray in the room. He was hit by the urge to rip open the kits, find a scalpel, tear open a vein and spray it into Dr. Lee's eyes. He'd infect her too and see if she could be so cold and uncaring then!

Suddenly out of the shock and rage came a brutal moment of clarity. *This was wrong.* He had to do something to stop it. Bill grabbed his medical file from doctor's arms and pointed it in her face. "You're not doing any more tests on me, you *bitch*. How dare you test me without my permission! Who the hell do you think you are?"

Dr. Lee grabbed for the file, but Bill lifted it out of her reach. "Gimme that! You ruin my study!" More strands of hair came loose from her bun as she swiped the air to try to recapture the file.

"You arrogant," she said bitterly. "You listen to me. You Americans. You good looks and the sex the sex the sex. In China, we take boy like you and put you where you hurt no one. Here you get medicine. No big deal."

No big deal? A few minutes ago he was just another student working hard to get his degree. Now he was irrevocably damaged. His future. What future?

He had to get out of there. He had to save himself – no one else must ever know.

"Listen to me…you little commie cunt," Bill said, his voice now eerily calm. "I'm walking out of here. And I'm taking this file with me. If you so much as breathe of word of this, I'll tell the school what you're doing. You'll be on the next rickshaw back to Shanghai!"

Bill hopped down from the exam table and nearly collapsed onto the floor. His legs were weak like a newborn fawn. He struggled to stand up straight, but then gained his strength and walked out of the white cubicle with the file tucked tightly under his arm. He felt the eyes of everyone in the clinic size him up as he headed for the door. He stared straight ahead, not wanting to see anyone. Maybe if he didn't look at them, they wouldn't really be able to see him and know who he was.

Outside the campus green looked surreal, as if he'd just stepped onto the surface of a planet he'd never visited before. He became acutely aware of each step and every breath he took, as if noticing these functions for the first time in his life.

His legs were still shaky. Once he was far enough away from the clinic he collapsed onto the grass. This part of the campus was empty. Everyone was on the other side at the football game. LSU versus Auburn. He could hear the crowd roar even from this distance. The stadium was nicknamed Death Valley because the careers of so many aspiring athletes and coaches died there. Football in Louisiana was serious business. You either won, or it was all over.

Today, Bill thought, Death Valley is on this side of the school. He lay on his back, clutching the file to his chest and gazed up into the sky. It was so blue. Not a shade he'd ever seen. This was more like a color in a painting – a pigment invented by man, not God. And the clouds – had they always been so bright white? Perhaps the world had looked this way forever and he just never noticed before. His eyes soaked it in, wondering how much time he had left to witness days like these.

And finally, he wept.

~

"Sir?"

Bill felt a gentle hand on his shoulder. It was a flight attendant.

One he didn't recognize – there must have been a shift change. The man had salt and pepper hair, but a youthful, smooth face.

"Sir, are you okay?" the man spoke softly with a comforting British accent.

"Sure, I'm fine." Bill rubbed his eyes and noticed his cheeks were wet. He hadn't noticed that he'd been crying. It wasn't the first time tears had come when thinking about that day at LSU. Ten years ago and he still wasn't over it. He'd grown up so much since then, leaving the small town Louisiana kid behind to evolve into a modern man of The City. And yet he still couldn't get beyond that day, his scorn and suspicion of doctors ever since, or the tears that inevitably came when he remembered. He felt ashamed, embarrassed that a stranger saw him this way.

"Really, I'm fine." Bill turned on his smile. He noticed that the flight attendant had an athletic body. The man squatted next to Bill's seat, his polyester blue uniform pants clung tightly to muscular legs and perfectly worked out glutes. His face was so close that Bill could smell the man, a mixture of recently used mint toothpaste and the unmistakable musk of desire.

"Why don't we open this thing up into a bed," the flight attendant offered. "You'll be more comfortable, and then maybe you can get some sleep."

"I don't sleep on planes. What I really need to do is keep myself occupied." Bill let his eyes search the contours of the man's body in an obvious way. "Where's the rest of the crew?"

"They're sleeping in crew quarters below," the man said and he gave Bill's body a long stare. "It's just me for the next three hours. I got the overnight shift on this flight."

"Maybe we can keep each other company."

"I'd like that," the attendant said. "You know, I looked you up on the manifest. I have to admit, I wasn't sure how to pronounce your last name. Soil-who?"

"It's from Louisiana. Acadian. It's pronounced *swallow*."

"Swallow?"

Bill nodded his head.

"Never heard that one before," the man said as he stood up. "Now why don't you come join me in the galley. I think I know a way to make the time fly."

4

The Armenian refinery was in worse shape than Bill Soileau imagined. On his clipboard he marked boxes off on a checklist indicating the equipment that would need to be replaced. Barely a box went unscathed by his pen.

When the Soviet empire collapsed, its victims took anything that wasn't nailed down. Half the pipes needed to make the plant run were missing. Bill suspected the metal was stolen, and then melted down and put to new use by the surge of capitalist entrepreneurs that plundered all of the former communist states.

He prayed to God that's what happened. He shuddered to think that some of the pipes were taken and used for plumbing in the local villages. There would be enough lead contamination to shave a hundred points off the IQ of an entire generation. Come to think of it, he hadn't seen a single child since he arrived.

The journey out to the site was stranger than he'd imagined it would be. The roads went from good to bad very quickly, weaving precariously along mountain ledges before winding down to a barren plain that looked like the surface of the moon. A short time later he got the first glimpse of his destination. The monstrosity of the refinery appeared in the distance as a dark fortress on the horizon, towering over an entire region.

Bill had seen countless refineries in his life. When he was a boy he'd stare in fascination as his family, all seven kids crammed into the old station wagon, drove by the plants in Louisiana. At night the speckles of tiny lights that covered the huge compounds made them seem like beautiful fairy kingdoms. He imagined they were castles playing host to a grand ball where Cinderella just noticed she'd lost a shoe. In the daytime, the refineries showed off rugged facades of steel and billowing smoke, exuding a toughness Bill admired. In those childish daydreams, the complexes were men by day, and women at night. He assigned the buildings personalities, believing the exteriors formed the faces of fanciful creatures. One plant he nicknamed "Old Grumpy" because a series of pipes made it look like two eyes with a perpetually scrunched brow. Another he called "The Professor" due to a smoke stack that reminded him of a bespectacled teacher puffing on a calabash pipe. While some boys played with toy fire trucks or soldiers, Bill took twigs and rocks to construct his own Exxon complex.

The oligarch had nicknamed the Armenian refinery Ararat One, after the mountain believed to be the final resting place of Noah's Ark. A fitting idea, since Noah's labors saved humanity from extinction. The oligarch contended that if he could get the refinery up and working again, he would be giving this beleaguered land and its people a second chance. But as Bill got closer to the plant on his drive in, the refinery didn't remind him of any rescue vessel. It looked more like a sinking ship.

Now that he was standing in the middle of it, seeing the details up close, his first impressions were confirmed. It was a wreck. The only thing that appeared to be in working order was the stench. That familiar acrid reek found only at refineries was still plentiful. Bill took in a deep breath to savor it. It reminded him of home. In his petrochemical classes at LSU they called it *the smell of money.*

"You there!"

Bill turned to see a petite dark-haired woman in a white overcoat marching in his direction. It was a commanding, forceful walk, almost comical coming from such a little person.

"You!" She barked again.

"Me?" Bill gestured to himself with his clipboard. He had a lot of notes left to take. He really didn't need any interruptions.

"*Oui,*" the woman said as she finally reached Bill. She was a little out of breath. "I mean, yes. I need you to explain something to me."

"I don't actually work here," Bill said. "I'm doing an inspection.

I'm not really in a position to answer any questions."

"I know who you are. You are of the team from San Francisco. Which is *exactement* what I need." The woman was French, Bill figured. They could be a bit too demanding. But he'd also found most fairly charming, probably drawn to them by his Acadian DNA. Sizing up the diminutive woman, he could already tell she was a little of both.

"I don't understand," Bill said.

"I have already spoken to the idiots who run this place and they cannot – or will not – help me at all. I have discovered a puzzle. A mystery. Perhaps it is something you need to see for yourself for your inspection."

Bill looked at his watch. There were only a few hours of daylight left and hundreds of components left to check. He didn't have time for detours, but he knew there'd be hell to pay if he missed any major problems. *A mystery?*

"Well, then I guess I should take a look. By the way, my name is Bill. Bill Soileau." He held out his hand.

The woman daintily clasped Bill's fingers in return.

"I am Quif."

On the south end of the complex stood a small, freestanding box-shaped building. It was pushed up against the exterior fence, which had been extended from the refinery to surround and secure it. The plant itself was a hundred feet away. In between was a dead zone of concrete.

"This is it?" Bill asked.

"Odd, do you not think?" Quif replied. "It is almost as if this little building was banished away from everything else. Perhaps with good reason."

"What do you mean?"

"Come inside. I will show you."

The door was unlocked. Apparently, the plant's owner was true to his word. The oligarch had promised the inspectors complete access to *anything* associated with the plant. He told them he had the money to fix every issue they found. He just needed to know what to repair. The company Bill worked for was all too willing to charge an astronomical consulting fee to help the oligarch with his reconstruction plan.

Just inside the door of the little square building was a dusty staircase. Quif flipped a switch on the wall. Powerfully bright fluorescents lit up the stairwell. Bill marveled that they still worked after so many years.

"Down here," Quif said as her high-heeled shoes tapped loudly on metal steps.

They went down ten sets of stairs before reaching the bottom and the only set of doors. They were heavily fortified with steel, but Quif pulled one open with ease and walked in, immediately flipping another switch. As the room became awash in light, Bill was stunned. From what he could tell, it was a vast underground complex once home to a sophisticated laboratory. Like the rest of the facility, it had been ransacked. He imagined where microscopes once sat. There were still test tubes and petri dishes scattered all around, most of them broken, cracked or shattered.

It might have been the plant's infirmary, too. At one end of the room were two exam tables sitting side by side. There appeared to be cabinets for storing drugs, although only a few scattered bottles remained. He picked one up. The label was in Russian.

"I was walking around the plant, trying to find the source of this… *cette odeur atroce…* when I saw the little building and came down here," Quif said. "They tried to tell me this was all here to study geological samples. Last time I checked, rocks do not need to be held down with leg and arm straps."

Bill hadn't noticed it before. The exam tables came with apparatus to firmly secure patients. It looked sinister, although Bill thought there might be some logical medical reason for that option. It didn't mean the handcuffs and leg cuffs had actually ever been used.

"Who are you?" Bill finally asked. He'd been a gentleman and introduced himself on the walk over. He spoke about the company he worked for, his background, and the inspection he was here to do, but the tiny French woman had remained curiously silent about her job on site. Why was she holding back?

"How badly do you want this plant to reopen?" Quif asked.

"What do you mean?"

"Well, what is your…I think the right word is *cut*?"

Bill wasn't sure where she was going with all this, but the tone in her voice revealed an anxiety just below the surface. She was hiding something.

"As far as this place is concerned, I'm just an inspector," Bill said. "So please, tell me, what's all this about?"

"You will make big profit when this refinery reopens, *oui?*"

"Me?" Bill scoffed. The French had one of the highest standards of living in the world, and yet they all acted repulsed by any notion of capitalism. The lies they told themselves were part of their charm. "The truth is, I don't make any additional money whether this place opens or not. This, thank God, will be my one and only trip here."

"*Oui.* It sounds like you and I are together in the boat of the same," Quif said, now appearing somewhat at ease.

Bill found himself amused at the way she mixed up her nouns and verbs. He could feel himself being seduced into liking this little woman.

"I am Dr. Quif Melikian." Quif explained her assignment for the Institut Pasteur. She worked for "the European equivalent of the Centers for Disease Control." She shared her fears about pollution from the refinery and what it was doing to the people who lived nearby. If the samples taken showed the results she expected, she was going to recommend the EU block the reopening of the plant.

"And the horrible smell!"

"That's actually normal," Bill explained.

"*Non!*"

"It's true."

"Well, it is sickening," Quif sniffed. "And this? It is not a place for studying the crude oil samples, is it?"

"It doesn't look like it," Bill agreed.

"I think they had to take people here to treat them because they were getting so sick from the pollution of the plant."

Bill scanned the room. He supposed anything was possible, but his bosses would require a lot more than paranoid speculation from some French doctor with such an obvious agenda. Oil was possibly the planet's most useful natural resource. He hated it when anyone tried to assign it morality. Fuel was a thing – it wasn't intrinsically good or evil.

"How would you prove that?" he asked.

"I have you," Quif said with a bit of pride.

"Me?"

"*Oui*. You are my witness. You came and saw this place and you will confirm that it is not a simple geological lab."

"Sure. I can do that. But so what?" Bill held up his clipboard. "I've already found millions of dollars worth of trouble in this place. This is just one more mess to clean up. It's no big deal. These people have lots of cash – enough to make anything go away."

"Good point," Quif nodded. "But what if all of this is – how do you say – *hasardeux*?"

"That's different. Any health hazard could be a big frickin' deal."

"What does this *frickin'* mean?" Quif asked.

"Let's just say it's something I need to report."

"Ah. Then we should get to work. There must be something in this lab that will reveal the truth. Start looking."

"*We* should get to work? Look, I don't..." Bill objected. The little French doctor and her mystery were intriguing, but she had to be kidding herself to think he was on her side. He still had a checklist a mile long and less than two days on site to get it done. He wasn't staying one extra second in this remote shithole. He'd already been counting down the minutes until he could return to San Francisco. Two days, fourteen hours and thirty-seven minutes until he returned *to men*. "I'm sorry. I wish I could help you, but I'm on a tight schedule. I have my own job to do."

"The welfare of the human race is the job of all of us, Bill Soileau," Quif scolded. "Besides, if you help me and we find something then I will give it to you for your report."

Bill had dealt with French scientists on a project in Libya. They could be remarkably persistent. He could tell this one was going to bother him until he relented. "Thirty minutes."

"*Quoi?*"

"Half an hour," Bill said flatly. "That's all the time I have to help you. Then I have to get back to my own work."

Quif looked Bill in the eyes. For the first time, he saw her composure relax, if only a little.

"Bill Soileau, you are a good man."

Good man? It was impossible to believe any doctor would ever say that about him.

"Let's just do this," he muttered.

Bill watched as Quif found an old cardboard box and began filling it with the remaining contents of the medical cabinets. She used a piece of paper as a scoop to gather up fragments of glass tainted with what looked like dried blood. An old battered coffee can with green goop dripping down its side sat on top of a heating vent. Something was written on the rubber lid in Russian. Quif put on latex gloves and pressed the lid snug, and then carefully wedged the can in the corner of the box so it wouldn't spill. It repulsed Bill to think what nastiness might be inside.

A nearby desk looked a lot safer for exploring. Bill opened a drawer to find a pile of papers. The text was in Cyrillic. They could be purchase orders for Frisbees for all he knew. He flipped through the pages, hoping he'd spot something that looked like a lab test slip – he'd recognize one of those, no matter what the language.

He turned to a page with faint green and white stripes. It appeared to be from an old dot-matrix printer. He didn't know what the words said, but the numbers seemed to correspond with the layout of a blood test report. What looked like a person's name was in the heading, leading him to believe it had to be that of a patient. This was it, he was sure. Someone's personal medical file. If this was just the geology department, then something like this should not be here.

He held it up to the light and stared. What were these crazy Russians up to? Who was the patient listed on the form, the person whose medical fate Bill now held in his hands? It's a man, he imagined. Were they anything alike? Bill wondered if the test results were bad news, like the kind he got at LSU. How did the man react when he heard it? Did it feel like a kick in the stomach? Maybe the patient was tougher and took his diagnosis more like a man than Bill had. His mind flashed back to that day at the university clinic, the traumatic confrontation with Dr. Lee, then lying on the campus green weeping until it got dark.

"Shit." As his thoughts submerged into the memory of that day, Bill's hand went limp and weak. He dropped the lab results and they fell to the floor, slipping beneath the desk. He bent down and crawled under. Where did it go? He couldn't see it, so he put his face as close to the floor as possible in order to peek under the part of the desk that held the filing cabinet drawers. There were about three inches of space between the floor and that part of the desk, and the report had slipped at least a foot in. There would be just enough space for his hand.

He reached under. His arm blocked his view, so he felt around blindly hoping his fingertips would feel the wayward paper—

Pain!

A sharp bite into Bill's index finger. A sting. His hand jerked back and his body instinctively recoiled.

"Fuck!" He hit his head on the underside of the desk. Agony shot through his skull. His finger throbbed. He held it up to his face. Whatever stabbed him left barely a mark – just a pinprick oozing a tiny droplet of blood. Bill put his finger in his mouth and sucked to soothe it.

"What is going on over there?" Quif shouted. "Are you hurt?"

"Uh, I just hit my head," Bill tried to shake off the pain. For a split second he thought of telling Quif about the prick to his finger. After all, she was a doctor. Weren't they supposed to help? Not in Bill's mind. It didn't matter that it had been nearly a decade since that awful day of diagnosis. He didn't trust doctors and never would. They had other agendas that put their patients last. He'd learned that lesson the hard way. Even these days when he required medication, Bill did all his own research and simply instructed his latest physician how he wanted to be treated. If the doctor objected, Bill would leave and find another.

He looked at his finger again. It wasn't bleeding anymore. Instead, there was a peculiar tingling sensation. Had he been jabbed by an old needle? God only knew what lurked in a syringe in a place like this.

"Do try to be more careful," Quif said from across the room. She was still piling items into a box and didn't stop to look over.

Bill crouched back down and pressed his face close to the floor to try to see what might have stabbed him. Whatever it was must have been pushed further under by his spasm. He looked at the structure to see if there was any way to pull the desk from the wall, but it was part of a built-in workstation that went the entire length of the room. Made of metal, it would take a blowtorch and a crew of five to demolish it for access.

"Find anything?" Quif asked. She stood in front of Bill holding a box brimming with items.

"Well, I thought I had found some paperwork that could be helpful, but it slipped under this desk." He scanned the room for a broom – anything with a long handle to reach underneath – but saw nothing.

"Leave it. I have plenty of evidence. Files, medications, old slides and test tubes. It should be enough."

The sensation in Bill's finger worsened. The tingling felt like it was crawling up into his hand, and then to his arm. Instead of pain, it was comforting in a strange way.

"Quif, I..." He wanted to tell her what he was feeling. Even though it wasn't hurting, he knew it wasn't natural – maybe she would know what to do. But just as the words for help were about to come out of his mouth, his eyes focused on Quif's white coat. It looked the same as the one Dr. Lee wore. The same color as the thin cotton curtains of the exam room at the campus clinic, the ones that offered a false cocoon of safety and privacy. White was the color of betrayal. Whatever was racing through his veins now could cause him no worse torture. Infection? He'd already been cursed with the most dreaded the world had to offer – the virus that came with the extra ingredients of condemnation, judgment and shame.

He'd handle this on his own. He'd come back tomorrow with something long enough to sweep under the desk and find out what cut his finger.

"You do not look right." Quif put the box down on the floor and squatted down next to the desk. "Are you sure you are okay?"

"It's just a bump on my head," Bill said as he crawled out from under. "I'll be fine. It's only my head."

~

Bill hid his hand under the table as they dined that night at the hotel's posh restaurant. It felt better. The sensation he first felt in his finger, and then his arm, now flowed throughout his entire body.

Or maybe it was just the wine they'd been drinking. They'd already finished two bottles and were on their third. That had to be it. The wine. It had nothing to do with the cut on his finger. Bill silently chided himself for being so foolish. Why create a stir over what was nothing more than a tiny pinprick that produced just one drop of blood? The tingling was his imagination.

Besides, he was having a wonderful time now, enough to even distract him from his urges and the lack of available guys. Quif turned out to be delightful company, especially after he told her about growing up in Louisiana.

"It is one of the few places in America that is tolerable," Quif teased.

"You only say that because you're French. You think New Orleans is still a colony," Bill joked.

"But I am not French. I am actually Armenian."

"From here?"

"I was born in France. My great-grandparents escaped when the atrocities started. My family has lived in France ever since. But in our culture, you are an Armenian above all else. I feel a great love for my people and my homeland, even though I am the first member of my family to actually set foot in Armenia in more than ninety years."

Bill sat spellbound as Quif began telling her family's tales of the genocide. It was a chapter of history they never studied in parochial school back in Baker, even though it was just as horrific as anything done by the Nazis. Why was he just hearing this now? Why not the same outrage as the Jewish Holocaust?

Quif's eyes teared over as she spoke about an underground labyrinth of caves only thirty kilometers away. They'd driven past the area on the way to refinery. During World War I, hundreds of Armenian men were herded inside. They all thought it was just another prison. Then the Turks lit huge fires at the entrances to suck out the air and asphyxiate the men. All those innocent lives were snuffed out.

"The world's first gas chamber," Quif sighed. "Hitler studied the success of the Ottoman Empire's killing of Armenians as a blueprint for his own Final Solution. He saw how war provided the perfect veil for the Turks to do their dirty work. The genocide happened in secret as the world was too busy to pay attention. When Hitler wrote his own master plan, they say he laughed and said *Who does now remember the Armenians?* And he was right. The world had turned its back and forgotten. It still forgets."

"I'm sorry." It was all Bill could think to say. He felt sad for Quif and her people, and understood why she felt so much anger. Still, he struggled to see why she hated the refinery so much. It was just an old plant, the same as any other. Bill liked Quif, but he could see she was an idealist, perhaps even reckless. Her agenda took precedent over everything. Considering another side was secondary to getting what she wanted, even if it meant using fear without facts. He should have known. She was, after all, a doctor.

"What is being done today to my people is like a form of genocide," Quif continued, her voice dramatically solemn. "This time they are being killed by greed. Instead of gas chambers, the weapons are pollution and disease."

Disease? Bill rubbed the tip of his finger, still hiding it under the table. "What disease are you talking about? Have you found something in your samples?"

"No. Not yet. It will take time for the technicians at Pasteur to analyze all the results. But I am sure of it. I see history repeating itself. I see it all the time."

Since working for the Institut for the past seven years, Quif explained how she'd become a type of "disease detective" traveling around the globe to suspected areas of illness and infection outbreaks. She spoke about the AIDS death camps in Africa, where the virus spread unabated because men believed in superstitions that said the way to cure themselves was by having unprotected sex with virgins. Tens of thousands of children now suffered from HIV.

"Intentionally infecting someone with HIV! Have you ever heard of anything so evil?" Quif threw up her hands in disgust.

Unprotected sex. The roulette party. No, it wasn't the same as raping innocent children. All the men at the party knew what they were doing. They *wanted* to tempt fate. To a doctor, though, it involved spreading a deadly disease. It was as immoral, and the differences would be irrelevant. Bill felt suddenly enveloped in guilt. Here was a woman hell bent on saving the world, and he was sure she'd see him as the poster boy for irresponsible, depraved behavior. Things weren't really that simple, but Bill now knew then he could never confide in Quif. Charming or not, she was still a doctor. He didn't need a doctor meddling in his life again.

He kept his hand hidden under the table. The tingling surged throughout his body. *God, this is great wine.*

5

Bill Soileau itched to get back to San Francisco. It would take nearly an entire day to return home, about the same brutally long journey it took to reach the refinery in the first place. The time zone changes made it look shorter on paper, but that was just the cruel trick of itineraries. He was bursting with energy, eager to be freed from the confines of the plane and back into the game. It had been nearly five days without sex. He wondered how his swollen testicles ever fit into his underwear when he got dressed that morning.

If not for the flight attendant on the way over, he'd have been starved for nearly a week.

The cut on his finger had completely healed. It went back to normal so quickly it was nothing short of miraculous. Maybe he should have returned to the lab to get under that desk and try to find out what had cut him, but by the next morning he couldn't even tell where he'd been jabbed. The mark was gone.

A small part of him regretted not saying anything to Quif about the cut. What if he did pick something up? It might prove she was right about the refinery. He pushed the idea to the back of his mind. *It was nothing.* He was due for his quarterly blood work anyway, an annoying requirement of being on medications. Anything awful would show up then. His regular doctor would catch it.

Besides, he felt *incredible.*

He'd always had high energy, especially sex drive, but in the past two days his whole body felt supercharged. It reminded him of when he'd taken ecstasy, yet it was even stronger – and without messing up his thoughts. If anything, he felt sharper, like he could take on the whole world. He'd breezed through the final inspections at the refinery. And for the first time on a transatlantic flight, he had fallen asleep. A deep, restful sleep for six hours with no bad memories. Then when he awoke, he jumped right into multi-tasking. He typed up his report for work on his laptop, while at the same time used an onboard internet interface – another great perk of First Class – to cruise a San Francisco sex hook-up website. Five days without men! Maybe the energy surge was the result of being so pent up, his libido on overload with no escape. He'd need to hit the ground running. Going online meant he could have someone waiting for him at his front door by the time he got there.

Normally, hooking up for sex online was a transaction that would take only minutes to arrange. He'd pre-screen listings for age and physical description. Picking from those, he'd make an introduction and describe whatever he was in the mood for. If that was agreed to, then the hunter and prey would swap photographs. Bill always sent two photos: a G-rated one where he was fully clothed that included his smiling face, and then separately a more revealing picture of his body, shot only from the neck down. If anything went bad, he never wanted someone to have a compromising photograph that might be used to embarrass him somewhere on the web. Bill was constantly amazed by the number of men who sent nude photos of themselves to anyone who asked. Some even had open-access websites that featured their smiling faces in the same full body picture as their erections. They obviously didn't have a mother like Bill's. Not that she was online. She was too poor to buy a computer. When he sent her money to get one, she ended spending it "on more pressin' needs," which he knew was code for gin tonics and cigarettes. Still, he'd always been careful to make sure his online life kept his identity and cravings secret from the general public. You just never knew who was surfing the web these days – or who they'd tell if they found something out.

After the photo exchange, if it was a match, then he'd send the guy his address. Maybe they'd exchange first names. The entire online transaction took about fifteen minutes. Bill had sealed deals in the past in less than two minutes.

There was no rush this time since he hadn't landed yet in New York and still had the whole cross country flight to get home. He could plan this time, maybe even be a little picky. Going without sex for five days made him something of a virgin again.

Hours later he had dismissed countless suitors. Too fat. Too nelly. Too tweaked on crystal mess. He had no doubt that any other day, he'd fuck them all regardless. Guys especially loved it when he exaggerated his Southern accent and told them *spit and shove or it ain't love* was the only way he screwed. But why settle for that old scene? He had a weird craving for something else, although he couldn't quite figure out what. It was like going to a restaurant and finding nothing appetizing on the menu, even though he was starving.

Then he found Ike.

Ike's online listing was the type Bill would have scoffed at in the past. It was one of those that shouldn't be on a website like this one. "I know this site is usually used for casual or anonymous sex, but I'm looking for more than that…"

More? What's with these guys who use sex sites to look for love? Bill started to click onto the next listing, but something about Ike's personal ad hit a nerve. Instead of writing it off as the misplaced plea of a lonely loser, Bill felt strangely intrigued and found himself devouring the entire text. Words like "feeling" and "companion" popped off the screen. In the past, he'd usually just scan the page looking for a guy's physical stats and numbers eight or higher.

Then there was Ike's online photo, shirtless in jeans with a friendly, sexy smile. He had dirty blond hair, blue eyes and a finely muscled body. They were about the same age, but Ike had a smooth hairless chest. Bill's features were darker, with a patch of hair across his pecs, which he kept neatly trimmed. Bill had always found the mixing of hairy and smooth bodies intensely arousing, as if they were opposites complementing one another – a perfect pairing, like his aunt Jenna's fiery jambalaya washed down with an ice cold Bud.

Yet it was what Ike wrote that kept Bill fixated on the screen. "Do you find yourself wondering how many tricks it's going to take to satiate that urge?"

Satiate. No one used ten-dollar vocabulary words on a site like this. *Who is this guy?* The truth was, Bill did think about his hyper sex drive. Even Mark Hazodo had told Bill it wasn't normal, and that was from a guy with levee spilling urges. Bill usually didn't give a shit about what Mark or anyone else thought. Sex was something he was good at. No one fucked more guys than he did – he might be the undisputed champion of the world in his weight class. Now all of a sudden came these feelings that he needed more than just sex.

Bill sent Ike an Instant Message. They began chatting back and forth, playing the online dance that precedes a hook-up. Ike's listing said he was looking for more, but it became clear pretty quickly that for the moment he was in as much physical need as Bill. Ah ha! For all of his high and mighty rhetoric, Ike was still a guy too.

ILikeIke: what's the address? i can cum right over
OilGuy415: uh, somewhere over the north atlantic
ILikeIke: great. i finally meet a great guy and he's an
           astronaut ;-)
OilGuy415: well, there are no good ones left on earth LOL

Bill explained exactly where he was and when he thought he'd be back to San Francisco. If the delay bothered Ike, he never showed it. They stayed online and chatted for hours. They talked about sex, the city and travel. They both marveled at how they could Instant Message as if they were next-door neighbors, even though one was 40,000 feet in the air nearly halfway around the world. The signal dropped a few times, but within moments they found each other again.

Ike seemed to know everything about current events, and could even talk politics without being a typical San Francisco left-wing narcissist. Bill had always believed it was impossible to discern tone from e-mails or chatting, but somehow he felt warmth emanating from the letters of Ike's electronic text.

OilGuy415: what do you do for work?
ILikeIke: i'm the executive director of project inform

OilGuy415: ?
ILikeIke: we run hiv prevention campaigns
OilGuy415: o

Bill wasn't sure what to type. He was the opposite of a prevention campaign. He thought back to the roulette party and his role as the bullet in the gun. He wished Mark had never talked him into doing that. How could he ever defend something like that with Ike? That everyone knew what they were getting into? That they were all consenting adults? *Damn!* He really liked this guy Ike. Why couldn't he just be a math teacher? Bill scolded himself for asking too many questions. He'd broken his cardinal rule about getting to know someone he fucked. It was stupid to read the entire personal ad and engage the guy in IMs for so long. Keeping things anonymous meant he never had to face these awkward dilemmas. HIV prevention? They'd never hook up now.

ILikeIke: i guess that's my opening to ask THE question
OilGuy415: ?
ILikeIke: poz or neg?

Bill stared at the words on the screen. It was a question hardly anyone asked anymore in San Francisco. He was pretty sure he hadn't even heard it mentioned for at least two years. It was assumed if you had sex that you were responsible for your own health. If you were negative, you made sure you protected yourself with condoms. If you didn't, then fear of infection wasn't an issue for you anymore. Therefore, you must be positive. Bill knew it was dangerous logic, but they were all men – this was the price of admission to the game. Besides, his ticket had already been stamped. There was nothing more that could be done to hurt him.

Bill considered disconnecting his laptop from the jet's internet interface. On the other end, Ike would think the signal dropped again and accept it as a blip of static. Bill could sneak away.

He knew it would look too suspicious. They'd been chatting for hours and then when Ike asks a question – when Ike asks THE question – Bill suddenly disappears? It would be so pathetic.

ILikeIke: u there?
OilGuy415: yup
ILikeIke: you don't have to answer that if you don't want to
OilGuy415: k
ILikeIke: we'll play safe
OilGuy415: k
ILikeIke: cuz i'm poz

Bill put his head back, staring at the cabin ceiling. *Poz*. Ike is HIV positive. And he's so open about it, almost nonchalant. Bill had never been with a man who was so candid about being infected. He thought back to his conversation with Quif, and her disgust with the African men who selfishly perpetuated the cycle of infection there. Was he as guilty as them? Or maybe he was worse because he knew better than some tribal superstition. He'd always shut his eyes to consequences because the world had been so careless with him. His parents. Dr. Lee. That night he was now convinced was the moment he'd become infected. No one had ever looked out for *his* best interests. Since discovering his fate, he'd been responsible, as per the rules. He'd only had unsafe sex with men who let him. Any notion of feeling guilty was ridiculous, right?

Now on the other side of the screen, connected by taps of fingertips on keyboards thousands of miles apart, Bill had randomly found a man who offered a path away from the game. For some reason, the prospect of changing suddenly didn't seem so daunting. Maybe the glow of energy he was experiencing was a sign he was ready to take a chance on some other way.

ILikeIke: ?
OilGuy415: i'm here
ILikeIke: u freaked?
OilGuy415: nope
ILikeIke: i understand if you don't want to now
OilGuy415: i still want to
ILikeIke: really?

OilGuy415: yup

ILikeIke: kewl. i'll bring condoms. it will still be hot. you'll
see

OilGuy415: no need

ILikeIke: ?

OilGuy415: we don't need condoms

ILikeIke: u sure?

OilGuy415: i'm poz 2

6

"The homo-sek-chewals want your children. Make no mistake about it," the Reverend Willy Warrant ranted from his imposing pulpit. "They are doing everything they can to lure your children and make them converts to their evil lifestyle!"

The congregation that filled the football stadium chanted in response. "Evil! Evil! Evil!"

"Yes! The homo-sek-chewals are looking for recruits. I say don't be fooled! They say they want marriage because they love each other. I say this is not love! That's why we need the president's constitutional amendment to stop this abomination they call gay marriage. They should never be allowed to marry like real people. What they do is the same as having intercourse with a horse!"

"Horse! Horse! Horse!" the crowd screamed in approval.

"They say they want to adopt children." The Reverend took out his handkerchief and wiped the sweat from his brow. His face turned crimson, a stark contrast to his slicked-back snow-white mane. "For what? They say they just want to love them. I say we don't want their kind of love!"

The crowd looked confused over what to holler back. A few sporadic mumbles emerged. "Horse?" "Evil?"

Bill Soileau rolled his eyes. Of all the television shows to have playing in the waiting room of his doctor's office, why in the world did someone have this crap on? Everyone knew the Reverend Willy Warrant was the nation's leading gay-basher. His best-selling book *The*

Straight and Narrow Life had sold 25 million copies and was considered a new testament for conservative Christians who thought Jesus and the Bible's Golden Rule were too permissive. Reverend Warrant embraced all the populist gay-hate ideas. *Homosexuality is an ideology of evil. Gay is just a lifestyle choice. AIDS is God's punishment.*

Not that Bill's own religious upbringing was much better. He's been raised Catholic, and attended the parish's parochial St. John's so he wouldn't have to mix with the blacks in public schools, the same as any of the other white kids. But after Bill's father died, his family couldn't afford the tuition and he and his siblings were enrolled as charity cases, something the priests and nuns never let them forget. His mother, already teetering on he verge of alcoholism, was made bitter from being so publicly an object of pity. She took her frustration out on those she determined her weakest children, namely Bill. Graduation from high school was the last time he'd been to church, though he still found himself using the word God, mostly in profanities.

He didn't care much for politics either, but he kept tabs on the Reverend Warrant's agenda. It was as if Warrant was out to get him *personally.* He supposed every gay person felt the same way after Warrant's campaign in the past election to pass laws against gay marriage in a dozen states. After a national constitutional amendment passed to ban gay marriage, what's next? Concentration camps?

On the issue of AIDS, Warrant was the worst type of hypocrite. He'd publicly taken an HIV test in order to show how his heterosexuality protected him from the disease. And he'd effectively fooled nearly everyone, even gay leaders, into thinking he cared about those who suffered from AIDS by sending money to Africa. But Bill had read an investigation by TheDailyBeast.com that showed how Warrant's money was only allowed for ill-fated, forced-religion abstinence campaigns. Some of the funds went to support tribal leaders who conducted witch-hunts to expose, imprison and abuse anyone thought to be gay.

Warrant's foot soldiers even put pressure on the U.S. Congress to suspend the 22nd Amendment, an unprecedented move that managed to get a terrible president re-elected to a third term, despite a deep recession and unpopular wars overseas. Power like that hat earned

Warrant a regular guest pass at the White House and influence with a naive, religiously devout commander in chief. If the Reverend and his mob had their way, Bill fumed, gays would be put down like rabid dogs.

"Where's the remote?" Bill asked the receptionist.

"Sorry," the young woman said. She picked up the clicker from her desk and switched the channel over to *Regis and Kelly*. The receptionist was watching the Reverend? It had to be a mistake. Maybe another program was on earlier and she simply forgot to change the channel once this shit came on. Still, someone needed to have a talk with her about sensitivity. This was San Francisco, and she worked for a doctor who specialized in treating gay men. The doctor himself was so flamboyantly gay he was only one lipstick shade short of being a woman. *The Straight and Narrow Life* shouldn't be allowed to stink up the TV here for even a moment. Didn't the woman know it was insulting?

"Bill...Soil-who?" the nurse called as he opened the entrance to the exam rooms. It was Barton, the same fey, skinny nurse who always greeted Bill.

"Barton, you know damn well how to pronounce my name," Bill ribbed.

"Of course I do, honey, but you don't go yelling the word *swallow* around here now, do you?"

After Barton checked Bill's vitals he ushered him into one of the private exam rooms. White walls. Bill felt the familiar pit in his stomach. Why did doctors' offices always have white walls? Why not paint them uplifting, bright colors? Maybe no one else had the same feelings about white walls as Bill, but he thought a gay doctor would want a bit more stylish decor.

At least on this visit Bill wouldn't have to worry about whether he had picked up an STD, one of the hazards of fucking strangers bareback. In the past month the number of his sex partners had dropped from somewhere around a zillion to just one. *Ike*. Bill felt giddy every time he thought of Ike. Who could have seen this coming?

He thought back to the day they met, after Bill took that horrendously long flight back from Armenia. As they had planned during their internet chat session from the plane, Ike was waiting outside Bill's building when the taxi rolled up. When Bill stepped onto the curb, their eyes met. Bill remembered thinking just one word. *Yeah.*

Ike was everything Bill had pictured during their hours of stratospheric instant messaging. Charming. Masculine. Handsome. He wore a pair of old jeans and a plain brown T-shirt that revealed a grounded confidence – he had nothing to hide with pretentious designer fashions. Here was a guy who was fine just being himself.

They spent the better part of the day together, most of the time quietly spooning. Bill felt a connection he'd never had with another man. His nose worked in overdrive - the scent from Ike was so powerful. The smell drove Bill to taste every inch of Ike's body, and at one point he climaxed without even the touch of a hand. Somehow Ike instinctively knew to nuzzle and kiss Bill's ears, his soft spot. Bill had never felt so fulfilled, both in the giving and receiving of pleasure. For the first time in ten years he didn't find himself thinking, *Who's next?*

When Ike finally had to leave that first night for a long-planned dinner with an important Project Inform donor, Bill felt a strange rush of anxiety. His heart raced. He'd been through this moment thousands of times with other guys – say a brief goodbye and never have contact again. This was different. He wanted a *second* date. And a third. And then a thousand more. He wanted Ike. *What do I say?* He had no experience with moments like this. He'd only tossed men aside before.

"I had the best time today," Bill finally stumbled. "You were, uh, awesome."

"You mean this?" Ike laughingly gestured to the bed. "You know, I also do dinners and movies." Ike placed his hand on Bill's shoulder and gently pulled him forward until they held each other.

"Come back tomorrow for a double feature," Bill said as he took in a deep breath of Ike.

"I felt it too," Ike said.

"Felt what?"

"I dunno exactly. A rush? It's like I'm tingling all over," Ike beamed.

Bill was overcome with a rush too, but it went beyond his flesh. He'd never spent hours just holding a man. But it felt normal, like it was somehow supposed to be this way. He'd lived most of his life without… He struggled to even think of the right word. Affection. His parents never showed any affection at home, although Bill now understood that they were victims of their circumstances. As a result, no one in the family, not even his siblings, connected on that level. The Sex Addicts Anonymous group leader said it was a common disorder to try to replace needed genuine affection with multiple sexual partners. It was hard to take that explanation seriously, especially after the leader sucked Bill off in the boiler room in the basement of the church where the group met.

So why this sudden feeling of affection for Ike? Not just *for* Ike, but *from* him too. It wasn't as if they'd known each other for weeks and had discovered endless common bonds. Inexplicably, it just happened. They were connected. Maybe love was a microscopic chemical reaction that happened unseen by the human eye, unheard by the ears – it just tackled you.

As soon as Ike was out the door, Bill called Mark Hazodo to tell him the news. After all these years, he had finally met The One.

"Dude, that's so cool. I hate losing my fellow degenerate, but hell yeah – that's great," Mark said. "You meet the guy on your trip? How long have you been seeing each other?"

"We met six hours ago."

"Six hours? What?" Mark laughed. "Bill Soileau! What have you been swallowing? You mean you fucked around with the guy *once* and you're trying to tell me you know this is the man you are going to spend the rest of your life with? Gimme a fuckin' break."

"I'm telling you, Mark. I just know. He's the guy."

"Right."

"Everything about him feels right. He even *smells* perfect."

"Not that bullshit about pheromones again," Mark scoffed.

"I'm telling you, it's true."

"Fine. Tell *me* all you want. But for fuck's sake, don't tell him. You'll scare him off. Hell – you're already scaring me!"

Bill didn't tell Ike how he felt, at least not at first. Within a week, they were spending every night together, split between their two apartments. The arrangement was such a radical change in behavior that more than once Bill awoke in the middle of the night to gingerly slide out of bed and quietly slip into his jeans to sneak out. His old instincts kicked in, as they had been trained to do for nearly a decade. *Don't be there when the guy wakes up in the morning.* He'd get as far as the top button when the epiphany of his new reality hit. He didn't have to leave anymore.

Why now? He always figured he was wired differently, unable to make the connections that came so easily to others. Now those faulty circuits were somehow repaired. Was the surge of power in his body responsible for the healing?

That morning Bill told Ike he had to go to see the doctor for his latest blood test results. On the surface it sounded like just a routine chat about that day's schedule, but when the words came out of Bill's mouth he realized it was the first time he'd ever discussed any details of his HIV with anyone other than a physician. Instead of being anxious about sharing a secret, Bill noticed how incredibly comfortable he was with Ike. Until this moment, he'd never let his guard down with anyone.

"I'm sure everything will be fine," Ike had said as he kissed Bill on the forehead. "I've never seen a healthier guy in my life."

Bill felt healthy, too. The rush of energy he experienced after the trip to Armenia had never relented, even a full month later. Maybe this is what love did to everyone. The thought startled Bill. That word. *Love.* Now waiting in the doctor's exam room, surrounded by stark white walls, it hit him. The pit in his stomach wasn't his latent fear of doctors predictably kicking in. It was something much stronger than that. *Love.* He was in love with Ike, wasn't he? That's what this incredible sudden vitality was all about. For the first time in his life, *he loved someone.*

"Fabulous!"

The doctor flounced into the exam room. He always said *Fabulous!* when he greeted people, rather than hello. "Hello? Ugh! The straights own that word," he had explained to Bill when they'd first met. "We can do better than that!"

"Fabulous!" the doctor repeated.

"Hey," Bill said cheerfully. He'd been seeing Dr. Doug Greene for the past year. Out of all the physicians he'd been through, Dr. Greene was the best informed, even if he had the mannerisms of an Orleans parish debutante.

"Oh. My. God." Dr. Greene pronounced each word as if it was its own sentence. He stared at Bill's face.

"What is it?" Bill panicked. "My test results? Are they bad?"

"Test results?" Dr. Greene reached over and laid a finger on Bill's cheek. "Oh, honey, I haven't even looked at those yet. There's a different crisis I'm worried about."

"What?"

"This dry patch of skin on your cheek. How long has it been there?"

Bill got up and looked in the mirror over the exam room sink. Dry patch? There it was, a little mark the size of pencil eraser only a fraction of a shade redder than the rest of his skin.

"I dunno. Honestly, I never noticed it before."

The doctor rolled a stool out from under the desk and sat sidesaddle. With a serious look on his face he said, "You know what causes that, don't you?"

"Uh, no." Bill had all sorts of thoughts racing through his head. Cancer? Some HIV side effect? An infection from Armenia?

"Soap," the doctor said flatly. "You've been using regular soap on your face, haven't you?"

"Well, I…"

"Tsk. What type of cleansing and moisturizing regimen do you use?"

Bill stumbled. "I don't really have a regimen."

Dr. Greene's jaw dropped. For several moments, it looked like he'd lost the ability to form words. "What type of gay man are you?" Dr. Greene shook his head. He took out his prescription pad and jotted down several brands, making sure Bill understood he was only to use facial cleansers on his face – never soap! "If you look forty when you turn forty, you can't sue *me* for malpractice!"

"Uh, thanks," Bill said. He thought of mentioning how Reverend Willy Warrant's gay-hate show was playing on the waiting room TV, but there had been enough drama already. "Do you have the results of my latest blood work?"

"I sure do," Dr. Greene said as he opened up Bill's chart and scanned the latest reports. "Well, that's messed up."

"What?"

"It looks like the lab made a mistake. None of the numbers make any sense."

"What do you mean?" Bill's mind raced back to the accident in the lab in Armenia. Did he catch hepatitis or something from that cut?

"Nothing bad," the doctor scratched his chin. "Or should I say, nothing at all. These tests show you're negative for everything. Everything is normal, or even better. Your T-cells are up. 1800? That's above normal. Your viral load is undetectable." The doctor flipped through a few more pages. "Okay, not just undetectable – it's non existent. Like you've never had it. Frankly, these are the test results of someone in perfect health who has never even been exposed to HIV."

"Oh," said Bill. For an instant he let himself fantasize about what it would be like to no longer be infected. He'd often wondered why no one had come up with a way to kill HIV. It felt like no one was even trying to work on a cure anymore. There was research on failed vaccines and new, more expensive treatments, but never a cure. What an incredible day that would be if they could rid the world of AIDS quickly and benignly. What a party that would be...

"It must be someone else's blood work, sweetie. Sorry about that." Dr. Greene closed the chart. "But whoever it is, I sure would like to meet him. His testosterone levels are through the roof. Woof!"

"So what do we do?"

"I'm going to send you right over to the lab for more tests, honey. I know it's a hassle, but mistakes like this happen. If I had a dime for every time the lab made an error, I'd be a queen."

The men eyed each other for a moment, then burst out laughing.

As he left the office Bill stopped at the receptionist's desk to write a check for his co-pay. Behind him he heard that unmistakable voice again.

"The homo-sek-chewals have an agenda. If they get their way, they will infect us all with their evil lifestyle! We must do everything to make sure that does not happen. A constitutional amendment is the only way to stop them – it is God's commandment!"

It was the Reverend Willy Warrant. The TV had been switched back to *The Straight and Narrow Life*. Bill glared down at the receptionist.

A scarlet rash of embarrassment washed over her face. She picked up the remote and clicked over again to *Regis and Kelly*.

"Sorry," she said.

7

Quif trotted down the long ornate neoclassical hallway of the Institut Pasteur, her heels clacking noisily on the marble floors. She much preferred to meet at her office in the more modern BioTop complex, but Benoit insisted on seeing her in person at the café in the Bertrand wing of the old main building. It was a daunting place, a converted mansion steeped in history. The original vaccines against rabies, yellow fever and hepatitis B all came from here. As did the first use of chemotherapy, and pioneering work on viruses. The discovery of AIDS. Her mind flashed briefly to her sister Natara. The greatest geniuses in medicine walked these halls, Quif thought, suddenly self-conscious at her absurdly loud footsteps.

Benoit had been so secretive when he called. He finally had the results from the samples she'd shipped back from Armenia. There had been such a backlog at the Pasteur lab it had taken two months to finish. She'd called and e-mailed repeatedly to try to get things moving faster. She couldn't allow the refinery in Armenia to reopen. Benoit claimed he'd put her research at the front of the line, otherwise she'd have to wait nearly six months.

Benoit. He was so charming over the phone. He didn't seem to mind her pestering. If anything, he appeared to enjoy it, and acted as if he loved receiving every nagging call. When they first met in person, she thought he was handsome with his black stubble and bright green eyes, even if he was too young for her. Young men constantly flirted with her. Maybe they thought as a doctor she knew some secrets of anatomy that made her a better lover, or perhaps they craved the experience a woman in her thirties was more likely to have. Or did they find her dark features exotic and somehow beautiful? It didn't matter. Benoit could turn on all his charms, but he was a fool to think this was anything more than work. With her job and caring for Natara, she didn't have time for a lover even if she wanted one. What was Benoit anyway? Twenty-five?

"There you are," Quif said as officiously as possible when she spotted Benoit. He had picked a table in the quiet far corner away from the rest of the patrons.

"Ah, Quif! You are more lovely than ever. Every time I hear your name, it makes me think of—"

"Armenia, I hope." Quif sat down. She folded her arms across her chest, hoping he'd see from her posture that she was there for business, nothing more.

"Well, that, for sure, *oui*," Benoit stumbled, looking a little bruised by Quif's abruptness.

"I would rather we met in your office, or mine. Why did we have to come here?"

Benoit signaled the waiter.

"I don't want anything." Quif waved away the man.

"Oh, come on," Benoit said with a mock pout. "I know you work too hard. A beautiful woman like you needs a break once in a while. There will be plenty of time for laboratories and conference rooms later. Based on what I've discovered, you'll be up to your neck in them."

"You found something?" Quif's eyes widened. "Tell me."

"Well, I could use some coffee first. I've been working very hard for you," Benoit exaggeratedly stretched his shoulders.

"Okay, okay. I give up. Yes, coffee."

Benoit held up two fingers to the waiter.

"Now, what is it?" Quif leaned in.

Benoit bent over toward the table and whispered, "Nothing."

"What do you mean, *nothing*?" Quif sat back, annoyed.

"I mean, *nothing*."

"Nothing? You brought me all the way over here to tell me nothing?" she snapped.

Benoit smiled and shook his head. "You miss the point." He reached down into a knapsack next to his chair and pulled out a thick manila folder. Gesturing with the report he said, "I think maybe you need to relax a little. Perhaps we should take an afternoon stroll in the *Parc des Buttes Chaumont*. It's not too busy during the week. It will be lovely and intimate, and the fresh air will do you good. As a doctor, I'm sure you know it's not healthy to be so—"

"Do you have results or not?"

Benoit placed the file on the table. He grinned broadly. "I'm sorry to be such a tease. I get the impression you could use a good tease."

"Benoit!"

"Yes, the report. Okay." He opened the folder. "As I said, the results are nothing. Well, at least as far as the blood samples are concerned. You took these from people who lived near the refinery?"

"Yes. Who else?" Quif said, her voice revealing how annoyed she'd become. She hated being manipulated, even though it was obvious Benoit was only trying to ingratiate himself with her in the immature way of most men his age. What did he mean *nothing*?

"Statistically, it doesn't make any sense. You collected hundreds of samples. There should be at least a few cases of diabetes. Or a patient or two exposed to hepatitis, maybe even TB or cholera. I found nothing. Do they smoke?"

"Like chimneys," Quif said flatly.

"Well, not one cancer either. Of any kind. Nothing! At first I thought maybe the tests were botched, so I ran the full panels again. Then a third time. The results came out the same every time. These are the healthiest people in the world."

It didn't make sense. Quif sat silently for a moment trying to piece together what Benoit said. She thought of the old woman with the crucifix and the elderly villagers, their sad cracked faces, lining up to offer their veins for her research. Had she bungled the collection somehow? She picked up the report and started leafing through the pages. The numbers backed up what Benoit had said. "What about the water and soil samples? Where are those? Any sign of contamination?"

Benoit pulled another file out of his bag. "That's the part I don't get. The environment there is as poisoned as you'd expect being so close to an oil refinery. Cancer rates alone should be elevated. But again...*nothing*. Any first year epidemiology student will tell you none of this is possible."

Quif grabbed the second file away from Benoit. She quickly flipped through the pages. The soil and water were contaminated just as she suspected. There were high levels of hydrocarbons, iron and benzene. Why wasn't any of this affecting the people who lived there? *C'est affreux!* So much for her mission to prevent the refinery from opening. No one would listen to her with zero proof of a major health catastrophe. The results of the tests could actually make matters worse. Now *any* industrialist could point to the research and make the claim that even the esteemed Institut Pasteur couldn't link refinery pollution to disease. It was a disaster. She could see her hard work being twisted to justify fuel production facilities being dumped into any Third World community. She thought of the poor people who would suffer as a result. A throbbing pain began to emerge behind her eyes.

"Want to hear the interesting part?" Benoit was still smiling. Such a fool, Quif thought. He has no idea what's really at stake.

"There's more?"

Benoit leaned back in his chair. "You know, I've never seen a doctor so rattled to find out that her patients are in excellent health. I'm worried about you."

Quif scanned the pages in the files, refusing to look up and encourage Benoit. "What do you mean *more?*"

"Maybe I won't tell you," Benoit said smugly. "Until you agree to go out to dinner with me. I know this incredible new Moroccan restaurant in Belleville—"

Quif peered up from the pages to glare at Benoit. Why did he have such a smirk on his face? "You said you had more. What is it?"

"Oh, come to dinner with me. Besides, I think you're going to want to celebrate."

"Why?" Quif was astonished. Couldn't young men think of anything except what's in their pants? Her work was in shambles, there was no reason for revelry. Dinner with such a juvenile – it was absurd.

Benoit reached down into his backpack again, this time retrieving a file in a green folder. "You can kiss me later," he said.

"What is it?"

"This, my lovely Quif, is a work of art. My masterpiece. Together, you and I are about to become the most famous scientists in the world. They'll be scratching the name Pasteur off the side of this building and chiseling ours in."

"Let me see."

"Ah, not so fast." Benoit held the folder snug to his chest. "What about my invitation to dinner?"

Quif thrust out her hand and scowled. "This had better be important."

Benoit used both arms to clutch the file like a loved one. "Important? We have just stumbled upon possibly the *most important* medical find in history. Something that could change the course of the entire planet."

"What in the world are you going on about?" Quif had to admit, Benoit now had her full attention. His green eyes looked brighter than ever. He was undoubtedly brash, but confidence made any man more handsome.

"Remember that trash you sent from that old abandoned lab at the refinery?"

Quif nodded, "*Oui.*"

"Well, how much do you know about *phage?*"

8

Bill Soileau sipped his café au lait. The cup was comically huge, like a prop from the old TV show *Land of the Giants*. Sweet Inspiration dessert shop was famous for its large portions, and the rich coffee was a perfect match for the mocha cheesecake melting in his mouth. The slice was enormous, too. Who could ever finish all this?

Out the window he stared at Beck's Motor Lodge across the street, a classic three-story motel from the 1950s spiffed up with a new coat of shocking salmon-colored paint with bright blue trim. Anyone driving by might easily dismiss it as nostalgic kitsch. Bill knew the truth.

A U-shaped complex on busy Market Street, Beck's rooms all had large windows that looked out onto landings that hugged each floor. A constant parade of visitors walked past the rooms and peered inside. Eager guests kept their drapes open and flaunted their naked bodies across their beds to offer themselves. If a passerby liked what he saw, he knocked on the glass to be let inside. After midnight, the displays became more outrageous. Hotel patrons ingratiated themselves for the window shoppers, or staged open-door orgies, all in an attempt to lure more men.

Bill had done the Beck's walk more times than he cared to remember. On nights when he felt an urgent need and wasn't too particular, he'd pick a room number in his head before arriving and fuck whoever turned out to be there. Other times he'd wander around each of the floors and take note of every turned-up bare butt until he settled on the one that appealed to him most. After the first, he'd need only a few minutes before he was ready to see what knelt behind the next door.

Now from the safe distance of the café, he watched men climb the stairs and circle the landings. Shopping malls have less foot traffic, he thought. Staring into the dollop of milk foam on his drink, he was suddenly glad for simple pleasures. Coffee and cake. If things were different, he might be one of those men across the street, condemned to pace in search of flesh.

"What are you thinking?" Ike said as he sat back down next to Bill.

Bill hesitated. *Why hold back?* He felt comfortable putting anything on the line for Ike. "I'm thinking about how happy I am."

"Cheesecake will do that to you."

"That's not what I meant."

"I know." Ike took a sip from the giant au lait. "I'm happy, too. I'm sorry it took me so long at the bathroom. I waited and waited, then a very large woman finally emerged wearing a *I Lost Weight, Ask Me How* button. I had to open the window!"

"You're such a romantic," Bill clanked his fork down on the plate, acting as if the remark made him lose his appetite.

"I'm sorry. It's just…you know how I feel about germs. I wish this place would get separate restrooms for men and women. I don't want to share. I like being able to keep a safe distance and still take a leak. Each time I use a public bathroom I thank God I'm a man."

"Were you always so phobic?" Bill wondered if Ike's HIV status made him especially paranoid about germs.

"I've always been a clean freak, type-A, super organized, things in their proper place and all that. When I got infected, I was truly shocked. I thought I'd be the last person in the world to get HIV, since I've always had a thing about cleanliness and germs."

Bill looked around the café wondering how many people overheard Ike blurt out his HIV status. It amazed Bill how open and casual Ike was about it. He didn't seem to care who knew.

"You have to understand," Ike continued. "I was all about condoms. And safe sex. And monogamy. I hooked up with guys, but it was mostly with an eye towards finding The One."

"So what happened?" Bill asked cautiously. He had been avoiding the whole *How did you get infected?* conversation. He wanted to know, simply because he wanted to know everything about Ike. It was part of the man he loved. But by asking the question, he knew it would then be his turn to tell.

"Well, I fell in love," Ike sighed. "I thought he was The One. I trusted him enough to stop using condoms. For a time, it was so wonderful. Working in AIDS prevention, I now have a better understanding why so many men give up on safe sex. I'd never felt the intimacy of skin-to-skin contact. I grew up in the age of AIDS. I'd been beaten over the head with all the warnings since I was a child. I'd never had sex without a condom – *ever*. Then there it was for the first time, without an artificial barrier. No plastic bag that everyone is supposed to pretend feels good. Without condoms, I couldn't believe how different it was. I thought, *This is sex?* All of a sudden I knew why sonnets were written about it."

Bill took a large gulp of coffee. He knew what Ike meant. He'd lived every waking moment of his adult life in pursuit of what Ike meant. He wanted to grab Ike by the hand and race back to his apartment right now and create the sensation he described.

"But I'd asked the wrong question," Ike said flatly. "I asked him if he was negative. He said yes. And you know, to this day, I truly believe he was being completely honest. He'd been tested and in his heart of hearts he thought he was not infected. As we made love, it was with a clear conscience. He never lied to me."

"I don't understand," said Bill.

"He was positive. He just didn't know it. His test was too old. And here I was, with a degree in social work dedicating my life to stopping the spread of AIDS, and I took the fool's bargain. And lost. I was so ashamed."

"But he had been tested. And came out negative. I'm not sure what else you could have done?"

"I've played this out a million times in my head, believe me. I should have insisted on monogamy and safe sex for six months until we both got tested together and received the results *together*. It's the only way. Over at Project Inform, the message is: protect yourself. Men are responsible for their own health. They can't blame anyone else. The other guy might be telling the truth when he says he believes he's negative. The problem is, he might believe the wrong thing."

"And positive guys who don't say anything?" The words just spilled out of Bill's mouth. He wasn't sure why he said it – something triggered in his head. He panicked. Would Ike hear it as a confession?

"I used to be militant about that," Ike shook his head. "Pure evil. Guys who know they are positive and have unprotected sex without disclosing. It used to make me so angry."

"Used to?"

"Then I had a client explain it to me. I'm not the only one who spent the last twenty years being hammered with the safe sex message. Everyone knows the risks they take by fucking without condoms, especially here in San Francisco. My client explained that it's become an unspoken language between sex partners. No mention of condoms is the same as confessing you're positive. Any guy who says he barebacks is really saying he's HIV positive. It's become as simple as that."

Bill said nothing. What Ike described was the philosophy Bill had lived by for the past ten years.

"But it's risky," Ike continued. "I pity the guy who's not clued into the semantics. That's why we created the *Watch Your Back* campaign at the Project. With the rules of the game always evolving, it's the only foolproof way."

Bill took Ike's hand. "You're not a fool for what happened. I hate the way a disease has been used to demonize and shame people. Like a virus has morality?"

"I'm okay. It was devastating at first, especially being the executive director of an AIDS prevention group," Ike sighed. "At least no one can accuse me now of making a living off of *other* people's misery."

Bill looked across the street at Beck's. He wondered how many of the men there tonight were playing the dangerous game of *Don't Ask, Don't Tell*. It wasn't his business to judge them, or make decisions for them. Ike was right – these days men had to watch their backs. They had to be responsible for their own protection…from AIDS, discrimination, and hatemongers like the Reverend Willy Warrant—

"And you?"

"Me?"

"You've never told me how you got infected."

"It was a long time ago," Bill whispered, wishing Ike would keep his voice down. "Back when I was in college in Louisiana."

"God. So young! That must have been terrifying."

"I..." Bill stopped. "Can we talk about it another time? It's something that I have trouble, uh..."

"Hey," Ike squeezed Bill's hand. "No problem. We don't have to talk about it ever, if you don't want to. I'm not here to bring back bad memories."

Bill looked into Ike's blue eyes. How could anyone be so understanding? He wished he could be as good a man as Ike. With all he had done, was it too late?

"I don't want to keep things from you," Bill said. "I really don't. Some day I'll tell you everything. It's just harder for me to be as open about everything as you. Maybe it's because I've never had the support around me that you obviously have. When I was diagnosed, I felt all alone in the world. There was no one there for me."

"What about your family? You have six brothers and sisters. And your mother! You couldn't talk to any of them?" Ike looked appalled.

His mother. Bill didn't have to wonder what she'd be doing right now. It was Saturday night in Baker, Louisiana. She'd be drunk on homemade daiquiris with her "lady friends" smoking Pall Malls and all complaining about the men who'd left them. His dad died when Bill was just ten, leaving Mom to raise and manage the entire brood. Five boys and two girls, with Bill invisible in the middle. Mom's drinking had started when Dad was still alive. It was always worse around the holidays. He remembered one New Year's when he was no older than five. All the kids were pulled out of their beds and plopped in front of the TV to watch the ball drop in *"Jew* York City." When midnight finally came, his parents went crazy and started banging the top of the set because an old episode of *The Tonight Show* was on. New Year's Eve had already happened the night before. They'd missed it because they'd both been on a 48-hour bender.

Then there was Christmas when he was seven.

All the kids raced downstairs that morning to see what Santa had brought them. Mom and Dad were passed out in the living room, a near-empty bottle of Gilbey's still sat on the ring-stained coffee table. Remarkably, they both woke up in fairly good moods as the kids hunted down their presents under the tree and ripped off the wrapping. Maria and Sheila beamed over matching Barbie Dolls. Frank couldn't believe he'd finally gotten a BB gun, and Dad proudly explained that it was a rite of passage for his eldest son. Four-year-old Sean loved his fire truck with sound effects mimicking a siren and the squawking voices of the dispatch radio. Baby Donald gummed his new teething rings. Bill looked everywhere for a gift under the tree with his name on it. The excitement of the moment was quickly replaced by shallow breaths of panic.

"Momma," Bill said. "I think Santa forgot me."

"What the fu—?" Mom said as she peeled herself off the couch. She bent down under the tree and started searching. She pushed gifts aside, but as her frustration grew she began throwing them against the wall. Bill put his arms over his head and started crying.

"For Christ sakes! Stop crying! You'll grow up to be a God-damn sissy," she yelled. "Sam! Tell him to stop crying."

"Stop crying," Dad deadpanned.

"Jesus!" Exasperated, Mom flopped back down on the couch. There was no gift under the tree for Bill.

She pointed at Sean. "You!"

"What I'd do?" Sean said defensively.

"That there truck," Mom continued to point. "That there is for the two of you to share."

Bill couldn't believe it. Share? No one had ever been asked to share in the history of Christmas. "Mom. That's not for me. That's a toy for a four year old!" The tears now started to come faster.

"Stop your crying, mister. You sit the fuck down and share that truck with your brother," Mom shouted. Then her expression changed to one of complete self-satisfaction with her decision, like she was Solomon and had just found a brilliant solution to the problem. She nodded her head in agreement with herself. "Santa said so."

Bill sat down next to Sean. How could Santa forget him? How could Santa want him to share with his kid brother? He reached over to touch the shiny chrome on the truck's ladder.

Sean seethed, "No! Mine!" Then in a whisper for only Bill to hear. "Sissy."

A loud clinking sound brought Bill out of the memory. It was Ike banging his fork on the side of the café au lait cup.

"Hey daydream boy, didn't you hear what I asked? What about your family? Why couldn't you turn to them in your hour of need? I've always heard that Southern families are so warm and loving, especially in Louisiana."

"Not all of them," Bill tried to force a smile.

"Well, then we'll make our own family," Ike said as he put his arm around Bill. "Even if it's just you and me."

"I'd like that."

"Besides, there's no reason to dredge up all this depressing talk about HIV. Didn't I tell you the good news?" Ike laughed.

"What?"

"It's silly, really."

"What?"

"Well, the funniest thing happened yesterday at the doctor," Ike said. "I go in to get the results of my regular blood tests, and he tells me that suddenly I'm *negative*. We had a good giggle about that. It was the weirdest thing. All of **my** tests came back with results that showed I'd never been exposed to HIV. *Ever.*"

"Are you serious?" Bill thought of the same strange conversation he'd had with Dr. Greene. He'd never heard of labs making such egregious errors, and now here was the second one in less than a week.

"No. I mean, yes. Oh, come on." Ike gave Bill a little shove. "It's just a stupid mistake by the lab. I have to go back in again on Monday. No big deal. Still, it was pretty hilarious at the time. You should have seen the look on the doctor's face. I think he thought someone had punked him."

9

Quif had attended the CODIS meeting only once before. The Collége de Direction Scientifique met six times a year, but Pasteur staff usually only went if they had a pet project up for discussion. As the Institute's scientific management oversight, the chairman and board members set the budgets and agenda for research. Two years earlier Quif spoke about a devastating outbreak of Ebola in the Congo. She remembered being impressed at the board's swift decision to intervene.

Surely they'll act even faster this time.

She sat far in the back of the room watching a colleague lecture on the latest dire predictions about the spread of AIDS in southern Africa. She grew impatient as the man rattled off the latest predicted death tolls. Every moment he grabs the attention of the board, another soul will die. Perhaps needlessly. What she had to say would change the course of the pandemic.

She scanned the faces of the board members. She knew most of them, but didn't recognize the man at the far end of the panel, the one with the slicked back snow-white hair.

"Who is that?" Quif leaned over and whispered to Benoit.

He stood up slightly from his chair for a clear view. "The one in the dark suit?"

"*Oui.*"

"You obviously don't watch much television."

Quif gave Benoit a perplexed stare.

"He's that obnoxious American television preacher. A friend of their silly president. The Reverend Willy Warrant."

"A religious leader? Sitting up on the panel with the board?" Quif was incredulous. "What the hell is he doing here?"

"He's hardly the only one. Look over there." Benoit pointed to the back of the auditorium on the opposite side. There in all his resplendent scarlet garbs was someone Quif instantly recognized. Cardinal Umberto Uccelli, the Vatican's infamous muscle. He'd become a hated figure in much of Europe with his inflammatory hardline comments about divorce. He publicly advocated for the church to bring back excommunication for divorced members who remarried. His statements were a shock to millions of casual Catholics who resented being branded unsalvageable sinners by a church that had spent decades covering up assaults by pedophile priests. Uccelli, nicknamed "the Uzi," was scorned in the press, his photo splashed across the front pages of newspapers. His face became synonymous with a new spike in criticism that the Church should stay out of people's bedrooms.

"Theologians," Quif moaned. "We do not need their voodoo. Why would Pasteur even allow their kind inside this room? It is an abomination to everything we stand for."

Benoit gently placed his hand on Quif's thigh. It felt warm and assuring, making her feel somehow calmed by his touch. In the weeks they'd been buried in their work, she'd grown more comfortable with him. He'd scaled back his juvenile advances, acting more like a man than a boy. She accepted his caress, hoping it would distract from the agitation she felt over what was about to happen.

"My beautiful Quif, you really do work too hard," Benoit said. "You don't even have time to keep up with the news. The Cardinal and the Reverend are here today sitting in as representatives for their governments. The board is finalizing a plan to fight AIDS in Africa. The Church and the Americans are putting up nearly a billion dollars to get anti-retroviral drugs to the millions infected with HIV."

"It's about time," Quif whispered bitterly. "They have blood on their hands for not doing it sooner. They had the money and resources for years, but only now they act?"

"Politics," Benoit sighed. "Pasteur is helping broker the final arrangements. The money comes with strings attached, of course. Their president says America will only help if Christian missionaries are allowed to accompany the drugs and teach the African people about abstinence as the only sure way to prevent the spread of the disease. No doubt they'll bring their Bibles along and try to convert the tribes."

"Awful."

"And the Pope wants to be sure that condoms are banned as part of the project, since the Church is against any form of birth control."

"Abstinence? No condoms? That is not practical. It is a recipe for genocide," Quif said in disgust. "All because one group thinks it has the moral high ground over another? While they plot their ridiculous agendas, millions will die. And where are the drug companies in all of this?"

"Sitting over there," Benoit said as he pointed to two rows of suits seated near the front. "They've made it clear they're not doing anything unless they get paid."

Criminals, all of them, Quif thought. For all their high and mighty pronouncements of superiority, the American government, the religious zealots, the Pope – they are all the ones who are truly morally bankrupt. To sit in judgment and let people die when they can stop the deaths was no different than committing the killings themselves. The drug companies were greedy crooks, but at least they made no pretense about it.

She'd never thought of herself as an idealist, but by comparison she'd happily accept that label. Looking around the room at the hypocrites all lined up to try to get their fair share from Africa's death rattle, the anger she felt confirmed that she was about to do the right thing. It was a brash move. Obnoxious. She'd be doing an end run around all the checks and balances the Institut demanded.

Yet she had no choice. It was *her* moral obligation.

"*Pardon,*" Quif spoke loudly. She gently brushed Benoit's hand from her lap and stood up. "*Pardon!*"

The presenter stopped speaking, the room fell silent, and everyone turned to look in her direction.

"May I have your attention, *please?*" She walked to the center of the room to stand in front of the board.

"Doctor Melikian, isn't it?" The elderly board chairman said as he looked down at his notes.

"*Oui.*"

"I don't have you scheduled to present today." "I know. But what I have to say is urgent." Quif's voice cracked, her nervousness making its way to the surface. The auditorium with its high ceilings and soaring columns was intimidating, even more so with so few people allowed inside. This was possibly the most exclusive club in medicine. She could hear the echo of her own voice.

"It will have to wait, Madame." The chairman's face became stern. "You are not on the agenda today. You can apply to speak at the next meeting in two months."

"With all due respect, sir, I cannot wait. Now is the time I will speak, and now is the time that all of you will listen. Here you are talking about the millions who are dying in Africa. You say you want to help them. What I am about to tell you will save their lives."

The board members murmured to each other.

"The little gal's got spunk, I'll give her that," the Reverend Willy Warrant said to his translator, loud enough for the entire chamber to hear.

"Reverend." Quif put her hands in prayer and touched them to her lips, her mind working quickly to grab the opening. She spoke in English. "Do you believe in miracles?"

"I do," the Reverend said without irony or hesitation.

"Then I have a miracle to report here today."

"That will be enough," the chairman chided in his deep baritone. "You know the rules, doctor. You cannot disturb our work with this nonsense. I must ask you to leave the auditorium at once."

"Hold on, hold on, hold on." The Reverend Warrant spoke with the animated cadence of one of his sermons. "I believe the little lady spoke of miracles. I for one would like to hear what she has to say. And I know *my president*," he emphasized strongly, "would be very disappointed if he found out that spiritual matters were dismissed without a fair hearing."

"My dear Reverend," the chairman said as he peered over the top of his reading glasses. "As you can see, this is a private meeting. Not a town hall. The doors are locked and our deliberations are secret and confidential. We take these precautions because we have very serious, urgent *scientific* matters to attend. We will not tolerate distractions."

"Are you saying that *God* is a...what did you say...a *distraction*?" The Reverend raised his voice.

"Well, no, of course not." The chairman retreated.

"Then I suggest you give this here doctor a few minutes to tell us about a miracle. I for one, and *my president*, and the very generous taxpayers of the United States of America, would greatly appreciate your indulgence."

The chairman pursed his lips. Without saying a word he gestured toward Quif, giving her the floor.

"Now doctor, are you going to tell us about how you have come to know Our Savior?" The Reverend smiled widely.

"Well...yes," said Quif. "I have, in fact, met our savior." Quif turned to the auditorium. "Benoit!"

Benoit raced from the back of the room, a stack of reports in his arms. He quickly placed one in front of each of the board members.

"Mr. Chairman, board members and...the Reverend. Please forgive me for the rude interruption. You will soon understand my urgent need to speak. While you have been meeting for the past hour, more than 700 people died who could have been saved."

Quif paused for a moment to gather her thoughts. She'd rehearsed her speech many times over the past few days, although it would be more of a challenge now to suddenly switch to English. She cleared her throat.

"Three months ago I traveled to Armenia. I went there to study what was feared to be pollution from an old abandoned oil refinery that is scheduled to reopen. I took all the usual blood and environmental samples expecting to find rampant illness. I *wanted* to find contamination and death. That is my job.

"Instead, I found *life*. A new virus." Quif paused for a moment. She noted a few of the board members flipping through the pages of the report, appearing rattled at what they read. Others continued to stare at her, their faces revealing their disdain for the interruption.

"On the site of the refinery was an abandoned laboratory. It was left behind by the Soviets when they pulled out. It did not look like a geological facility. Instead, it looked like a medical lab where research and experiments were carried out, possibly on human beings. I knew it made no sense for medical research to be done at an oil refinery. The fact that it was in one of the remotest parts of the world made me fear something heinous was at work. The lab had been robbed and vandalized, but I managed to find remnants of the experiments that had been done there. Blood samples, petri dishes, old test tubes and files. I sent it all back here to the Institut where it was analyzed, checked and rechecked by my colleague, lab specialist Benoit DuCharme. My worst fears were realized.

"The Soviets were doing experiments *on people*. They injected the local villagers with living organisms to see what effect they would have on their health. There were no safety protocols. From the translations of the documents I brought back, the results were barbaric. Many died. The local population was decimated."

"Organisms?" The chairman interrupted. "What type of organisms?"

"Phage, Mr. Chairman," Quif said solemnly. "Phage."

"You mean bacteriophage?" Board member Dr. Helen Mangeur interrupted. Mangeur, a director at Pasteur, was well known for her high opinion of herself. Whenever Quif had spoken with her in the past, she always felt like she was being addressed as a first year medical school student. "Félix d'Hérelle made that discovery back in 1917, right here at Pasteur. You really should do your homework, Dr. Melikian. There's no news here."

"The Soviets have been experimenting with phage for years," François LaFontaine, another board member, chimed in. "Germs that are trained to kill other germs, so to speak. It's a primitive concept, but it works. The Soviets thought it could be a cheaper way to fight common infections. They started fiddling around with it back in the time of Stalin. Once drugs like penicillin became inexpensive and widely available, phage research was abandoned. There have been attempts to restart it here and there because of concerns about antibiotic resistance, but it's really just a weak alternative. Last I heard they were using phage in the Republic of Georgia to treat gastrointestinal infection. Really, Dr. Melikian, you are wasting our time by acting like this is some great discovery."

"Stop! I do not need to be lectured like some school girl." Quif scolded back, then continued with a more determined tone. "I am not finished. I agree that I would be wasting your time if this was only about bacteriophage. It is not. If you look at the report placed in front of you, you will see that I am talking about something different. The Soviets found a way to create *viral* phage."

"Indeed," the chairman whispered. He skeptically flipped through his copy of the report.

"As you all know, bacteria and viruses work differently in the human body. A virus splices in on the DNA level. A virus is remarkably adaptable, making it so much harder to eradicate from the body. Killing bacteria is like shooting at a target. By comparison, we cannot see the target of a typical virus. And when we think we do, it moves, changes or hides.

"The Soviets have created a virus that can kill another virus. It is able to mutate like a retrovirus at the RNA level. It *learns* to seek out and destroy any other virus it determines is doing harm to the body. Hepatitis. The common cold. *AIDS*."

"How do you know this?" A voice called out from the back of the room. Quif turned to face a woman standing in the audience. She wore an American sports team baseball cap, her blonde hair pulled back in a ponytail. The casual dressed-down look was probably meant to obscure her identity, but there was no mistaking one of the biggest celebrities on the planet. It was the pop music icon Milana. *What is she doing here?* Quif lost her train of thoughts. She remembered recently seeing a picture of Milana on the cover *Le Monde*. She was part of the huge Live 8 concert to bring attention to the problems of Africa. Quif recalled thinking how ironic it was that after a career of promoting promiscuity in her music, the aging star had suddenly made the fight against AIDS in Africa her personal crusade. *She must be well into her forties now, but she is still so beauti—*

"Dr. Melikian, please continue," the chairman intoned, his eyes never leaving the pages of the handout.

Quif did a double take for another look at Milana. "I met the survivors," she hesitated, then got back into the rhythm of her speech.

"I took their blood. They had no signs of any diseases. Nothing. Statistically, that is not possible. Not even one type of cancer. The viral phage the Soviets created worked. The proof is in the patients."

"You have considerable gaps in your research here, doctor," the chairman said, his voice now infused with restrained professorial curiosity. "You have documents that show the Soviet's plans for viral phage, and you have the end result. This analysis of the phage in the patients' blood is very impressive. What you are missing is everything in between. How did they make this leap? It defies logic to go from simple bacteriophage to the type of miraculous *viral* phage you're talking about."

"I agree. We do not know exactly how they did it. What I have pieced together so far is that they found a way to speed up mutation and evolution. The Soviets *forced* mutation until they created this super-virus."

"They forced mutation," the chairman asked. "How?"

"I believe they used the best possible laboratory on earth – the only place we know that has all the tools and ingenuity to defeat a virus, knowledge developed over countless millennia that we still barely understand. I am talking about the human body itself. For all the wonders of modern medicine and our miraculous drugs, the truth remains that the best we have been able to do is provoke the body to heal itself. The Soviets used the ultimate incubator. I think they used the immune systems of the local people. Trial and error. They kept pushing until they found a person whose natural immunity could be mutated into this viral phage. They shrunk hundreds of lifetimes of evolution into a matter of decades."

"Evolution? Trial and error?" The Reverend Warrant asked. "What type of error?"

"People were murdered by these experiments, Reverend," Quif said. "There were no safety protocols. The Armenians, like they have been for more than a century, were considered expendable. It was like a death camp."

"Those Godless bastards," The Reverend shook his head.

"If this phage is such a miracle," the chairman jumped in, ignoring The Reverend, "then why did the Russians leave it behind?"

"I can only guess that they did not know they succeeded," Quif said. "The scientists shut down the operation and abandoned the lab when the old Soviet Empire collapsed and they stopped receiving their paychecks. They knew the last people they injected with their phage did not die – the elderly villagers I met – but the Soviets fled before they saw the long-term results."

"What about side effects?" Dr. Mangeur looked down at Quif. "Injecting a live organism into people is a dangerous business. I don't like it."

"With all due respect, doctor, the patients have already survived for at least fifteen years. That is long enough for any side effects to show up. I cannot find any. And while I agree it needs to be studied, I also know there are millions in Africa who will not live another ten years without a miracle like this. More than eight thousand people die each day from AIDS. Are we to deny them?"

The auditorium became silent. Quif knew it was best to stop talking, and she watched as the dozens of brilliant minds processed the significance of what she had said. For ten minutes, no one spoke a word. The only sounds in the great chamber were the wisps of pages turning as the board members consumed the report. They squinted and shook their heads. The arrogance was gone from Dr. Mangeur's face, replaced with astonishment.

"What you have here is the potential to eliminate dozens of diseases," the chairman said. His usual professional distain was suddenly replaced with an emotion Quif had never seen in the old man – enthusiasm. It was clear he struggled to manage it. "A virus that can hunt down and kill other deadly viruses. Healthcare as we know it will be transformed. Instead of chronic illnesses and endless expensive medical care, you're talking about *cure*. Actual cure. We *must* find these scientists and get them to share their research."

"That won't be easy," Benoit stood up from his place in the audience. "These are killers. They murdered countless innocent people in their work. Are you going to give them the Nobel Prize, or put them on trial for crimes against humanity?"

Quif looked to Benoit and nodded. He had come to her aid.

"With what's at stake here, young man, medical ethics might have to take a back seat," the chairman said. "Finding cures inevitably puts lives at risk. With each new drug that's developed, some patients get the treatment while others are given a placebo for control. Some die. We long ago accepted the inherent cruelty of this approach, knowing there would be losses for the sake of science and the overall benefit of mankind. Like when we put our feelings aside and welcomed Nazi scientists back into our ranks after the War."

"Maybe, but not *Mengele*," Benoit said, referring to the reviled concentration camp physician.

The chairman frowned.

"Look, this wasn't just some blind study of an antibiotic," Benoit stood his ground. "These patients were slaughtered. Just read the transcripts of the research and you will see how people suffered the most painful and horrible deaths. Some were eaten alive…from the inside! The scientists knew what they were doing. They were careful to never use their real names in any of the paperwork we found. They signed everything with numerical codes. We haven't found a single name to pursue in what we've discovered so far."

The chairman looked to Quif. "Based on the passionate words of your associate, I'm assuming you have a different idea for how to approach this."

"Yes, Mr. Chairman. Please turn to page fifty in the report. We propose that a team of investigators be allowed to return to the site of the lab. Not just myself, but a much larger crew. My first visit was just cursory. We need to go back and turn that place upside down. This time nothing can be overlooked. It is possible that traces of the pure phage could be sitting somewhere in an old syringe, slide, or dish. That is all we need to help us create more."

"What about in the blood of the survivors you found?"

"We must study them, too. We need to see if the phage infection can be transmitted from person to person. If it is like any other virus, blood and bodily fluids might be the perfect host. We cannot forget – this phage is a living organism. In many ways, it is the same as HIV – a powerful deadly force inside the body, but it quickly dies when exposed to the outside world."

"Bodily fluids?" The Reverend scowled. "What type of bodily

fluids? Are you saying this *cure* is transmitted by *fornication?*"

"I...I do not know," Quif stammered, thrown off by the strange question. She had never thought of it this way before.

The chairman placed his finger on a page in Quif's report. "Helicopters?"

"There is no time to waste. As you see in my proposal, I would like the team assembled by next week."

The board members conferred for only a few minutes before giving their approval. Benoit came over and took Quif's hand as they stood together to hear the verdict. Quif nodded to Benoit, grateful to feel his firm grip. They were in this together.

"You've got your helicopters, Dr. Melikian," the chairman finally spoke. "And you've got me, too. I'm going with you. Meet me in my office in one hour."

"*Merci,*" Quif said. In the excitement she embarrassingly tilted her head in a slight bow.

The chairman canceled the rest of the session, making it clear that CODIS and Pasteur needed to act immediately on news of the phage. With all the force of his powerful voice, he reminded everyone that they were never to speak publicly of what they'd learned.

"A discovery like this could lead to great..." The chairman paused. He appeared to grasp for the right word. Then he looked at the Reverend Willie Warrant and continued, "...misunderstanding."

As the meeting broke up and she walked out the back of the auditorium, Quif passed Cardinal Uccelli. He had a copy of the report in his lap as he furiously scribbled into a small black notebook.

Why should he be so interested? Quif thought. After all, this is now in the hands of science. God has nothing to do with it.

10

"Fabulous!"

"Dr. Greene?" Bill Soileau didn't expect to get a phone call from his doctor at work. He got up from his desk and shut his office door. "Uh, what can I do for you?"

"Good morning, Bill. Look, I hate to bother you, but I just got your latest lab results."

"And?"

"I really don't know how to explain it."

"What do you mean?"

"Well, baby boy, for the second time in a row we have a screw up by the lab. I'm as embarrassed as someone wearing white shoes at a cotillion after Labor Day, but you're going to have to come in and have them done again. I'm sorry."

"What do you mean screwed up?" Bill thought of telling the doctor about Ike's lab tests. Maybe there was something wrong with the entire lab system.

"Once again, I got the results of someone who's HIV negative. Perfect health. Not to be a sour puss, honey, but this just can't be you."

"You sure?"

"Hello?" The doctor tapped on the receiver. "Do we have a bad connection or something? Is this Bill Soileau I'm talking to?"

A strange thought entered the back of Bill's mind. What if these weren't just coincidental blood test errors. What if something else was going on? He knew the idea was absurd. If there was one thing he knew about HIV, it was that he'd be infected until his last breath. It remained a death sentence, even if it took longer to be carried out these days. Still, he couldn't deny that he'd felt physically invigorated lately. Maybe his body was learning to fight back in some new way.

"Listen, I would love to have my patients miraculously cured. I really would. But this is just another mistake by the lab. That's all."

"But, Dr. Greene, I have to tell you. I feel *incredible*. I mean, I have this non-stop energy pulsing through my body. The last few months I've been like a new man. Look, I know this is going to sound ridiculous, but has anyone…you know…"

"What?"

"Has there ever been a case where it, uh, went away?"

"You mean a cure?"

"Yeah. I mean, I've heard of cases of cancer where the person woke up one morning and the cancer was gone. And no one could explain how it happened. Has anything like that ever happened with," Bill whispered, "*this?*"

"Doll, have you been reading that Deepak Chopra crap?"

11

Quif gazed over the busy tarmac. She breathed in the moment. Dozens of white coats darted back and forth from the luggage trams to the helicopters. They shouted out the names of the items they carried to a supervisor who checked off a list on his clipboard as the cargo was transferred onto the choppers. If not for the white uniforms, it might look like an army preparing for an invasion. In a way, it was an army. Her army. Her invasion.

The workers at Yeveran's Zvartnots International Airport weren't sure how to deal with the onslaught at first. The World Health Organization and NATO had flown in the six NH90 helicopters ahead of time to rendezvous with the chartered jet from Paris. The NATO soldiers insisted on being armed, claiming it was their standard operating procedure. Quif could see how the small machine guns the soldiers carried unnerved the staff at the airport's cargo center, probably because the weapons were too reminiscent of the bad old days of Soviet occupation.

"Dr. Melikian?"

Quif turned to see a NATO officer behind her. She was never very good at recalling the insignias of rank, but she thought he might be a colonel. He was definitely French.

"Yes. Are we ready to go?"

"It's not that," the man said. "There's a problem."

~

They spotted the plume of smoke spiraling up into the clouds from fifty kilometers away, as soon as they cleared the peak of Mount Aramazd. Benoit clutched Quif's hand as they stared in disbelief. The chairman held onto the seat straps as he had the entire flight, with his eyes closed, enveloped in a minor state of panic. He'd told everyone he hated the idea of taking a helicopter. They terrified him.

"Do you think it was an industrial accident?" Quif yelled to the colonel, straining to make herself heard over the din of the chopper's swooping blades.

"We don't know yet. I think we'll have a better idea soon. The ground team that drove in the trucks said the entire place was fully engulfed when they got there this morning. There was no way for them to get close enough to tell how it started." The colonel gestured to the horizon. "It looks like mostly smoke now, so it should be burned off enough to give us a look."

"I do not understand," Quif shouted. "The refinery was not operational yet. There should not be any fuel. What is burning?"

The colonel shrugged.

The helicopter landed on a barren plain of dried, cracked mud nearly a kilometer from the smoldering plant. The pilot said he wanted to be sure the aircraft was far enough away to avoid falling debris if there was an explosion. Quif and Benoit helped the elderly chairman off the chopper and began hiking toward what remained of the refinery. The colonel led the way, flanked by two armed soldiers. Moments later two NATO jeeps emerged from around the south side of the compound, racing out to collect the team.

"Thank goodness," the chairman wheezed. "I don't think I could have walked all that way."

By the time they arrived near the perimeter of the plant the smoke had dissipated to a thin trickle, a dramatic change from what they'd witnessed from the air only minutes earlier.

"I think it's safe now," one soldier said to the colonel. "It's been dying down for the last hour. I don't think there's much left to burn."

Quif tried to get her mind around the scene before her. What had once been a monstrosity of industry, towering at least ten stories into the sky, was now a wreck of twisted, melted metals reduced to a heap no more than twenty meters high. She took a handkerchief from her pocket and held it over her mouth and nose. The acrid stench that repulsed her on her first visit was now many times stronger. It made her eyes tear.

Or maybe the tears came from the emotions she could feel surfacing. The place was a complete loss. If anything survived in the underground lab, it would now take months to excavate. How many thousands of innocent souls would perish in that time? Would her sister Natara be among them? Worse, the fire meant the greatest medical discovery to end the pain and miserable deaths of millions might *never* be found. How could such a thing happen? The refinery had been idle for so long, and now it suddenly bursts into flames?

"Doctor," the colonel said after being briefed by the drivers. "I think you should all come with me."

They boarded the jeep and drove around to the far side of the plant to the site of the underground lab. As they turned the corner, Quif gasped. The little square building that once served as the entrance to the underground labyrinth was no longer there. In its place was a hole the size of a Parisian city block. She stood up in her seat, steadying herself with the rollover bar, but she still could not see how deep the crater went.

"Is this the location of the laboratory?" the colonel asked.

"I do not understand." Quif wanted to be strong, but her voice cracked. "What could cause something like this?"

The jeep came to an abrupt stop. Quif's chest slammed against the roll bar. She lost her grip for a moment, but steadied herself in time to keep from falling.

"An explosion. Do you see how the concrete is torn at the edges?" The colonel pointed to large slabs of cement turned upward around the rim of the crevice. His demeanor was serious, the tone of his voice impressively controlled. He acted as if he saw destruction like this everyday. "That means this wasn't because the refinery caught on fire. Whatever happened started right here at this spot. Debris shot up from underground, ripping a hole in the earth. Maybe a kiloton of blast. I'm guessing it was HMX."

"HMX?" Quif stared at the immense wasteland of cement and metal. Gone. It was all gone. The hole went far deeper than where she'd stood in the lab. There was nothing there now except a haze of lingering soot.

"High Melting eXplosive. Very dangerous stuff. Anything in that lab would have been completely incinerated."

"Who would do such a thing?"

"Whoever it was, it was certainly no accident," said the colonel. "This was the work of professionals. Someone wanted to make sure that lab was obliterated."

"Colonel, this HMX – is the smoke toxic?" Benoit asked. "There's so much of it in the air. There's even a plume over there." He pointed to a dark cloud that hovered on the horizon to the east.

"What the hell?" The colonel said as he turned and squinted into the distance.

"What is it?" Quif asked.

"That's not from this explosion. The wind is blowing west. That's a different fire."

~

The helicopter touched down just outside the mouth of the cave. Wisps of smoke drifted out, the sign of a fire dying somewhere inside.

"Tire tracks," the colonel said as he studied imprints in the ground. "Transport trucks, from the look of it. And hundreds of –"

"Transporting what?" Quif interrupted. "Who would bring something all the way out here just to set it on fire?"

The colonel shook his head slowly, his face grim. He signaled for two soldiers now wearing full chemical warfare protection suits and gas masks to head in.

Quif waited by the chopper with the colonel, the chairman and Benoit. As she studied the stone entrance, she suddenly felt light-headed. Was the smoke making her dizzy? No, that wasn't it. The wind was blowing the other way. She leaned back against the fuselage to keep her balance.

Then it hit her. She knew these caves. They were home to one of the horrors of her childhood bedtime stories – the entrance to the underground caverns where Armenian men were slaughtered during the genocide! The same caves where innocents were herded inside and asphyxiated in the world's first gas chamber. Quif put her hand to her mouth, suppressing a gag of sickness in the back of her throat. What twist of fate brought her here? This was supposed to be the greatest day of her life – a day that would lead to saving the lives of millions. Now this?

Her eyes blurred and she envisioned the handsome faces of the Armenian men, most of them really still just boys, as they were sent into these caves ninety years ago. The horror they must have felt. Did they know? Or was it only when there was no more oxygen to breathe that they finally realized what was happening? The will to survive would have forced them to try to find any means of escape. Without air, their desperate clawing of rock walls would have only lasted a few minutes. She'd heard that decades later, historians dedicated to fighting debunkers and documenting the forgotten genocide would find remnants of fingernails still stuck in the stone.

Quif felt something snap. In an instant the overwhelming grief from seeing the caves was replaced with an even stronger feeling. *Rage.* Where does the evil needed to commit such atrocity come from? In her work for Pasteur she'd seen too much of it. Darfur. Uzbekistan. The Philippines. In tracking outbreaks of disease around the globe, the machination of men all too often had a hand in the suffering. They were complicit by turning their backs on misery, or setting in motion events without concern for the consequences. Refugee camps were epicenters for illness and death. She'd heard too many stories from weeping women clutching their dead babies that just months earlier had been happy, healthy, and well fed. Then one day armed thugs showed up in their village to tell them it wasn't their home anymore. A child's life snuffed out, all because of a conflict where most of those fighting couldn't even recall how it started.

The Turks who killed the Armenian men and boys. The bomb that destroyed the lab and the millions of lives its secret would have saved. The anger grew to boiling as the images pounded Quif's mind. *Lives lost. So many lives lost.*

One of the soldiers emerged from the tunnel. He took off his gas mask. It dropped from his grasp and fell onto the ground, as if he no longer had the strength to hold it. He put one arm on the side of the chopper and bent over. Quif saw pain in the man's face.

"Are you okay?" Quif asked as she rushed to the soldier's side. He was young, like so many soldiers. Not too long ago he was a just a boy.

"They're dead," the man said. He was crying. "All of them."

"Dead? Who's dead?" She turned the soldier toward her. He was weeping like a child now, unable to catch his breath. She grabbed him by both arms and shook him. "Tell me!"

"Doctor..." the colonel started to speak but his words faded out.

Dead. All of them. Somehow she knew who was dead inside the cave. Their faces flashed in her thoughts. She picked up the soldier's gas mask from the ground and ran toward the entrance of the cave.

"No!" the colonel shouted.

Quif darted into the tunnel, struggling to get the mask over her face. A few meters inside, the ground took a steep slope down. She tumbled hard into the dirt, falling face first, landing on her hands. Her palms throbbed with pain. As she brushed herself off, she stared into the blackness ahead. She wasn't sure where she was going. She stood up and took tentative steps. The light from the entrance behind her dimmed the farther she went. Far in the distance, she caught sight of the other soldier, his flashlight inspecting an area deeper in the cave.

She heard someone behind her. She turned. It was Benoit. He'd grabbed a mask and followed her in.

Unsure of the footing, together they crept slowly up to the flickering light. Even with the mask, the smell was overpowering and eerily familiar – a combination of burned fuel and a nauseating odor Quif had come to know all too well from her journeys to the world's death camps.

"You shouldn't be here," the young soldier barked through his mask.

Quif could only shake her head at what she saw. Benoit ran over to the wall of the cave, lifted up his mask, and vomited.

The mound of bodies was larger than any she'd seen before. There were hundreds piled atop one another, the mass still smoldering. The cadavers were stacked so they would burn easier, not too high and with enough space to allow air to feed the flames. The pyre appeared endless, reaching as far into the cave as she could see in the shaking beam of the soldier's flashlight.

She knelt next to the nearest body. The flesh had been burned away, leaving little remaining but bone. She wondered what type of fuel was used that could be so thorough. She'd seen mass graves where bodies were burned to try to stave off the spread of disease. None looked like this. Human flesh, filled with water, was not this easily dismissed. She looked at a skull. The mouth was shut. At least that meant this victim was likely already dead before the flames consumed – there was no sign of screaming in agony in those final moments.

Bits of clothing, jewelry and shoes somehow still survived. How could flesh be consumed by the flames, and these objects weren't destroyed? It didn't make sense. She spotted a small, ornate crucifix in the debris. A silver image of Christ, his mouth slightly ajar. It was the one that belonged to the old woman who persuaded the others to help Quif with her blood samples.

Heesoos Kreesdos mér Purgee'chuh.

Holy Savior, Jesus Christ.

The local villagers.

Quif closed her eyes. More than anyone, these people knew the ghastly history of these caves. As Armenians, they grew up hearing the same terrifying stories she knew from her childhood. It was a legacy shared by all Armenians – tell the tales, remember the holocaust, imprint it in your very being. Do whatever is necessary so you never forget – never allow others to make the genocide disappear from history. As a people, they'd pledged to be the living keepers of the truth. If all the books and documents were destroyed, what happened to the Armenians would still survive *in them* and the stories they would pass from generation to generation. The truth had to live on, so that evil like it would never be repeated.

It *had* happened again, in this very same place. Quif's body convulsed when she thought of the terror the men and women must have felt as they were marched inside. She recalled their cracked, sad faces. Were they gassed first? Did they go quickly? Did they suffer?

Heesoos Kreesdos mér Purgee'chuh.

Christ, where were you to save the Armenians this time?

She could hold it in no longer. The sound of her wails, trapped inside the mask, bounced back at her in damnation.

This was all her fault.

12

"The roses are quite lovely," the florist said. "They just came in this morning."

Quif stared at the deep red petals. They reminded her too much of blood.

"No, I think I will take the sunflowers. A nice bouquet, *s'il vous plaît*."

The yellow flowers might cheer up Natara. If not for her sister, then for herself. Since returning from the atrocity in Armenia, she'd walked the streets of Paris in a fog. She'd dealt with death before, even on a large scale. In Rwanda, she'd seen mass graves. That was different. Those poor souls didn't perish because of something she did.

As she paid for the flowers, she studied the face of the matronly florist. The woman's make-up was impeccable. She wore a perfectly tailored dress with her hair elegantly pulled into a classic twist. As Quif stared, the woman's face blurred into the cracked aged skin and dowdy gray locks of the peasant from the village near the old refinery. The ornate crucifix hung around her neck, now stained in blood. She held out her hand to Quif, pleading.

Why did you murder me?

"What?" Quif said, alarmed.

"I said, here is your change, *Madame*," the florist's coiffed image came back into focus, her hand held out with fifty centimes. She looked bewildered by Quif's rattled demeanor.

For the past month, visions of the massacre haunted Quif. She'd stayed away from Pasteur, with the excuse she needed to care for

Natara. That was true, but she also found it too devastating to face Benoit and the others. She'd set into motion a series of events that ended with the murder of hundreds. She was responsible. How could she ever look anyone in the eye again?

When not tending to Natara, she tried to bury herself in the mundane. She found herself failing at even the simplest tasks. Today she went off to distract herself by running errands in the markets around the corner from her Square de Clignancourt apartment in Montmartre. The *boucherie*, the *fromagerie*, the wine merchant. Maybe she'd prepare a nice dinner tonight, if she had the energy. She'd done much of the same shopping three days earlier, but threw out most of the food after leaving it to rot on the kitchen counter. Natara was too sick now to help and Quif hadn't bothered to put the groceries away.

Maybe it was part of her therapy to recover from the massacre, but Quif found herself needing to be among the living, thrust into busy crowds. It was increasingly difficult to be around Natara. She'd been bedridden for the past week, now exhibiting undeniable signs of HIV wasting. The medications no longer worked and Natara's blood counts revealed she was quickly declining toward end-stage AIDS. Quif had the nurse working full time now to help, but Natara had lost the will to eat. She'd sunk into a near catatonic state. Random bursts of lucidity convinced Quif that care at home was still preferable to a hospital, but her last days were not far away.

The few times Quif checked in with Pasteur, no one still had any solid answers. Benoit was sure the old Soviet scientists had somehow returned and destroyed everything and everyone to cover their murderous tracks – no witnesses left to their savage experiments. The NATO colonel told the CODIS board it could be the work of terrorists, since Armenia and Azerbaijan had been feuding for years over the Nagorno-Karabakh region. For its part, the Armenian government promised a full investigation, but the scope of what happened was clearly out of its league. After so many weeks had passed, there were no leads and no clues.

And no sign of the miracle phage.

Quif climbed the four flights of stairs to her third floor apartment. The elevator was in perfect working order, but Quif didn't feel she deserved such comforts. She closed her eyes and prepared her mind before putting the key in the door.

"*Bonjour!*" she said as she walked in, her visage suddenly transformed into a chipper facade for her audience. She couldn't convey her misery to Natara. That was the last thing her sister needed.

"Quif!" Natara sat with her feet up on the couch. It was a good day. The nurse had been able to get her out of bed. But the television was not on, or music, and Natara had nothing in her lap to read. What had she been doing there? Staring at the wall? Quif made a mental note to tell the nurse to make sure Natara was always mentally engaged in some way. It could help thwart the onslaught of dementia that was inevitable.

"Ah, *ma chérie*. I can see you've had a busy day today," Quif said as she walked over and kissed Natara's cheeks. "You made it all the way out here to the sofa."

"*Oui.*"

"And look what I brought you!" Quif held the bouquet in front of Natara's face.

"What kind are they?" Natara asked. Her eyes wandered to something on the other side of the room.

"They are sunflowers!" Quif enthused. "Surely, you remember sunflowers. When you were a little girl they were your favorite."

"Were they?" Natara's thoughts were suddenly elsewhere.

"Where is Mademoiselle Dominique?"

"Who?"

Quif held her composure, even though she was annoyed. The nurse was always sneaking out, probably to smoke a cigarette since Quif forbade it in the apartment.

The phone rang.

"Quif Melikian à l'appareil," she answered

"I know you're taking time off, but I need you to come in next week." It was the chairman. "We're having a special meeting of the board to discuss the phage disaster and I'd like you to be there."

"Why?" The idea of rehashing everything depressed Quif. The Institut and several government agencies had already debriefed her. Why did she have to relive the tragedy yet again?

"It's a bit of a formality. We're closing the books on it, so to speak. Certainly the investigation of the massacre continues – the American CIA is now on the case. But as far as a medical research project is concerned, I'm afraid it's over. The blood samples you brought back from your first trip aren't viable to grow new phage. I'm sure they'll be fascinating to study for years to come, but...."

"I know." Quif thought of the millions whose certain deaths could have been prevented had they been able to reproduce the phage. She looked over to study her sister's pallid face. Natara would be among those to perish because Quif had failed.

"Doctor, did anyone else have access to that lab besides you?" the chairman asked. "Did anyone else see what you saw?"

"What do you mean?"

"Well, it's a question you're bound to be asked at the inquest."

"Inquest?" Quif didn't understand. "I thought you said it was a meeting of the board."

"It is," the chairman hesitated. "But some on the board are raising some serious concerns about your actions in this matter."

"*My* actions?" Quif felt a little of her urge to fight return. She was guilty enough already about what had happened, but that didn't mean others had the right to convict her of anything. "I am not the one who blew up the refinery. Surely you do not think I had anything to do with the murders of the villagers!"

"Calm down," the chairman sighed. "Of course no one believes you were involved in that. But...."

"What?"

"Well, frankly, you were the one who got everyone stirred up in a fuss about all this. For example, no one ever saw this mysterious underground laboratory...except you."

"*Pardon?*"

"We spoke to the owner of the refinery. This Russian oligarch you mentioned. He claims to have no knowledge of any such lab."

"*Impossible!*"

"And according to the Armenian government investigation – which I'll admit is shoddy at best – no one who ever worked at the refinery has any recollection of such a place ever existing."

Quif's felt the stab of betrayal. *Where is this going?*

"Mr. Chairman, with all due respect, you were there."

"I know, I know," the chairman's voice offered reassurance. "Look, I'm on your side in all of this. Really, I am. But I never saw any lab. All I saw is a hole in the ground."

"And the bodies. Those hundreds of people who were murdered. Did I just imagine that as well?" Quif's voice began to reveal her anger.

"Of course not. No one's accusing you of being delusional."

"Those people were killed to keep this secret from coming out!" She yelled into the phone, her composure now completely gone. Quif looked across the room to Natara, still sitting in her stupor, not reacting to a word of what was being said.

"Stop screaming," the chairman commanded. "Dr. Melikian, belligerence is not going to help you in this matter. I know you're upset. Seeing all those bodies was horrific for all of us. Do you think I wasn't affected?"

"No. Of course not." Quif remembered how frail and visibly shaken the chairman appeared that day.

"The truth is, we don't know that the massacre was related to the refinery. Investigators found tire tracks of transport trucks and the footprints of hundreds who'd marched into the cave, probably at gunpoint. They were apparently gassed and their bodies set on fire as a way to destroy the evidence – typical tactics used in ethnic cleansing, a tragedy that goes back centuries in that part of the world. It could be completely unrelated."

"That does not make sense. The timing is too coincidental. Besides, what about the blood samples? You have seen evidence of the phage with your own eyes. Am I accused of making that up, too?"

"No. It's a remarkable find, without a doubt. There's just no proof where it came from."

"No proof? I brought that back from Armenia myself! Just ask Benoit. I handed it all over to him."

"We did." The chairman was silent for a moment, as if collecting his thoughts. "Now, doctor, we should talk a bit about Benoit. You have to admit, he's more than a little infatuated with you."

"So?"

"It's clear that he'd believe anything you told him."

"I cannot believe this!" Quif's voice rose again. Natara turned to look over from her haze on the couch. "Are you calling me a liar?"

"Not me." The chairman sighed. "Like I said. I'm on your side. But others…well, they think you've caused irreparable damage to the reputation of the Institut."

Quif's thoughts churned to tally the consequences of all that had happened. The greatest medical discovery in history had been in her grasp and now it was lost. Her poor sister was in her final days. She'd been witness to another Armenian genocide. And now her career as a doctor, perhaps all she had left, was about to be ruined.

"What can I do?" she asked, forcing herself to calm down.

"Is there anyone else who saw the lab? Another witness?"

Quif thought of the petrochemical engineer she'd met. From Louisiana, if she remembered right. Now living in San Francisco. He'd helped her that day gather the evidence from the lab. She'd promised to keep him informed, but with all that had happened since then she'd completely forgotten. She was sure she'd kept his business card somewhere.

"Yes. There is someone else who saw the lab."

"Really? Who is that person? How can we find them?" The chairman's voice suddenly became insistent. It didn't sound right to Quif. *Why is he being so demanding?* It was her career on the line, not his. Quif thought of the hundreds who had already died because they knew the secret of the phage. They were murdered because she'd revealed their identities. It wasn't paranoid to be more careful this time.

"Actually, I am not sure."

"Yes. No. Which is it?" the chairman chided.

"More of a theory," Quif stammered. "I *think* there might be someone else who saw the lab. I need to check it out and get back to you."

"I see. Well, think hard, Dr. Melikian. A great deal depends on it."

13

Bill Soileau sat in his SUV in the company parking lot. He kept the engine idling, shuffled papers on the passenger seat, and rifled through items in the glove compartment.

It was all an act to kill time. Dorothy was staked out by the front door, as she often was first thing in the morning, chain smoking. She said she needed to store up on nicotine before she could start work. It seemed more like an excuse to corner Bill as he tried to head up to his office. She always refused to let him pass.

Dorothy's smoking reminded Bill of his mother. When he was a child, Mom loved to talk on the kitchen phone for hours. It was the wall-mounted type, with a cord on the receiver that only stretched six feet. Mom would yell for Bill to come into the kitchen, hand him one of her Pall Malls, then tell him to go across the room and light it for her off the burner on the gas stove. He remembered dreading the chore. He usually inhaled the smoke, causing him to choke.

"Don't be such a frickin' little girl," Mom would berate. It didn't matter that Bill was only five.

Bill hated being around smokers ever since, but that wasn't the main reason he avoided Dorothy. Nearly fifty years old and fifty pounds overweight, she looked like a slightly heavier version of that amateur British singing sensation Susan Boyle, the ugly woman who surprised and delighted the world with her angelic voice. But with Dorothy, there was no such charm. Instead, she flirted relentlessly with Bill. She was so explicit and aggressive, it was like a contact sport.

Her latest tactic was to share sexually graphic anecdotes. Did she think this would turn him on? Instead, her tales made him wonder how anyone could ever have sex with a woman.

Poor Dorothy. She had no idea Bill was gay – he'd never come out at work. Not that he was ashamed. But he always figured that in the world of oilrig roughnecks, he'd be asking for trouble. So he'd kept his personal life private. He'd managed bigger secrets for so long, it wasn't a big deal.

Of course, that was all before he met Ike. That morning Bill awoke to find himself embraced, Ike's arms draped around him from behind. Closer than fried oysters and French bread in a po'boy. Or maybe they'd melded into a single being, bound somehow on the cellular level. In the past when he'd heard silly songs on the radio about love transforming two people into one, he'd roll his eyes at the absurdity. And yet it had happened. Just like the love songs said.

How could you hide something like that? He'd never come out at work before because he'd never had a good *reason*. He wondered if he should march into the office and tell everyone. Or perhaps he'd wait until the next company party. He wouldn't avoid going, like he usually did. He'd bring Ike with him. After all, Ike was now the most important thing in his life. How could he not share that, or act like it didn't exist?

Bill looked over to Dorothy, still puffing and standing sentry. She must be lonely. She didn't have an Ike. That's why she acted the way she did. If she knew he was gay, she'd have to stop pursuing him.

Bill got out of the SUV and made his way to the entrance.

"Hello handsome," Dorothy said, her voice raspy like a lounge singer.

"Dorothy, I have something important to tell you. I—"

"Lose something in your car?"

"What?"

"It looked like you were searching for something. I thought you'd never come over here to ravage me with your Southern charms."

"Oh, I was just…" Bill tried to regroup. This was going to be more difficult than he thought.

"I gotta tell you a funny story."

"I'd love to hear, but—"

"It's about this guy I've been seeing," Dorothy continued. "Get this – we only have sex if I cook him dinner."

"That's—"

"And I noticed that if I cook Italian, then I get *the oral.*"

"Uh…" Bill's eyes instinctively glanced at Dorothy's fupa.

"I'm telling you, Bill. I've made lasagna every night for the past two weeks!"

Bill shut his eyes to somehow block out the conversation, but the vision of Dorothy's plump cottage-cheese thighs spread wide popped into his head. He saw her gorging on a plate of pasta while her labia pouted and then somehow mouthed the word *marinara.* Bill stifled a gag.

"Is that weird or what? I mean, if *you're* into that, then I'm sure it's perfectly normal. It's just the first I've heard of a guy getting turned on that way. You know, I also make a mouth-watering sausage and peppers if you'd like to come over some night."

The alert beep on Bill's cell phone went off. "Look at that," Bill said as he desperately flipped open the receiver to study the text. "Reception needs me right away. Gotta run!"

Bill careened past Dorothy and raced up the stairs. As soon as he reached the floor, the receptionist called out. "You've got a call on line one. Overseas. Says it's very urgent. Wouldn't leave a message and insisted on staying on hold."

Bill unlocked his office door and grabbed the receiver. "Hello?"

"Bill Soileau?"

It was a woman's voice. It sounded foreign and vaguely familiar. "Yes, who is this?"

"It is Quif calling from Paris."

~

Bill had heard about the explosion at the refinery. Accidents were common in the industry, but not at plants that hadn't been operational for more than a decade. From what he'd seen during his inspection, there wasn't enough fuel on site to light a backyard barbecue, let alone cause the type of destruction reported.

"I saw the damage. It was not an accident," Quif said.

"Then what was it?" The reports Bill read said the cause of the fire wasn't known.

"It was a bomb."

"Damn terrorists," Bill lamented.

"Terrorists? Why did you say that?"

"Isn't that who it always is these days?" Who else could it be? "Bombs don't plant themselves."

"Do you remember the lab?" Quif asked.

"Of course. It was creepy." Bill instantly thought of the moment he reached under the desk and was stabbed in the finger. He was so panicked when it happened. Thank God it turned out to be nothing.

"I found something."

"What?"

"Bill Soileau, that day at the refinery I felt you were a good man. Am I right?"

Bill tried to process such a strange question. *A good man.* No doctor would believe that, especially one who specialized in infectious diseases. Someone like Quif would never truly accept him – especially the man he used to be before Ike.

"Good? Sure, uh, I guess so."

"I am going to tell you something few people in the world know. That means I must trust you."

"This sounds serious." What did she know about the refinery explosion?

"Many people have died because of what I am about to tell you. You must swear to me that you will tell no one. *Promettez-le moi.*"

"Died?" Bill walked around his desk and pushed the door to his office closed.

"All the local villagers...murdered," Quif's voice cracked. "Hundreds of them. Executed and their bodies burned in nearby caves – the same caves I told you about from the Turkish holocaust."

Bill remembered the story and the role those caverns played in the original Armenian genocide. He was stunned to learn the same place had been used as an arena of death again. "What's going on? Some sort of local war?"

"It is a cover up. The villagers were all witnesses."

"Witnesses?"

"The Soviets used that lab we saw to conduct medical experiments *on people,*" Quif explained.

Bill thought of the examination tables, the ones with straps to secure arms and legs. He envisioned patients screaming in agony. "What did they do to them?"

"They were working to create a super virus."

"You mean, like a weapon?"

The line went silent. Bill wondered if the connection had been lost. "Are you still there?" he asked.

"*Oui.*"

"What did you mean? Is this some sort of biological warfare?"

"You remember the lab?"

"Of course." Why wouldn't she answer his question?

"I need you to help me. You and I are the only ones left who can report what we saw. Will you testify?"

"Testify?"

"I know it sounds crazy. No one believes me when I say there was a lab. All that exists now is a big hole in the ground."

"Well, sure. I can say what I saw. First you have to tell me what this is all about. Testify where? Was there something dangerous there I need to know about? Was I exposed?" Bill's mind jolted back again to the drop of blood from his finger that day. He'd been jabbed with a needle or bitten. Then the tingling sensations throughout his entire body. A super virus? Had he been infected?

"No, no, no," Quif assured. "There was no danger to you. The Soviets experimented with something called phage. *Viral* phage, to be precise. It is a type of virus that kills any other virus it sees as a threat to the human body. A bug that can destroy another bug. But there is no need for you to worry. It is not contagious. It is like an infection. You would need to be injected with a needle."

14

As Quif emerged from the Denfert-Rochereau Métro station she looked around the dreary neighborhood. She didn't care for this part of Paris. Far beyond the narrow, charming lanes of the rest of the Left Bank, here the streets were wider, there were too many cars, and everything was worn and sooty. The gray skies and light drizzle didn't help. It was an odd place to meet.

She hated leaving Natara, even for a few hours. Throughout the night she'd heard her sister whimpering in bed. The depression was making the wasting worse, and vice versa. If she didn't improve, Quif would be forced to place her in hospice. She couldn't let that happen. Even if the care was loving and eased Natara's suffering, no one ever left hospice alive. It was a death sentence.

Quif glanced down the sidewalk, then looked in the other direction. There was no one around. Across the street, a man waved, beckoning her. It had been months since she'd seen his face, but she knew who he was. She popped open her compact black umbrella, waited for a break in the traffic, and rushed across, carefully stepping to avoid the many puddles.

"*Bonjour!*" Quif said as she kissed the man back and forth on both cheeks twice. She wondered if as an American he understood the significance of the gesture. Four kisses meant they were close friends. At least that's what she wanted. She needed him to be her ally.

"Quif," Bill Soileau beamed. "I'm so glad you could make it. I'm sorry for calling you at the last minute."

"I have to admit I was surprised to hear from you so soon. Just yesterday we spoke on the phone. And then today...here you are in Paris. I do not understand."

"You said you needed me."

"I do, but I did not tell you to jump on the first plane." When Quif received the call from Bill only two hours earlier she was startled. He knew something about the Armenian plant he wouldn't tell her over the phone.

"Let's go inside," Bill said, as he gestured to a gleaming black wall with an arched doorway. It had a strange formality that made it stand out on an otherwise drab block. Quif noted the small sign above the entrance. *ENTRÉE DES CATACOMBES.*

"Here?" Quif had heard of the catacombs, but she'd never been. Like most native Parisians she went out of her way to avoid most places frequented by tourists.

"It seems appropriate," Bill said.

"A bit morbid, I think," Quif scoffed.

"I've been a few times. It's private."

Bill paid for their tickets and they stepped down onto a dark, stone spiral staircase. The deeper they circled, the more Quif wondered when the stairs would end. They must have gone several stories beneath the ground when they finally emerged into a long, dimly lit tunnel.

"Are you scared?" Bill asked.

"Not at all," Quif quickly replied, suspecting the caretakers purposely kept it eerily dark to create a mood. She wouldn't have her emotions manipulated by such theatrics. Besides, she'd been to medical school, worked in hospitals, and been on the frontlines of health catastrophes. Nothing down here could possibly compare to what she'd already seen of death.

"The remains of six million Parisians," Bill said, talking like a reassuring tour guide. "The bodies were moved down here starting in the 1700s from cemeteries all over the city to free up the land for people to live – and to stop the spread of disease from poorly buried rotting corpses."

"I know the legend," Quif cut him off. She didn't need some American to tell her about Paris. She buttoned the neck of her jacket and tightened her scarf. The farther they walked, the colder it became.

The stone floor changed to gravel. Quif was glad she'd put on practical boots instead of the heels she usually wore. Why had Bill insisted on meeting here?

"It goes on for three hundred kilometers. Amazing." Bill said, excitement in his voice. He stopped and placed his hand on the stone wall. "Don't worry. It's all been reinforced."

"Bill Soileau, why do you like this place?"

"Growing up in Louisiana, you develop an appreciation for the macabre," Bill said. "You've really never been here before?"

"No. Why?"

"You'll see."

The tunnel took several sharp turns until it straightened out and Quif noticed a bright light ahead. At the end of the hallway they emerged into a large chamber. A lamp sat on the right side of the room, causing Quif to squint and put her hand up to block the glare. When her eyes adjusted she turned to her left to see what the beams illuminated.

"*C'est impossible!*"

The wall on the opposite side of the chamber looked back at her with hundreds of empty eye sockets. Instead of rock or brick, there stood a vast fortification of human skulls. It went on for as far as she could see.

Quif stared at the bone faces. The skulls didn't simply sit in a pile. There was a design to their placement, like a work of art. In between the skulls were other bones. All femurs, she noted, precisely lodged to embrace the skulls and hold them in place. No glue or cement appeared necessary – the construction and gravity held it snugly together. Like expert masons did their work with slate, grim artisans two hundred years ago created a immense necropolis using only human remains. Quif found herself fascinated by the ghastly beauty.

With silent reverence, she walked further into the crypt. Around one corner she read a plaque. Here were the bodies taken from the Cemetery of St. Nicolas des Champs, placed in the catacombs on August 24, 1804. Bill followed as she roamed the tunnels and found a section dedicated to those who gave their lives in *Le Révolution*. There were occasional tombstones and altars of bright white limestone.

An empty metal chair sat where Quif concluded a caretaker was supposed to be on duty, but she and Bill had not seen a living soul since they entered the tomb. She pulled the chair closer to the skull wall and stood on the seat for a closer look. She gently touched a forehead, noting the bone was cool and dry. It was no longer white, but had taken on a brownish tint, like that of an old sepia photograph. Now high enough to peer over the top of the wall, Quif could see what sat behind the crafted skull facade. The skeletal walls were ten feet thick, reaching deep back to the original brick-enforced quarry bulwark, the space packed solid with the remains. Arms, hands, teeth, and ribs, along with additional skulls apparently not beautifully intact enough to make it out to the front. *Six million people* rested here, their remnants now linked until eternity reduces them to dust.

People. Her training as a doctor was supposed to make her dispassionate about the dead. Corpses were empty vessels – human anatomy in its final curtain call. Yet Quif had never been able to shrug death off so easily, not in medical school, and especially now after what she'd seen in the tunnel in Armenia. The old woman who had helped her get the blood tests from the reticent villagers – she was in that billowing heap of incinerated flesh in the cave. That old woman died because of the events Quif had put in motion. They were all murdered *because of her.* The images rushed back, making Quif taste the soot of the burning pyre in her mouth. She began coughing, the same as she did that day. Soon she was hyperventilating, unable to catch her breath.

Bill rushed to her side and helped her down from the chair. "Are you okay?"

"Why," Quif wheezed as she sat down in the chair. "Why did you bring me here?"

Bill softly rubbed her back. Soon her lungs began to fill normally.

"I'm sorry. I didn't mean to upset you. On the plane trip I had a million different thoughts race through my head about what you told me. About the lab in that refinery. About the Soviets creating a super virus. It made me think of this place. It's perfect."

"Perfect?" Quif breathed deeply to pass any danger of gasping for air again. "For what?"

"Look, I lied when I made that crack about being from Louisiana and how we had a thing for the macabre. That's bullshit. The truth is I come here almost every time I visit Paris."

"Why?"

"It's hard to explain. I think about my own death. I have for the past ten years. Then you told me about the lab in Armenia...and there was that call from Dr. Greene...and Ike..."

"Death? But you are such a young man." Quif struggled to follow what Bill was saying. He was all worked up, not at all how she remembered him from Armenia. He was almost blasé then, even after discovering the lab. Had she misread him? Was this what he was really like? "You are not making any sense."

Bill looked like he wanted to speak, but something held him back.

"Okay, let us start with an easy question." Quif tried to soothe with her voice, hoping to draw Bill out. He'd flown all this way on a moment's notice, but whatever he had to say was clearly too difficult. Why her? Why here? "Maybe it will help if you start by explaining why you insisted on taking me down to this underworld of death."

The expression on Bill's face changed to be more at ease. He relaxed his hands. "Yes. That's a good place to start. I couldn't stop thinking about this place on the flight over."

"Why?"

"Well, when you look around here you see the bodies of so many people. And that got me thinking. How did these people die?"

Quif looked down the corridors of skeletal remains. There were so many, representing countless generations of Parisians. "Some of these bones date back nearly a thousand years. At that time, most died from disease."

"That's it!" Bill looked exhilarated. "Don't you get it? I have it. I have that thing you spoke about. What did you call it? The *phage*. I have that phage thing in me."

"What?"

"It's all I could think about after your call," Bill's voice became louder, nearly shouting. "I mean, this incredible energy! It's like nothing I've ever experienced in my life. I've never felt so alive. I'm changing. I threw away my pills. All those medications costing thousands of dollars. I flushed them! I don't need them. I'm cured. And so is Ike. Don't you see? Look around you. Millions of people won't have to die because I...I can make them live..."

"Stop! Calm down. Cured? Of what?" Quif studied Bill's face. His cheeks were red. He could prevent millions of people from dying? She regretted ever mentioning the phage virus. It was a curse. Now just speaking of it had transformed this American oil worker into a ranting lunatic.

"The plane ride over!" Bill ran his fingers through his hair, his face appearing as if struck by a sudden vision. "I *slept* on the plane. Don't you see? I don't have to deal with that fucking memory anymore! That goddamn day at LSU. It doesn't own me. I'm cured of that too!"

"Bill Soileau, you are making me—"

"I have the phage in me," Bill insisted.

"Okay. Listen to me. Slow down. How? You did not even know about the phage until I told you about it yesterday."

"Remember when we were in the lab and I hit my head on that table?"

"*Oui.*" Quif vaguely recalled the moment.

"The reason I hit my head is because I had dropped a piece of paper and I was reaching under the desk to try to grab it. Something stabbed me in the finger as I stuck my hand under. It hurt like fuck, so that's when my body jolted and I hit my head."

"Why did you not tell me, I would have—"

"Whatever jabbed me was sharp enough to make me bleed. That freaked me out. Then I got this strange tingling feeling. First in my finger, and then all throughout my body."

"You should have had me look at that cut right away," Quif scolded. "What if it got infected?"

"It *did* get infected," Bill said, sounding exasperated. "That's what I'm trying to tell you. That's why I brought you here! I think there was a needle under that desk – and I was injected with that phage stuff. Now I'm cured, and so is Ike."

"Cured? You keep saying that. Of what? And you think you passed along the phage to this someone named Ike? How would you do this?" Quif rubbed her forehead. It was too much to consider. The miracle phage was still alive? In Bill Soileau?

"Quif…"

She looked up into his eyes. Even in the shadows of the crypt, she could see they were a common brown. She'd always liked brown eyes, thinking they imbued a type of quiet strength. She studied Bill's pupils. They weren't abnormally dilated. The whites in his eyes appeared clear, not bloodshot. Could it be? Was it possible he was telling the truth?

"Before I went to Armenia, uh, I was HIV positive," Bill said, his voice halting. "Now it's gone. I'm cured."

HIV. *AIDS*. Bill was HIV positive. Quif tried to make sense of it all. Bill was from San Francisco. Gay? She'd never considered that before – he was such a masculine man, a petrochemical engineer no less. Was this Ike he mentioned his lover? A needle in the lab. Now cured. And passed it onto someone else. Living proof the phage infection can spread by human-to-human contact? If true, the cure was not lost after all.

In the corner of her eye she thought she saw someone peek at her from around a nearby wall of bones. She whipped her head to look, but no one was there. Had someone been listening to their conversation the whole time? Perhaps a tourist. Maybe she was simply spooked by the eerie place. She brushed the thought aside. It didn't matter. If Bill Soileau was right, a twist of fate had given her a second chance. Not just for her, but millions dying around the world. Including Natara.

She would not fail this time.

15

ILikeIke: paris? what r u doing there?

OilGuy415: sorry i didn't get to reach you before i left. it was all very sudden

ILikeIke: ?

OilGuy415: get my voicemail?

ILikeIke: just that you were heading out of town on urgent business. last time i checked there are no oil wells in paris ;-)

OilGuy415: it's not about oil this time. it's about hiv+

ILikeIke: are you sick?????

OilGuy415: not any more

ILikeIke: ?

OilGuy415: and neither are you

ILikeIke: ?

Bill Soileau looked up from the IMs on the computer screen. Across the room on the far side of the lab he spotted Quif and her colleague Benoit frantically fiddling with microscopes and blood samples. They looked agitated. He heard bits of sniping in French.

Bill had been in constant motion ever since explaining everything to Quif in the catacombs. From there he and the doctor grabbed a taxi and raced over to Pasteur. Quif spent the whole ride barking orders at someone on her cell phone. Bill couldn't keep up with his limited Acadian French, but from the tone she sounded excited, or panicked.

Possibly both. He now had second thoughts about breaking the news in the crypt. Perhaps the setting was too dramatic for her. He'd forgotten how high strung she was when they worked together in Armenia.

Whatever she commanded into her phone made things move quickly. As soon as they pulled up to the Institut he was whisked inside to meet Benoit. Within minutes the two doctors began drawing vials of Bill's blood. They siphoned at least a dozen test tubes. He'd lost count, leaving him a little woozy.

He understood their excitement. He'd been obsessed with the revelation for the better part of a day, and it still sounded unbelievable.

He didn't want to tell Quif about being gay and HIV positive. She was a doctor, after all. And he'd never revealed his orientation or health status to *anyone* associated with work. Roughnecks weren't exactly known for their progressive view of the world. Just being openly gay in the petrochemical business would be like riding a bicycle nekkid through his home parish. Add to that being HIV positive? Might as well jump off an oil platform into the North Sea, because he surely would be pushed.

What choice did he have now? He had to trust Quif, and he needed her on his side. Somehow he knew the virus that swam in his veins could prevent the deaths of more people than the millions who rested in that Parisian tomb. That's what the doctor had to see – to have the same epiphany he'd had.

He'd been imagining the implications as soon as Quif told him on the phone about the old Soviet lab. That's when he heard that miraculous word for the first time. *Phage.* Suddenly so many things started to make sense. The changes he felt. The intense energy. The strange blood test results. He had the cure in his body. *He was the cure.* And he could pass it along to others. He knew it worked - he'd already given the cure to Ike.

Through love.

There was no other explanation. He didn't share needles with Ike. They had sex. Unprotected, bareback, politically incorrect, fluid-exchanging unsafe sex. How else could it be said? They fucked AIDS right out of their bodies. Now sex, the same passion that led to the disease in the first place, would be used to end the world's worst plague.

On the eleven-hour flight to Europe he'd played out all the scenarios in his head, like a chess match plotted out to checkmate. With relatively few moves, the game could be won. The end of HIV. The destruction of AIDS. He knew it sounded crazy, but the fastest way to cure the dying meant that governments and their health departments would be forced to encourage those carrying the phage to pass it onto others. The sickest people would need to be fucked first. Then the world would become a virtual unsafe sex orgy until everyone had the cure. He imagined how conservative politicians would react to such an idea. Maybe they would waste critical time trying to turn the phage into some politically correct pharmaceutical. While they took years to figure that out, tens of millions would die. Perhaps they'd argue it was justifiable homicide in order to keep their dubious moral code intact.

No. He would not let that happen. He wouldn't let inaction kill any more than it already had.

The Catholic Church would have a meltdown. The new pope started a witch-hunt against homosexuals within months of rising to power. The Church stood firm in its belief that sex was supposed to be only for reproduction, and only in marriage. Now it would be impossible to make the case that sex was a sin. Instead, it would become the ultimate gift from one human being to another. Sex would mean *life*.

Bill thought of the Reverend Willy Warrant and his bigoted TV show. A gay man and gay sex spread…a cure! How would he explain this one in his sermon?

If the airplane had offered internet service, Bill would have chatted about it with Ike. He needed Ike. But buying a ticket to Europe with only a few minutes notice meant he couldn't be picky. The next seat to Paris was no-frills. How many might die needlessly if he waited another day for first class?

Of all people, Ike would understand the urgency. He was so filled with compassion for others – he worked in HIV prevention no less. Bill couldn't wait to tell Ike about the miracle phage. It would be an overwhelming moment of joy, and hard not to break down crying. The plague was over. The disease that had tormented them both was gone. They'd become so close so fast it was difficult for Bill to imagine an intimacy greater than the one they already shared, and yet he felt the phage was now a bond between them that transcended even the most passionate love. Bill had given Ike the gift of life. It was too bad he couldn't tell him in person and see the look on Ike's face.

After the blood was drawn in the lab, Bill asked for the nearest computer so he could finally reach Ike. Now that he was typing it was clear his fingers and instant messages couldn't keep up with all that was in his head.

ILikeIke: ?
OilGuy415: i can't explain it like this. where r u?
ILikeIke: home

Bill looked over to Quif and Benoit to ask if he could use the phone next to the computer. He saw they were in another heated exchange. Rather than interrupt, he picked up the phone and dialed. There was odd static on the line at first, but after a few seconds the call went through.

"Hey," he said to Ike.

"What's this all about?"

"Did you ever get the second round of blood tests back?"

"Yes. I saw the doctor yesterday," Ike said. "And those were messed up, too. Once again there's no sign of HIV or anything. And I went to a different lab this time. You'd think it would be impossible for the same testing mistake to happen twice."

"It's no mistake," Bill said.

"Of course, it's a mistake. What else could it be?"

"Remember that trip I told you about to that old oil rig in Armenia?"

Bill explained everything. The Soviet experiments. The phage. Quif. The Institut Pasteur. The massacre of the Armenian Villagers. He didn't stop until he finished the entire story, pausing only a few times to make sure Ike was still on the line. All Bill could hear was silence.

"You still there?"

"Yeah," Ike said, sounding tentative. "Are you okay?"

"I'm great! Haven't you been listening to everything I told you? I'm better than I've ever been. I'm cured!"

"About that…" Ike stopped.

"What?"

"Well, honestly Bill, you sound almost…delusional. I mean, a Soviet conspiracy? A virus that turns out to be a cure? Hundreds murdered to keep the secret? It sounds like Tom Clancy's gone queer."

"I'm serious." Bill was devastated. Ike didn't believe him. Ike, his rock, the man he needed most, now more than ever – *he* questioned the story. *Delusional.* He never expected to be doubted by Ike.

"Look, I'm not making fun of you. You know I love you. But I'm worried that you're losing it. Maybe all this travel is too stressful. Can you come home right now? I don't like hearing you ramble like this."

Maybe it was too much to comprehend. Bill had lived the events. Ike was only hearing what happened for the first time.

Wait. *Did Ike just say he loved me?* Bill felt it, too, but had been holding back. He'd never said I love you to anyone, and they'd only been together for a few months. Up until now he hesitated to say the words himself for fear he'd go too far too soon and ruin what they had.

"I love you, too," Bill sighed.

"Oh, fuck," Ike said. "We're having a big moment here, and I've screwed it up by saying the wrong thing."

"It's okay," Bill said. "I understand. It's a lot to digest."

"Look, it's just that I work in the world of AIDS and I've never heard of this thing. What did you call it? Phage? I'm not sure that's even a word in the dictionary."

"I know it all sounds far-fetched."

"But I *have* heard of people experiencing all sorts of weird side effects from their medications. One client used to refer to something he called *Sustiva dreams.* He said his mind played tricks on him. He couldn't tell the different between reality and the wild visions induced by the drug."

"This is not a dream," Bill said flatly. Ike was treating him like a mental case.

"Isn't it? I mean, what you've just described is pure fantasy.

Imagine...AIDS is finally cured the same way it became a pandemic – through sex. Any gay man who says he isn't haunted by the specter of AIDS is a liar. We all are, whether we're infected or not. Hell, maybe even straight people feel the same way. But what you've described is an alternate universe to the one we live in. As much as I wish it was true, I'm afraid this is all in your head."

Bill didn't know how to respond. Ike wasn't with him. As the only other person in the world who Bill knew was also infected with the miracle phage, there was no time to waste. Ike needed to act, just as urgently as Bill did. There were too many lives at stake.

"Do you really love me?"

"I do. I said I do. I would never lie to you."

"And I would never lie to you." Bill's voice cracked.

"Don't misunderstand what I'm saying. I believe that you *think* you're telling me the truth. Just like my old Mr. Right who told me he was negative. He never lied, remember? It didn't matter. He was wrong. He simply believed the wrong thing."

Bill looked across the lab to see Quif and Benoit had moved to a desk with a three-foot tall metal cylinder and two computer monitors. How could he convince Ike? Everything depended on it.

"Okay, that's fine. You've been hurt in the worst possible way, and you don't want it to happen again. I get that. So don't take my word for it. Go out and get new blood tests. Do it five times at five different labs if that's what it takes for you to see the truth. All of them will come back negative. They will show that you have never even been exposed to HIV. In fact, each time you will come back the healthiest person your doctor has ever seen..."

"I'm sorry," Ike interrupted.

"What?"

"You're obviously all worked up, and I've hurt you. I'm sorry."

"Don't apologize," said Bill. "Just promise me you'll do this for me. Promise me you will go out and get new blood tests. What time is it there?"

"It's morning. Just after nine. Why?"

"Go to the lab and get tested as soon as you get off the phone. Not just one lab. Go to many as it will take for you to believe me. Ask for a rush on the results. Hell, go to the health department and get one of those instant tests where they swab the inside of your cheek. Promise me you'll do it!"

"Okay, okay. You need to calm down."

"And when you get the results, and you finally believe me, you'll need to do something else."

"What?"

Bill paused. He needed to choose his next words carefully. This moment had gnawed at him, but he had no choice. He'd let the doctors do their work, but even without their tests he already understood the power of the phage. There was no time to waste – the cure had to get to as many people as possible. He and Ike might be the only two people in the world who carried the precious virus. It was irresponsible to wait for the doctors to figure it out. Bill turned to make sure Quif and Benoit were still too far away to overhear.

"After you get your test results," he whispered into the phone, "you'll believe me about the phage…uh…then I need you to go out and fuck every man possible in San Francisco."

"What?"

"Bareback."

"Are you joking with me?"

"It's no joke."

"I can't believe this. The man I love just told me to go and fuck other men."

"Ike, when you come to believe as I do that you're infected with a virus that kills HIV, then what other choice do you have? You must spread it! That means fucking other men. As many as you can!"

"I'm going to hang up now."

"No! You need to promise me! Ike, I need to hear you say the words! You must promise!"

"This is sick, Bill. I mean, if you want to break up, just be a man and tell me. Don't say you love me, then a minute later tell me I need to go sleep with other men."

"I'm not breaking up with you!" Bill panicked. He should have known better. Ike wasn't the type of guy who'd have sex with just anyone. He wasn't like Bill. That's what Bill loved about Ike. Yet he'd asked him to do the one thing Ike never could – to be promiscuous.

"Okay, I know all this sounds nuts. If you don't believe anything about the phage, just believe that I love you. Can you do that?"

For a few torturous moments Ike said nothing. Then, "Yes, I can do that."

"And get tested again, okay?"

"And if I get all these tests done, and they come back the way you said, then you think I should…what?"

"Nothing. Just forget what I said. You don't have to do anything you don't want to. I'm sorry I said that. Please, just erase that."

Out of the corner of his eye Bill saw Quif and Benoit waving from the other side of the room. They motioned for him to come over.

"I gotta go," Bill said. "Get the tests, okay?"

Bill hung up the receiver, wondering if he'd just ruined everything with Ike. What good was being a savior if he lost the only person he ever truly loved?

"Hurry!" Quif yelled.

"It's there," Benoit said. "It's…amazing."

Bill walked over. He noticed the machine had the manufacturer's label CS3000 Scanning Electron Microscope. He stared at the strange images on the computer monitors. The scenes appeared to be from a different universe, yet it was a world that existed in his own veins. In the center of one screen was a monster with what looked like a large head, long neck and six spindly legs. It was hideous.

"*C'est incroyable*," Quif said.

"*That's* living inside of me?" Bill felt a wave of dread, followed by prickliness on the back of his neck. He'd seen many movies with creatures more frightening and vile, but this one was real. In a strange way, he was its parent.

"More like *was* living inside you," Benoit explained. "Since this picture was recorded, it has already died. From what I can determine, the ability of this phage to reproduce is astonishing. I suspect there's very little incubation period. Perhaps within minutes an entire army of phage is at work. But outside the host of the body, it's probably the most fragile virus I've ever studied. Remarkable. The Soviets must have figured some way to sustain what was in the needle, something we must do as well."

"It looks, uh, scary." Bill wondered how many of those were inside him at this very moment.

"Scary? Well, it is *vicious*. You see this round part here," Benoit tapped the screen with his pen. He was almost giddy.

"The head?"

"Sure. Okay. You can call it that. Inside that sphere is RNA."

Bill gave Benoit a puzzled look.

"You've heard of DNA, right? Well, DNA looks like a very long ladder made of rubber that's twisted into strands. RNA is like that, only one side of the ladder is missing. You have the rungs searching for the other half of the ladder to create the structure. Understand?"

Bill nodded.

"That's how a retrovirus works," Benoit continued. "To complete the ladder, it couples with the structure of another cell and rewrites its DNA to make more of itself. That's how the infection spreads. This phage's head, as you call it, is filled with RNA. It's coded with a message to rewrite the DNA of diseased cells back to that of their original configuration. The HIV cell is transformed back into what is was before, a T helper lymphocyte cell."

"A T-cell? I know about those. That's the immune system, right?"

Benoit nodded his head, clearly pleased to see his student learning.

"So how does the RNA get from the head into other viruses?" Bill had received a C in biology at LSU, but he thought he was beginning to understand Benoit.

"Ah! Yes, that's why the Soviets named this thing a phage. You see this long shaft and what looks like six legs? Well, think of it like a spacecraft landing on the moon. Or a mosquito. It lands on other cells and then injects the RNA down the shaft and into the cell. The technique is classic phage. We know this from years of studying *bacterial* phage and the spread of common infections. This is the first *viral* phage ever discovered. It's rewriting DNA! Very aggressive. Very…beautiful."

Quif looked lost in her thoughts, hypnotized by what she saw on the screens.

"Are we heroes again?" Benoit asked her.

"What?"

"Should I call the chairman? I think he will want to see this immediately."

"No," Quif said, emerging from her haze. "We must wait. Last time we rushed and hundreds paid with their lives."

"We don't know that had anything to do with the phage," Benoit protested. "The reports suggest it was ethnic cleansing. Besides, this time is different. We're in Pasteur. Nothing can happen to us. We are not running off to the middle of nowhere looking for some mysterious needle. The truth is here." Benoit gestured to Bill. "It's standing right in this room!"

Bill flinched at Benoit's raised voice. He looked at the image of the viral phage on the microscope screen. What had he gotten himself into? In putting the pieces together, he'd failed to think every detail through. He didn't anticipate Ike's reaction. And now Benoit explained something that should have been obvious. From this day forward, Bill was no longer just himself. He was the parent of these tiny monsters. Patient zero. He'd be studied, poked and questioned. They would want to know everything about his life. He couldn't deny the scientists what they wanted – to walk away would be the same as allowing genocide. Still, until this moment, he'd never grasped the entire truth. His life was no longer his own. He had just donated his body to science. The problem was, he was still using it.

"Benoit, calm down," Quif demanded. "We are in this together, *oui?*"

"Of course," he said solemnly.

"We can not go to the Institut with another half-baked plan. Our credibility is shot. They do not even believe me that there was ever a lab in the first place."

"I know."

"When we go to the board for the inquiry next week, we must bring irrefutable proof. We will not only reveal that the viral phage is still alive, we must also show them how it works as a cure. Until then, no one must know. I want this lab sealed tight. Tell them it's quarantine conditions due to a cholera study – something that will keep everyone out. We are the only ones who know the phage is alive and it must stay that way. We'll do all the tests ourselves."

"In five days?" Benoit shook his head. "That's not enough time to do a proper clinical trial."

Five days, Bill thought. Why wait that long? He already knew it worked. How many people died from AIDS in a day? Thousands? He knew they needed proof, but it was wrong to wait.

"I don't understand," Bill said. "Why don't we just fu—"

"I am not talking about a full study," Quif interrupted, ignoring Bill. "We just need to document how it works in one person. From infection to cure."

"Are you crazy?" Benoit nearly shouted. "You can't go around injecting this into patients! You'll never be approved for that. You're going to get us both fired...and sent to prison!"

"No one ever said anything about patients. We only need one. Just like Salk did with the polio vaccine, testing it on his own son. Once we can prove our theory about the phage is correct, then I am sure Pasteur will give us everything we need."

"But who would do this?" Benoit asked.

"I know someone," said Quif.

16

Bill Soileau opened his eyes to an unfamiliar living room. Light beamed through the tall wood-framed windows onto his face. He tried to remember what he'd been dreaming. Fragments of it still lingered in his head. It was something terrible about Ike. He'd lost him in a forest of sad trees. No, not a forest. *A grove*. And men in dark sunglasses with hearing aids. The images evaporated. It was just a dream. Ike was still his. Wasn't he?

Bill's hand brushed a coarse wool blanket that covered him. The couch in Quif's apartment was too small for him to lie completely flat. He'd slept in his clothes. He couldn't recall getting the blanket. Someone must have draped it over him during the night.

He got up and walked quietly down the hall toward the bathroom. The door to Quif's bedroom was open. On top of the still-made bed slept the two doctors, also in their clothes. Neither had bothered to remove their shoes. Benoit spooned Quif. Bill couldn't quite figure out the relationship between the two. He thought he caught glimpses of affection, but Quif was so bossy with the younger man. When she awoke, would she kiss Benoit, or give him a hard elbow in the ribs to push him off?

Bill looked in the other bedroom. Natara lay flat on her back, her arms at her sides. Poor thing. People tended to look at peace when they slept, but not Quif's sister. Natara was so sickly thin it was difficult for Bill to even look at her face, the cheeks sunken as if they were deflated beignets. The eyes were hazel blanks. When open, they didn't seem to register anything in particular. The only specific reaction Bill had witnessed was a horrible wince of pain when she was injected. There was so little flesh left on her bones, the prick of the needle must have had the impact of a stab from a knife.

The procedure had taken only a few moments last night. The two doctors decided they'd do it together to share the responsibility if anything went wrong. Benoit drew a syringe of blood from Bill's arm, and then Quif injected it into Natara's vein. All they could do was wait.

After using the bathroom, Bill stood in the doorway of Quif's room. "It's been six hours," he said.

The two doctors awoke, rolled apart from each other with indifference, then swiftly gathered their wits and headed to their patient. Bill wondered if they'd been trained from medical school to grab catnaps and then move at a moment's notice. At Natara's bedside Benoit carefully inserted a butterfly needle and began filling test tubes.

"She does not look any better," Quif said. She put two fingers on her sister's wrist and looked at her watch to take her pulse.

"Maybe it hasn't been enough time for the phage to incubate," said Benoit as he filled a fourth tube.

"When I was infected, I felt it immediately," Bill offered. Perhaps Natara was too far-gone, the HIV too strong to be conquered by the phage. "Something should have happened by now. I felt the tingling in seconds, then throughout my entire body within minutes."

Benoit filled the fifth and final vial, placing each one delicately into a slotted black sleeve for transport. "I'm off to the lab. I'll call you."

Without a goodbye Benoit was out the door. Bill thought maybe he'd misread the relationship with Quif. No smiles. All business. Moments ago they embraced in bed while sleeping. Here in the conscious world they were distant and somber. *Professional.* Of course, they had to be serious now. The life of Quif's sister was on the line, as well as their careers.

Quif placed her palm on Natara's forehead. "There is no fever. Her pulse is still lethargic. I do not see any change in her condition from yesterday."

"Quif," Natara whispered, her eyes opened slightly.

"*Ma chérie,*" Quif said, filling her voice with exaggerated ebullience. "It is a beautiful day, *oui?*"

Natara's eyes moved over to stare at Bill.

"And you see, we have a visitor this morning. It is our friend Bill. The American. You met him last night. Natara, say hello to Bill."

Natara continued to stare. Her mouth opened a fraction and a glob of drool oozed down her cheek until it landed on the pillow. Bill had never come face to face with someone dying of AIDS. As many times as he'd contemplated his own death from the disease, he never imagined it would look this ghastly. Withered away to nothing, the final days were a slow, dreadful waiting game. Why wasn't the phage performing its miracle? It had cured him, and Ike. Now that it was needed more than ever, it had failed to take hold.

"Natara? Say hello to Bill," Quif coaxed. "He is from San Francisco. You remember San Francisco, right? We had such a wonderful time when we went there. We rode the cable cars, ate the chowder of the clam. Remember?"

Natara turned her attention back to her sister. "No," she mumbled.

Bill wasn't sure if Natara was refusing him, or simply failing to recall.

"So it is going to be one of those mornings, eh?" Quif said. Bill could see the doctor strained to keep a cheerful guise for her sister.

They spoke little for the next few hours, worried they'd disturb Natara's rest. Quif held her sister's hand most of the time. Bill found some bread and strong smelling cheese in the kitchen. They ate in silence. Bill thought this must be what a bedside vigil was like when someone died. Would Ike be there for him when his time came? How long would that be, now that he had the phage? Perhaps with the phage they could live to be one hundred. What disease could kill them now?

The blare of Quif's cell phone ended the wake. Bill listened as Quif spoke on the phone. He only picked up a few words of the French, but her face said all he needed to know. At first she was serious, asking questions in a very officious tone. Then her eyes rolled up and Bill could see she was blinking back tears. She abruptly hung up.

"We have failed," Quif said. "The phage did not transmit into Natara's blood. Her viral load remains at end-stage levels. Her immune system is still gone. No T-cells. There has been no change. The phage died before it could infect her."

"I'm sorry." It was all Bill could think to say.

"Benoit believes the phage is so fragile, it cannot exist outside a human host for even an instant. It needs to remain in the body to survive."

Quif went on to explain about experiments they'd done with every conceivable *nutrient agar* and hundreds of different Petri dish tests. Bill quickly became lost in the medical jargon. Still, no matter what the lab results said, logic trumped science.

"That doesn't make any sense," Bill said. "I mean…it got *into me*. I was jabbed by a needle or something in the first place. Whatever lurked under that desk. The phage survived there somehow, possibly for years."

Quif sat silently for a moment, her face revealing her consternation. "You are right, of course. We now must assume that whatever pricked you contained something other than phage-tainted blood. It must have been the pure isolated virus the Soviets created, perfectly suspended in time by some process we do not know. Benoit thinks the phage is so delicate that even a blood transfusion would not work. We are lucky that you are blood type O, the universal donor. But even if we make your blood flow directly into another person, pumped through a tube, Benoit believes it would not survive the trip. We most conclude that blood is not the way this virus is trans…"

Quif stopped in mid-sentence. Bill felt uncomfortable at the way she stared at him, her head tilted to one side examining him head to toe.

"You are sure you passed the infection to this Ike person?" she asked.

"Uh, yes. He was also HIV-positive, and now there is no trace of the disease at all. He's been tested at least twice, and both times came back negative. I'm sure he also has the phage."

Quif twisted her lips. "And you do not share needles?"

"No."

"But you have what you Americans call the safe sex, *oui?*"

"Uh," Bill felt his face get red, "not exactly."

"*Pardon?*"

"We don't use condoms, if that's what you're asking."

"Do you do the fellatio?"

"Well, I…"

"I do not know the slang word for the tongue in the—"

"Look, I think I know what you want to know," Bill interrupted.

"Bill Soileau, I will put this bluntly. Did you ejaculate your semen inside of the anus of this Ike person?"

Bill had to stop himself from laughing at the way Quif phrased it, her questions so clinical and awkwardly mixed up in the way of someone who spoke English as their second language. But she was finally zeroing in on what he already knew. The phage was passed to others through sex. It was the only way he could have given it to Ike.

"Doctor, I will tell you every detail of my sex life with Ike, if that's what you need for your work." Bill looked over to Natara's limp presence on the bed. "We will save your sister's life. I know we will. All I ask is one thing."

"What?" Quif's voice now took on an eagerness.

Bill's mind flashed back to the memory of that day at LSU. The day he was diagnosed by the callous Dr. Lee. The image only flickered this time, perhaps finally being displaced by a new imprint, a different feeling now emerging about physicians. "You must never judge me."

For the next half hour Bill recalled every sexual act performed with Ike. It felt like something he was born to do, as if he were a great artist, and sex was his canvas. He recounted every caress, kiss and climax. He thought he saw Quif blush when he told of how he and Ike took turns in the dominant role and would sometimes begin their days inside each other so they could "take part of him with me to work."

She asked for his sexual history before Ike. Bill hesitated, but then it all began gushing out. He couldn't recall every face and scene, but he didn't hold back. He even told her about the roulette party. If Quif judged him, he didn't see it. She just dutifully wrote everything down in a small spiral pad. When she finally asked how he was infected with HIV in the first place, Bill stopped.

"No," he said. "I don't talk about that."

Quif opened her mouth to say something, but just then Benoit came back into the apartment.

"Do you have a specimen cup for urine?" Quif asked him, never saying hello.

"Yes. It's in my kit."

"Give it to Bill," she demanded.

Bill was puzzled. "You want to test my urine?"

"No, I need a sample of your semen."

"Oh…"

"What is it?" Quif asked. "Do you need some help getting started? Perhaps Benoit should assist you?"

"I don't really need—"

"Quif! What are you suggesting?" Benoit snapped.

"I am only thinking of sensory stimulation," she said casually. "After what I have just listened to, it is clear the photos of models in Vogue will not be…*inspiring*. Benoit, on the other hand, is a very handsome man. If that is what it takes to get this done…"

"No," Bill protested. "I can handle this on my own. *Really*." He took the cup and headed down to the bathroom. Just like in Armenia, he thought, the little doctor was aggressive beyond common sense. Pimping her colleague to get what she wanted? Someday a passion that strong could have consequences. As he closed the door he looked back down the hall. He could see in Benoit's face how deeply wounded he was.

Quif looked at Benoit, shrugged, and said, "What?"

~

Bill awoke to the sound of Quif shouting into the phone. He'd nodded off on the couch again. Outside the city was now dark. He looked at his watch. It was nearly midnight.

"What is it?" he asked as soon as she snapped her cell phone shut.

"It is exactly as we suspected. Benoit says the tests show the highest concentrations of the phage virus exist in the seminal fluids. The levels are hundreds of times higher than those found in the blood stream. You were right, Bill Soileau. That is how the phage infection is passed."

"But…why? I mean, HIV is spread through blood. Why would this be any different?"

"Ah, perhaps that is a question for *Monsieur* Darwin, *oui*?" Quif said.

"I don't understand."

"We do not know everything. We found papers that indicated the Soviets were trying to make mutation happen at a faster rate than in nature. If that is how they succeeded, then this phage virus is concentrated in semen due to evolution. Natural selection determined that was the safest and most effective way for it to do what it was destined to do."

"It's bizarre."

"But not unheard of. We know that HIV levels are highly concentrated in some bodily fluids, more than in blood. It also explains why the phage never spread beyond the villagers. It cannot be transmitted casually by breathing on someone, or in saliva. Intimate contact is the only way, and the Armenians were isolated from the rest of the world."

Quif put her hand up to her mouth and shook her head in disbelief. Bill felt a sudden rush, happy for the doctor that she'd finally figured it out.

"So, are you ready?" Quif asked.

"Ready?"

"It is time."

"For…?" Bill wasn't following where this was going. Ready for what?

"Well, you must now infect Natara with the phage."

Bill knew he was here to save Natara, but until this moment hadn't thought through the details. His mind had been too preoccupied with the drama of seeing the phage virus with his own eyes, the failure of the blood tests, and whether he'd bungled his relationship with Ike. Natara needed his semen. Of course he would give it to her. "Do you want me to use another specimen cup? Are you going to do it the same way they do artificial insemination?"

"Have you not been listening to anything I have said?" Quif looked incredulous. "This virus cannot leave a human host for even a moment.

No syringes, no tubes – it must be done person to person."

"So I have to…" Bill didn't want to complete the sentence.

"You have the sex with my sister."

Sex with a woman. It was something Bill had not considered in years, except when forced to by his brief encounters with Dorothy at work. Her constant, sexually graphic flirting had killed off any latent remnants of heterosexuality, if there were any left at all. Since his teens, he'd only desired guys. He knew how it worked with men, the intricacies of their bodies, the areas to touch to create pleasure. To Bill there was nothing more arousing than a lightly hairy chest that tapered down to a trail from the belly button to below. He loved to breathe in the scent of a man, to allow the musty smell to overwhelm him, to devour every inch of rough flesh. His was a world of beloved firm pectorals. What did he know of breasts? The thought of labia unnerved him. He knew there were men who craved all these things, some perhaps as much as he desired men. Bill wasn't one of them.

He could never have sex with a woman.

"I don't know if I can do it," he said.

"Why not? Are you unable after giving the sample?"

"No, it's not that," Bill said, knowing his unusually high sex drive allowed him to climax several times a day. Performance wasn't an issue, as long as there was lust. With women he had none. "I haven't had sex with a woman."

"Ever?"

"Well, when I was in high school. That was a long time ago."

"The sex is still done the same today as it was then," Quif said, beginning to sound impatient.

"No, it's not that. I know how it's done. It's just that…I have no desire to have sex with women."

"Desire!" Quif exploded. "This is not about your pleasure! This is about saving the life of Natara! This is about saving the life of millions!"

"Hey! Look, pressure does *not* help. Okay? I get it." Bill grasped for an idea, any other way to do what needed to be done. "How's this? How about you get Benoit to come back. I'll have sex with him, infect him, and then he can have sex with Natara." Bill could fuck Benoit, even if he was straight. The technique for taking a straight man took more time, more care, but he'd done it so many times.

"Are you crazy? I am already risking everything to infect my sister – and then to pray it works. She is dying. I can justify this. To infect someone who is not HIV-positive as an experiment…it is unconscionable! What if you end up killing Benoit? We do not know enough yet about all the ways the phage works. All we are absolutely certain of is that you cured Ike of HIV with the sex. And now you must cure Natara."

She was right, of course. But how? In all his fantastic notions of how the phage would cure the world, how he himself would spread the miracle, Bill had only envisioned himself with men. He knew women were dying from AIDS as much as men, possibly even more so in Africa. He figured someone else would do that work.

A woman. He'd had sex with strangers more times than he could count, where passion and intimacy were shared for only as long as it took to reach those few moments of release. Could he take such a dispassionate approach with a woman? Since they didn't arouse him, could he simply use their bodies as a tool to bring himself to climax? He thought he could close his eyes and think of someone else, perhaps pull up a memory of a particularly hot encounter from his past that would arouse him enough to forget he was inside a woman. He could just think he was feeling the flesh of a man. If a vagina were wet and tight enough, would he even feel the difference?

He'd only think of sex he'd had before he met Ike. He refused to use imagery of their love as the means for spurting his semen into a receptacle. No, his sex life with Ike was too precious. Fucking women was only about passing the cure, not because of love or even lust. He had so many passionate, anonymous past encounters he could draw upon to make him ejaculate. *He could do this.* He just had to trick his nature into believing he was fucking a man.

"You're right," Bill finally said to Quif. "It's the only way we know the phage works. I'll do it."

"*Bon.*"

Bill and Quif stared at each other for a moment, an embarrassed silence now between them. Bill didn't know what to do next.

"I don't know either," Quif said.

"What?"

"I can tell that you are wondering how to begin. Honestly, I have no idea."

Bill had watched Natara for the past day. The illness made her appear catatonic, barely dabbling with consciousness. If she could just lie there, he could get in and out without too much distraction. What if she suddenly startled and began fighting, trying to push him away? How much could she understand about what this was really all about? He couldn't even convince Ike that the phage was real. What chance did he have with Natara?

"You need to speak to her first," Bill said. "Tell her what's going to happen. Maybe she'll understand if you explain it to her."

"I will try."

Bill went down the hall to take a shower. It had been two days since he washed. For Natara, it was the least he could do to prepare. If he smelled pleasing, it might help quell any apprehension she had, if she noticed him at all. It struck Bill as he soaped himself that Natara might sleep through the whole thing, since she was so far gone at this point. Was she too sick to be cured? What if he pumped her full of his fluids and still nothing happened?

He dried himself off and wrapped the towel around his waist. With a lover, removing clothes was part of the foreplay. He figured he wouldn't need that type of opening act when fucking a near-comatose woman. When he reached the bedroom he saw Quif stroking Natara's hand, whispering gently in French. The covers had been removed and folded down to the foot of the bed. Natara wore only a pajama top, pulled up slightly to reveal a thick bush of black hair. The room was dimly lit, the lamp on the nightstand turned to its lowest setting. Still, Bill could see Natara's bony limbs, the skin on her thin legs unnaturally pale from being indoors so long. Although he'd never seen one in person, Bill was sure this was how a fresh corpse would look. Only the slightest heaving from Natara's chest revealed she was still alive.

"She is ready," Quif said. "I tried to explain to her what you are going to do. I cannot tell if my words are getting through to her. She does not react. She just looks at the ceiling." Quif's voice scratched. Bill could tell her heart was breaking.

"You've done the best you can," Bill said. "Who can explain something like this? Even for someone fully aware, it's irrational."

"I took off her panties."

"I see that." The situation was painfully uncomfortable. Bill was naked except for a towel, now expected to mount a dying woman and screw her back to health.

"I thought I would stay and hold her hand, in case she has a bad reaction."

Stay? Quif would be there to watch? Bill had struggled to come to terms with the idea of having sex with a woman. He thought he could rise to the occasion. The idea that the woman's sister would be right there was too much. "Uh, I don't think I'll be able to do this if you're sitting there."

"But I am a doctor! I will treat this as very clinical."

"Quif, I am about to fuck your sister. I'm gay. All of this is too weird to begin with. To have a sibling in the same room watching and taking notes, well, it's…" Bill tried to find the right word, "distracting."

"*Mon dieu!*" Quif said in disgust. "Americans are such *puritans*." The doctor walked past Bill to the door and gently pulled it to close. "I will leave you to your privacy," she whispered.

Now alone with Natara's cadaverous body, the magnitude of the daunting task fully enveloped Bill. He considered the tuft, knowing it was the target he needed to hit. If it was only as simple as pushing in and pulling out.

He let the towel drop to the floor and climbed aboard the bed. He crawled up next to Natara and placed his hand gently on her arm. When he began to caress, the expression on Natara's face changed. Her eyes opened wide and she jerked to turn in his direction. It was the most he'd seen her move since they met. The sudden burst of energy rattled Bill.

"Natara," he whispered as he brushed her arm. "Natara."

Was he getting through to her? Clearly she'd reacted to his presence, and it appeared she felt his touch. Yet as he studied her eyes, he could tell they were as vacant as they'd been the entire time he'd been in the apartment. It was as if there was only emptiness behind them, like she was sleeping with her lids open. He moved in closer and kissed her softly on the cheek. "Natara," he said again, hoping the tone of his voice would sound soothing.

If he looked at her any longer he knew he'd never be able to do what he had to do. He turned onto his back next to her and shut his eyes. He moved his right hand down to grasp himself. He was flaccid, but it only took a few tugs to get blood flowing. He wet his fingers in his mouth and massaged the spit into his flesh to increase the sensation. As he began to engorge, his thoughts offered the image of Ike. He felt Ike's breath on his neck, he saw the thin hairs at the bottom of his spine, the crevice that led to...

No! He could not think of Ike. Not now. That would be a betrayal of their love, not to be tainted by *this*. No. He had to think of a stranger, a past encounter that meant nothing other than the climax. He thought it best to reach back to a time long before Ike, when sex was driven only by lust, filling whatever random hole offered the means to release.

He pushed his thoughts to his days in Louisiana. Long before the destruction of Katrina. New Orleans. The French Quarter. Beyond the Lavender Line. Taking the dark walk off riotous Bourbon Street, far beyond the crowds. He envisioned his footsteps up to Burgundy Street, leading him to the rough, blue-collar men of the Rawhide bar. The jeans and leather crowd, where there was little pretense of socializing. Talking happened only as a brief prelude to sex.

Bill was far too young then for mixing with these men. They sized him up when he walked through the door, and he couldn't help being thrilled by their hungry glares. He liked the idea of being wanted. He wondered if their sexual appetite was anywhere near as powerful as his.

The bar's walls were painted black and the place smelled like a mixture of sweat and spilled booze. He ordered a beer and took a swig from the bottle as he leaned against the pool table in the back. A few moments later a rugged young man with a shaved head and thick dark razor stubble stood before him. The man's intense blue eyes locked on Bill's as his hand cupped the front of his prey's jeans. The man didn't blink as his fingers pulled down the fly. He kept the steely eye contact as he knelt and took Bill into his mouth. Bill stared back as the man skillfully brought him over, their eyes never leaving each other. Bill suppressed a moan, but the change in his breath revealed his climax. "Fuck, yeah," he heard someone nearby say. The other men in the bar had all been watching.

Recalling the bar room blowjob made Bill fully erect. He wet his fingers several times to further lubricate. Without opening his eyes he turned to put himself over Natara and pressed himself up to her. He could feel the sensation of an opening beneath the tuft. He pushed. It was dry and uninviting.

He forced his thoughts back to the Rawhide bar. Now he was in the bathroom, many beers later, shaking himself off at the wide trough urinal after a long piss. Several men had followed to watch. He was young and a star with this crowd. He wasn't embarrassed for them to stare at his body. He was ready for more fun. The beer he'd guzzled had gone to his head and emboldened. He became aroused in his hand in anticipation.

He pressed harder at Natara. Finally, the lips relented and allowed him inside. He tentatively pushed further, pulling back slightly, then incrementally entering a bit more. Back and forth. It was how he had sex with men. Few wanted to be impaled in one fell swoop. The sensation with Natara was different than with men. Less welcoming. He could feel no want. Instead, parched flesh twitched at his intrusion. He had to ignore that. He had to somehow finish.

He threw his thoughts back to the bathroom at the bar. How cocky he was then. Literally. He turned and showed his arousal to the half dozen men who now crammed inside the room. One of them locked the door, while another grasped Bill in his hand and pulled him forward. They lifted Bill's T-shirt off and tossed it onto the filthy floor. They yanked his jeans and underwear down to his sneakers. Six mouths explored his bare flesh, their goatees and stubble scratching and tickling places Bill didn't even know existed on his body. The sensation was overwhelming. So much stimulation in so many places all at once.

He felt his breathing increase. A guttural moan. Was that his? Or Natara's? He felt detached, like his body was on autopilot. He kept his eyes closed and he returned to the Rawhide.

Something wasn't right. For the first time, his mind was playing back in detail what he'd only previously remembered in bits and pieces. Until now, the memory stopped at the urinal in the Rawhide. Beyond that, all he could recall before were pieces, like a film that had run off its reel and flickered a few frames before dying. He'd never gone as far as to summon up the image of being in a locked bathroom with six men stripping off his clothes. Somehow his brain decided now was the time to reveal the rest of what happened that night. Why? There must have been a reason it was blacked out. He felt a terrible sense of dread. He tried to force the memory to stop, to think of something else, but he'd lost control.

He was that young man again. Drunk. Anything goes. Too naive to know what was really at stake until too much had already happened. A college boy, yes, but in those days still too redneck, too backwater Louisiana, too innocent about the world. He suddenly felt the powerful excitement of being bent over the urinal, his cheeks spread, and hot breath…down there. *Down there?* Then more than breath. A mouth. A tongue. He was dripping wet. How much of it had come from the man's mouth and how much was the drench of his own desire? No one had ever done that to him before. He wanted more. He begged for more.

Then pressure and entry. He'd been taken before, but never like this. In the back of his head, something told him that he should tell them to stop. He wasn't sure they were wearing condoms. It felt too good, so intense. One man after another was inside. *Don't do that.* The words surfaced inside his head, yet he was somehow powerless to make the sound come out of his mouth. Another part of him had taken over. The animal part. The want. The need to be so wanted. To be loved? He felt unbelievable pleasure and revulsion at the same time. It wasn't brutal. The men weren't trying to hurt him. In their own way, they worshipped him. He was paralyzed, unable to say or do anything to get them to stop. His body reacted with its own spasms onto the tiled floor. The men cheered. They were finished. They all told him he was the best. He should come back anytime. When the final man left, Bill locked the door. Now alone he sat his bare wet ass down on the cold soaked tiles. He picked up his shirt and pressed it to his face. He should have said no. Why didn't he say no? He wept into the shirt. Had he just signed his own death sentence?

Bill felt the tears drip down his cheeks. He opened his eyes. Natara stared back at him, her eyes searching his face. She looked aghast, as if struggling to figure out why she was the subject of such savageness. He looked at the tears on Natara's face but couldn't determine if they were hers, or his own that had fallen.

He pulled out. She was moist now. Not from her own accord, but from him. He had done what he set out to do. His seed – the miracle phage – was inside the dying woman. Would it save her? Had it saved him? In the end, despite everything, maybe he was still the damaged kid from that night in New Orleans.

17

Quif wandered the neighborhood shops in a daze. At the florist, she stared at the rows of tulips, but didn't really see them. Her mind was elsewhere. She couldn't stop thinking about what she'd done – and it was all for nothing.

It had been a restless night. At first she waited by Natara's bedside, holding her frail hand looking for any sign of improvement. At three in the morning she went to her own room to try to sleep, but stayed awake staring into blackness. *What had she done?* She'd let a man she barely knew force himself sexually onto her sister. Her dear, dying sister, who could no longer fend for herself.

The phage had failed.

Quif wondered if she could live with guilt of what she'd done in Natara's final hours. She'd turned her sister into a victim of rape.

Rape. Quif could try to justify her actions with scientific rationale, but it was rape nonetheless. Natara had never consented. She was taken without permission, no matter what the intention. As a doctor Quif had failed in her commitment to "do no harm." As a human being, her act was deplorable.

She couldn't continue to sit there and see her sister rot. She felt like she'd been trapped in the apartment for days, now suffocating and unable to face what she'd put her Natara through. Quif had to flee and get some fresh air, if only for a few hours. *Damn that nurse Dominique.* Quif had told the nurse not to come in yesterday for fear she'd witness what they'd done and report them. In a huff over learning she'd not be paid for a day, Dominique quit. Now Quif had no choice but to ask Bill to watch over Natara.

Bill Soileau, the same man she ordered to rape her sister.

Quif tried to shake off the thought. She wasn't being logical. The sex was for a good reason, Bill was a good man, doing a good thing. She couldn't blame him. Rationally, she knew science was about trial and error. But with the stakes so high this time, her efforts were wrapped too tightly in emotion. It was no way to be a doctor, but with her sister as the patient, she couldn't be detached in the way her profession usually demanded.

If the phage had worked, would she be less of a monster? Then would the ends justify the means? She realized this was the same thinking the Soviet scientists surely used when they experimented on the Armenians.

She dreaded going back to the apartment. She told Bill she needed to do some shopping, but bought nothing. She was too distracted to think of something as banal as picking the oranges with the tiniest pores, as they had the sweetest juice inside. *Oranges?* What a ridiculous thing to think of at a time like this.

Quif left the shops and made her way to a bench on the Square to sit and watch Paris wake up. Children in their uniforms ran off to school. Well-dressed young men and women executives hurried to the Métro. The city burst with life, renewed as it was every morning. She tried to absorb the energy. It was no use.

She raked her hand through her long dark hair. It felt oily and made her fingers smell musty, like an unclean room. When was the last time she washed her hair? She couldn't remember. Maybe a long hot shower would soothe her. With leaden steps she headed home.

She opened the door to the unexpected and delightful smell of breakfast. Eggs cooking, perhaps a light fluffy omelet. Dominique had not quit after all! The shower would have to wait. Quif couldn't remember the last time she'd eaten either.

"That smells *délicieusement bon!*" Quif said, trying to make her voice sound as genial as possible. As she hung up her coat she vowed to better manage her relationship with the nurse from now on. With Natara still dying she needed Dominique's help more than ever. Was that coffee she smelled brewing, too?

"Dominique, you are full of wonderful surprises this morning," Quif said as she rounded the corner and headed into the kitchen. "It is so thoughtful of you to prepare breakfast for –"

"Quif!" Natara said as she turned away from the stove. Her hair was pulled back from her face into a ponytail. It was impossible! Her cheeks remained gaunt, but now beamed with fresh pink color. "You are home at last!" Natara rushed to her sister and embraced her hard.

Quif was too stunned to move. *This couldn't be Natara.* Last night she was a shadow of a person, a creature more than a human being. She heard Natara's sobs smothered in her shoulder. She was crying. It *was* Natara. She knew the sound of her sister. She recognized her scent and the curve of her neck. Quif hugged back and finally let her own emotions free. They held each other and wept. It was the first moment Quif could remember *sharing* with Natara in years. She'd heard of tears of joy, but thought them only the things of fairy tales. Now she knew such tears were possible.

"Is it really you, *chère Natara?*" Quif took Natara's face in her hands. The flesh was warm in her fingers. The eyes were no longer blanks. A soul once again filled them.

Natara kissed Quif on the cheeks, over and over, then wiped her eyes with her sleeve. Natara had put on a lovely print dress, draped in an apron. Quif stepped back to soak in the astonishing sight. He sister was still frighteningly thin, but somehow vibrant.

"I borrowed it from your closet," Natara sniffled. "None of my clothes seem to fit anymore. I couldn't bare the thought of wearing pajamas for another day. I think I'm going to burn those pajamas."

"It is okay," Quif said as she grabbed Natara and clutched her against her chest. She was still fragile beneath the dress, a waif compared to what she once was. There was barely enough flesh to cover the bones, but Quif could feel something else. Life had returned. "You can wear anything I have. All I have is yours."

"I hope you don't mind that I started cooking breakfast without you," Natara apologized. "All I could find were eggs. I'm starving! I don't think I have ever been this hungry in my entire life."

Quif put her hand to her mouth and shook her head. She couldn't help herself. The tears rushed out again. *The phage worked!* It was the miracle she hoped it would be. Natara was saved. Now millions more would be, too. But, the cost…

"Natara… what we did to you…you understand…we had no choice. I hope you can forgive me. There was no other way…"

Natara embraced Quif again. "I know, my sister. You should not feel sorry. My new brother explained everything to me."

"Brother?"

"We are of the same blood now, *oui?*"

Quif heard a cough behind her. She turned to see Bill Soileau in the doorway sipping a cup of coffee and smiling. "She woke up just after you left," he said.

"And I was not here. I am so sorry," Quif said to Natara. "I thought it had failed. I could not take one more moment of sitting there, watching you suffer. I had to get some air. I abandoned you." Quif agonized about the horror Natara must have experienced as she awoke and found a stranger by her bed. Worse, the man who had forced himself on her during the night.

"Oh, Quif," Natara said as she took Quif's hands in hers. "I knew you were there all night long. I remember."

"How *much* do you remember?" Quif felt enveloped in dread.

"Do not worry, my sister. This thing – you call it the phage? – it has a way of making sense of things."

"What do you mean?"

"The moment the phage came inside my body, it was like an awakening. I felt a burst of energy, and a tingling sensation in my arms and legs and face." Natara looked over to Bill. "And I looked into Bill's eyes. He was crying. My face was awash in the salty tears from those angelic brown eyes. Somehow I knew instantly that this was not a man attacking me. It was a person in pain, fighting to give me this gift."

Quif turned to Bill. Why was he crying?

"And I understood. *Everything.* That this was the beginning, not the end. So powerful was the surge, the battle inside me, I let my consciousness be pushed to the side. It was as if my body was so far gone that I just had to do nothing but let it heal. All the time, I kept thinking of you Quif, and how I would tell you soon about this miracle."

"I felt the tingling too when I was first infected," Bill said.

"And then I finally opened my eyes, and I saw Bill. I was not afraid. We had a bond. That might sound crazy, but I don't know how else to explain it. It was instant. I knew that I loved him. Like I said, I immediately became aware that this was my brother."

Brother? Was Natara delusional? Maybe this was a form of posttraumatic stress disorder, or perhaps it was Stockholm syndrome. Quif had heard of people falling for their captors, or having a mental snap after surviving a horrible catastrophe. She studied her sister's face. No, this was not insanity speaking. It had be so long since, she'd almost forgotten. This was the true Natara, resurfacing after so many years — the whimsical, free spirit who believed in karma, fun, and love. When AIDS had destroyed her so completely, those things were stolen one by one until only the shell of her being was all that remained. Her sister was finally home. The real Natara had returned.

"You know what we have to do now," Bill said.

18

Bill Soileau dreaded making the call. What if Ike still didn't believe him? Bill had witnessed the miracle with Natara, but Ike was six thousand miles away. Their first conversation about the phage was a disaster. As he dialed, he prayed Ike had gone out and had the new blood tests done.

"Hey."

"Hey, you." Ike sounded groggy. It wasn't even dawn yet in San Francisco. "I'm still in Paris."

"I figured."

Ike always woke up in a good mood, and Bill hoped that would hold true today. "I woke you, didn't I?"

"That's okay," Ike said as he took a deep breath. "I wanted to hear your voice. I miss you. All night long I clutched your pillow in my arms, making believe it was you."

Yes, Bill thought. Ike was back to his old self. If he held any grudge from their last talk, it wasn't in his voice.

"I miss you, too," Bill said. "You can't imagine how much." He thought of all that had happened. The disturbing sex with Natara, and then her miraculous rebirth. All he had believed about the phage turned out to be true. Now he needed to convince the one man in the world who meant more to him than anyone else, the only other person he knew capable of passing the phage.

"When are you coming home?" Ike yawned.

"It's going to be a little while. They want to do more tests."

Bill remembered the bitter argument he'd had with Quif a few hours earlier. Despite the proof of her own sister's recovery, the doctor insisted on something she kept referring to as "proper protocols." Instead of organizing a massive effort to spread the miraculous phage to as many people as possible, Quif and Benoit would prepare a report with their findings and present it to a special inquiry board at Pasteur. The meeting would be in a few days. In the meantime, Bill and Natara would be put through an innumerable array of tests. Benoit even woke Dr. Greene overnight to get Bill's medical records sent immediately from San Francisco.

"This time we do things of the book," Quif said.

"You mean *by the book*." Bill frowned.

"*Oui*."

"That's fine. I understand your fellow scientists need proof. But it's crazy to delay getting this out to the rest of the world, even for just a week. Don't you understand the power of this virus? The ability to cure millions is at our fingertips. It's…" Bill struggled for the right word. "It's *immoral* to keep it from those who need it."

"You do not need to lecture me, Bill Soileau." Quif sounded annoyed. "I am the one who has been chasing this phage, *oui*? People were murdered because of this cure. Things are not so simple. Besides, it is not exactly, as you say, at *our fingertips*." Quif gestured to the front of Bill's pants.

Bill felt a twinge of embarrassment. "I'm not suggesting you stop your research. I promised to help you in every way, and I will. But it is reprehensible to wait. What do you want to do? Take years to figure out how to turn the phage into a pill?"

"No, I do not mean that. I know the world would accept this eagerly if it was as simple as taking a tablet. Such research might take decades. I agree with you that this is not the answer. But to do anything with the phage without the approval of the medical community, well, that would be a disaster. Believe me, they will help us spread the phage. First we must prove to them that it works."

"I don't need anyone's approval. How many will die in the meantime?"

"You will wait," Quif said sternly. "It is no longer your choice."

She was wrong. Now that he was on the phone with Ike, Bill could put plans into motion without involving Quif. If only he could get Ike to understand.

"What do you mean they want to do more tests?" Ike asked.

"Some pretty dramatic things have happened here. I'll tell you all about it. First I need to know. Did you get more blood tests done?"

"Yes."

"And?"

"Okay, you've got me officially freaked out. I went to three different places and the results were all negative. I don't have HIV anymore. According to the tests, I never did. It's just like you said it would be."

Ike should sound more excited, Bill thought. To learn he was cured – shouldn't he be excited? Full of joy? This was a moment that should draw then closer, but instead…

"You still sound skeptical."

"I have to admit, I'm confused," Ike said. "It doesn't make any sense. Your story about this phage thing is just too fantastic. Still, it's the only explanation that fits. I don't know what to believe."

"You have every right to be confused," Bill said. He forced himself to remain calm. He had to nurture Ike through this. "I found it very hard to believe, too. We've been taught our whole lives that a virus is evil. That it kills, or makes people sick. The idea that a virus can also be the mechanism to cure seems like it can't possibly be true. But I've seen it with my own eyes. It is true."

"Seen it?"

"Under a microscope. It's the strangest creature. Long legs, a big head, and this thing that looks like a needle that jabs into its enemy. It's a vicious killing savage."

"Sounds horrifying."

"To look at, yes. I've also seen what it can do. A person on the verge of death is up and walking today, instantly healthy."

"How? I don't understand. I thought you and I were the only ones who had this phage virus? Did you give someone a blood transfusion?"

Bill took the phone away from his ear for a moment and clutched the receiver. He had to tell Ike everything. Otherwise, how would he truly understand what needed to happen now?

"We tried a transfusion. It didn't work."

"Then how?"

"Ike, you know I love you, right?"

"How did this other person get the phage from you?" Ike said, his voice impatient.

"Well, it turns out the only way we know the phage can be transmitted person to person is in semen. That's where it's concentrated enough to infect someone else, so I…"

"You fucked him. You fucked some guy to infect him. Is that what I'm hearing?"

"Ike, it wasn't—"

"I can't believe this!"

"Ike, calm down. It's not what you think. I mean, it wasn't even another man. It was…a woman."

Bill waited for Ike to respond. Nothing. He knew Ike hadn't hung up because he could still hear the faint sound of breathing.

"Ike, you've got to believe me. It was for the sake of medicine. It was awful. I didn't even know if I could finish. But I had to. I had to save this woman. She was end-stage AIDS. The sister of the doctor I came to Paris to see. The thing is…you've got to listen to me. It worked! This woman, her name is Natara, she's cured. Just like you. Just like me. In just a short amount of time, the HIV was gone. She felt that tingling sensation – that's rush of energy. Now her body is healing. She was up walking and talking. Ike, are you there? Are you hearing what I'm telling you? The phage. It's real. I saw it work with my own eyes!"

"A woman." Ike's voice was eerily calm. "You had sex with a woman."

"Yes, I did. I'm sorry. There was no other way."

"Bill, do you have any idea how insane this all sounds?"

"I know. But I need you to believe me. Do you?"

Ike was silent for a few moments. "It's getting harder and harder. But then I look at my own test results and…"

"You do! You do believe me!"

"For the sake of argument, let's say I believe you. I mean, let's face it, I just don't see you going around having sex with women for fun. What happens now?"

"They want to study me. And the woman. We'll be at the Institut Pasteur here in Paris for the next few days being poked and prodded like lab rats. I just don't think we should wait that long."

"Wait?" Ike asked. "For what?"

"To cure others," Bill explained. "I mean, you're in AIDS prevention. How many people die each day from the disease?"

"At last count, about 8,500 die each day. Mostly in Africa. But I'm not sure what you're suggesting."

"I don't think we should wait for the French doctors. What if something goes wrong? There's no time to waste. We need to spread the phage infection immediately and plant the cure in as many people as possible. Then get them to pass the virus to others. We need to cause a pandemic...of cure."

"I guess that's the right thing to do." Ike sounded wary. "But how?"

"That's the problem. I can't. I'm here in Paris. I'm now a prized possession. I can't leave. It's really up to you."

"Me?"

"Ike, I know you don't want to do it, but you need to go out and infect others. Have unprotected sex with men. Find men you know are HIV positive. And make them promise to have sex with other HIV positive men. Single-handedly, you need to start a massive outbreak!"

"Bill, I...I can't do it. I'm not like that. I'm not promiscuous. I never have been. You're asking me to change my nature. I can't."

"You must!"

"I wouldn't even know how. Look, I don't hang out with men like that. The world of orgies and unprotected, anonymous sex is so foreign to me. I don't have a single friend who does those things."

Bill swallowed hard before answering. "Yes, you do."

"Who?"

"Me."

"What are you talking about? You're my handsome Southern gentleman. You're not a...whore."

"Ike, I did many things before I knew you." Bill panicked. If he told Ike everything he'd done with men, it might end their relationship. But if he didn't tell Ike right now how to enter that world, then the phage cure might never get to those who needed it.

"Look, I know a guy who can help. He's a player, so to speak. He understands how the scene works. I'll call him and set it all up. He'll be your chaperone."

"But I don't want to have sex with other men."

"Ike, you can't think of it that way. Can't you see how important this is?"

"Who is this guy?"

"His name is Mark Hazodo."

"Mark Hazodo? I know that name! He's that freak who was involved in that internet porn scandal!"

"Uh, it wasn't exactly porn..."

Bill had known Mark and his antics for so long he'd almost forgotten what a public nightmare that video caused. Mark had been one of the earliest victims of so-called *upskirting*, where a video cell phone recorded someone in a compromising position, and then the recording was put on the web for millions to gawk at and forward. In Mark's case, the video showed him performing an extreme sex act. A man in a leather hood had his fist inside Mark. Unfortunately for Mark, he wasn't wearing a mask. The whole world saw his euphoric face in the same week his company launched a line of videogames targeted to children. It was front-page news, and right-wingers like the Reverend Willie Warrant had a field day with it, smearing the entire gay community.

"You know that degenerate?" Ike was suddenly furious.

"He's a, uh, friend of mine."

"He set our fight for equality back a decade with that video! What type of man has Mark Hazodo as a friend?"

"It wasn't that bad..."

"Not that bad? Bill O'Reilly named Mark Hazodo THE WORST PERSON IN THE WORLD! Who the fuck are you, Bill Soileau? Honestly, I don't know anymore. This phage story. You fucked...a woman! Then you want me to go out and have unprotected sex with strange men. I can't...I just can't."

The line went dead. Then bursts of a loud high-pitched whine assaulted Bill's ear. The French dial tone.

19

Quif had never been on the Métro at 5:30 a.m. before. She eagerly waited for the first train of the day to arrive at the Jules Joffrin station. Only a few others boarded with her. They looked especially tired. She studied their yawns and weary eyes.

Two men at the far end of the car stood out from the rest. They were young with short haircuts and dressed in nearly identical neatly pressed dark pinstripe suits. They had a certain vibrancy, as if somehow they were already fully engaged in the day. That's more like it. She'd been up for an hour already, bursting with energy. She couldn't wait to get back to the Institut.

The special CODIS meeting was just two days away. It would be a race to the finish to make sure her presentation was flawless. Anything less would bring doubt on the findings, and there were too many lives at stake for that to happen. Tests she and Benoit had done four times were repeated again to confirm the results beyond question. That meant working nearly non-stop for days. The few hours of sleep last night were the first she'd had in her own bed all week. But she wasn't tired. All the good she'd ever dreamt she could possibly do in medicine – with her entire life, for that matter – was now happening for real. Sleep? She was too excited.

The tests on Bill and Natara corroborated all their theories about the phage. They'd documented how the phage was passed from one person to another, and its perplexing fragility outside of the human body. They'd been able to calculate the speed at which the phage replicated, estimating that complete infection of the body happened within two hours. Nothing had been shown to work so quickly since the Ebola virus. Yet instead of death, the phage virus brought life.

DNA from the blood samples of the Armenian villagers confirmed the strain of phage was identical to the virus in Bill, and now in Natara. That meant the phage was no temporary fix. The cures in the villagers had lasted nearly two decades without any side effects. Before their murders, they were possibly the healthiest people on the planet.

Quif daydreamed of standing before the CODIS board this time. The chairman would be hesitant, of course. After all, he'd been held somewhat responsible for the tragedy at the Armenian oilrig. Not that he had anything to do with the massacre or the destruction of the refinery, but the chairman had vouched for her and mounted a mission ending in piles of corpses, not cure. That smoldering pyre – if she'd had kept her mouth shut, they might all still be alive. Even the phage can't bring them back, but as the cure spreads, it will carry a message.

Redemption. Not just for her, but for her people.

She vowed to make sure the world knew how the villagers gave their lives. This was one Armenian genocide that would not be forgotten. Perhaps she would even insist the phage be given a name that noted the sacrifice of those who had made it possible. ArmeniaViroPhage had a nice sound to it.

AVP. Yes, that would look strong on the handout to the board. She shut her eyes and imagined the expressions on their faces as the report was placed in front of them. Would the pop star show up again? Dr. Helen Mangeur, Pasteur's bitch director who tried to belittle Quif at the last meeting, would finally be put in her place. That foolish bigot, the Reverend Willie Warrant would get the "miracle" he craved. And when he learns the only way known to pass the cure *is through semen*…

Quif became giddy at the thought. She giggled aloud.

She opened her eyes. The other passengers on the train stared at her, including the two young men in the dark pinstripe suits.

"Nothing is more lovely than the laughter of a beautiful woman," one of the men said to her.

Quif began to respond, but caught herself. She didn't know these men. People didn't talk to strangers on the subway. It just wasn't done. And they'd spoken to her *in English*. Tourists? She decided to ignore the remark and looked down to the floor, like everyone did on the train.

By the time she reached the stop for the Institut she'd pushed the encounter with the young men from her mind. She had no space in her thoughts for such frivolity. She was due to meet Benoit in the lab at six to review the final round of tests and complete the report. Bill and Natara were told they could sleep in and enjoy a few hours of freedom. Their days of living in the lab as guinea pigs were over – at least for now. Once the CODIS board read the report, Bill and Natara would no doubt be put through the rigors of examinations all over again.

The grounds of the campus were still dark when she stepped through the main gate. When she reached the lab the lights were already on and the door ajar. Benoit must already be hard at work.

She smiled when she thought of him. With all of his previous adolescent advances toward her, she'd misjudged Benoit. The past week had revealed just how much of a dedicated scientist he really was. He'd lived in the lab with her, never once griping about all that needed to be accomplished. He was as passionate about the phage discovery as she was. She'd never seen this side of him before – he'd become so serious. She found herself gazing into his dazzling green eyes the previous day when he reviewed the negative staining protocols of the electron microscope with her. She felt a growing bond with him that went beyond the discovery of the phage.

"*Bonjour, Benoit!*" Quif said cheerfully as she removed her coat. She looked around the lab. Benoit wasn't there. Perhaps he was in the back.

She sat down at her computer and typed in her passcode, eager to see if Benoit had entered the latest data. There was no reason to think these tests would be any different than the previous four. Still, she was eager to see it with her own eyes. This was going to be a great day – she could feel it.

She tapped the keys. Then again.

That's strange, she thought. The passcode worked and got her into the system, but the files with all the raw data were gone. She clicked on another part of the screen. Bizarre. The draft of the report for CODIS was also missing.

Don't panic, Quif told herself as she took a deep breath. Benoit said he was worried about someone else accessing the results. For days he'd vowed to move the files out of the Pasteur computers and onto secure discs. Maybe he'd already done that.

She got up and walked to the back of the lab and down the corridor to Benoit's tiny personal office. If he wasn't in the lab, she could always find him there.

"*C'est affreux!*" Quif slipped and nearly fell. As she steadied herself with the wall she noticed the floor was slick and wet. She looked down to see a thick puddle on the linoleum. She immediately knew what it was.

Blood.

She bent over to study the puddle. Shards of glass revealed the remains of test tubes. She used the tips of her fingernails to carefully pick up a large piece with writing on it. It was Benoit's scrawl. "Patient Zero – Bill Soileau."

Bill Soileau's blood! Dozens of test tubes had been dropped and smashed. She spotted what looked like the remains of vials from Natara, and Bill's semen samples, too. Who could have done this? This wasn't some random tray dropped in the hallway. It looked like all their work was deliberately smashed! It was ruined. The lab was supposed to be under quarantine lockdown. No one from Pasteur would dare break such a protocol.

A feeling of dread cascaded down her in the chest. The phage. Someone had found out they had the virus and had come here to destroy it. Just like in Armenia, where they bombed the lab and killed anyone who knew any—

"Benoit!" Quif called down the hallway.

No answer.

She stayed to the side to avoid stepping in any more of the spill.

"Benoit," she pleaded.

She felt her body begin to shake. She slowly pushed open the door to his office. The lights were off and Benoit was in his chair, leaning back. For a moment she allowed herself to believe he'd simply fallen asleep. She prayed that was true. She flipped on the light switch.

"Ben—"

Quif put her hands up to her mouth. She felt light-headed, as if all her strength had suddenly rushed from her body.

Benoit. No. No. No!

Benoit green eyes were open, looking up to the ceiling. They no longer sparkled with life. His throat had been cut, ear to ear. His head tipped back, held on only by a flap of skin in the back.

No. No. No.

The cut had gone right through the bone. The front of his shirt was soaked in blood. It was already dried. He'd been murdered sometime overnight.

Quif couldn't catch her breath. As she bowed to force herself to inhale, she noticed how Benoit's hands were duct-taped to the arms of the chair. He'd been captured, restrained and then killed.

Why? Who would?

She gasped. In short breaths, air started to fill her lungs. It was happening again. The phage. Like the villagers, those who knew about it were killed. Benoit. Whoever had done this would want to kill her, too. And Natara and...

No, not Natara!

Quif ran from the office.

"Ah!" she screamed as she slipped and fell in the puddle of blood. As she struggled to get back up, she looked at her hand, now drenched in crimson. Tiny splinters of test tube glass stuck in her palm. *Pain!* Tears began to come. She'd done it again. Another was dead because of her and the phage. *Benoit!*

She raced down the hallway and back into the lab. As she ran for the exit two men appeared in the doorway. *Them?*

It was the two young men in the dark pinstripe suits from the Métro.

She turned and ran back into the lab and down the hall towards Benoit's office. She slid in the blood spill again, but caught herself so she didn't fall. She looked back, but the men were not chasing after her. She had a chance. She had to escape. She had to find Natara and make sure she was safe.

Just beyond Benoit's office was the exit from the lab into the main building. Someone else had to be here. Once she got beyond those thick metal doors, designed so not even a microscopic germ could escape, she'd find help. Or she'd just keep running – to anywhere but here!

Quif pushed the metal release bar to open the doors. Nothing. It wouldn't engage! She tried again. And again. She slammed the bar up and down. Then she threw her shoulder into the door. It wouldn't budge! Her tiny body couldn't even get it to rattle.

The quarantine! The mechanisms to open the door had been disengaged under her orders. On the other side was a blaze of warning signs to make sure no one would dare come in. Not even sound could penetrate the seal.

Or maybe it could. She had to try. She pounded at the door and shouted as loud as she could, "*Au secours! Au secours! Au meurtre! Au meurtre!*" The blood from her hand left red blotches where she struck the metal, she felt the glass splinters go deeper into her flesh.

The only way out was the same way she came in. As she turned back to see if there was any chance to backtrack she saw the two young men. They simply walked toward her. They didn't run. There was no worry in their faces. They *knew* she'd be trapped.

"*Je vous en supplie,*" Quif begged. "*Je vous en supplie.*" Her body trembled so hard her knees buckled and she found herself kneeling. She noticed that one of the men held a gray oval in his hand. She wasn't sure what it was until he tore off a small piece – enough to cover her mouth.

Duct tape.

20

Bill Soileau stretched back in his seat and let the sun beam onto his face. It wasn't the full embrace of God-fearing Louisiana heat, but the warmth brought a familiar, calming comfort. Water lapped against the side of the boat, little waves stirred up by the passing of a sister *Bateaux-Mouches* river shuttle headed in the other direction. Like the boat he was on, it swelled with tourists, many snapping pictures at the architectural icons that sat atop the stone embankments overlooking the Seine. The Louvre, the Musée d'Orsay, the Eiffel Tower. Even the bridges were ornate and magnificently crafted.

In addition to the catacombs, riding the river shuttles was always on his agenda when visiting Paris. The boats connected many of the main tourist stops, and for only fifteen dollars he could ride all day, getting on and off as many times as desired. The journey was remarkably serene, a completely different world from the noisy, congested city streets only meters above. Yet he'd never taken the boats for the calm or to sightsee landmarks before. In the past, he'd discovered the shuttles were the most productive way to cruise for men.

He would get on board and look for the most handsome man traveling alone. With the seats so close together, he'd nestle in next to his target and let his leg gently brush up against the man's thigh. With all the sights to behold, an uninterested man would think nothing of it – Bill would seem like any other eager tourist fidgeting in his seat trying to take in as much as possible. Bill didn't often make the mistake of pursuing the unwilling. His sense was uncanny, led by that musky smell he believed identified desire. When his leg brushed against the other man, the smell would become more pungent, as if somehow signaling the hunger to connect. Bill used the rubbing of his thigh to make the man aroused to the point where he'd need to cover his lap to hide his enthusiasm. Without ever speaking, Bill would gesture for them to disembark at the next stop and head for whoever's hotel was closest. Back when he was single, Bill fucked tourists by the dozen. It was the perfect arrangement – there was no chance he'd ever see them again.

He looked around the boat and saw several attractive men. Some had been glancing at Bill since he boarded. A year ago, he would have eagerly pursued them all.

But now, when he needed to have sex with strangers more than ever before, he simply could not do it.

It wasn't because he'd spent much of the past week masturbating into specimen cups. Quif and Benoit had demanded so much of his semen he felt like a cow herded off to the barn for milking once an hour. No matter how quickly they worked, the virus died as soon as it was out of the cocoon of Bill's body. At one point Benoit stood in front of Bill as he released directly onto a Petri dish, accidentally splashing Benoit's sleeve. The young Frenchman didn't flinch. His only reaction came later when the test once again revealed the phage had failed to survive for even a moment.

Most men would be sexually drained after a week of that, but that's not what held Bill back. When he found out he had the day off, he got on the boat to pick someone up and start spreading the phage himself. He'd come to adore and respect Quif, but she was wrong about waiting to get the cure out to the world.

Here, with so many men within reach, Bill found himself unable to complete the mission. He had no desire for other men. The only man he now craved was Ike.

Bill prayed that mentioning his friendship with Mark Hazodo hadn't ruined everything. Ike needed to know that Bill wasn't the man he once was. He wasn't a player anyone, even though the future of mankind would be better off it he could return to his old promiscuous ways. He'd explain it all to Ike when they reunited in San Francisco.

He saw friends walking and chatting along the banks of the river.

He wished he'd brought Natara along. Without the game of hunting for men, the river trip became tedious after the second time around the Ile de la Cité and Ile Saint-Louis. Natara would have been good company, especially since he felt a strange desire to be with her – to protect her. He couldn't forget the terror in her eyes the night he implanted her. It didn't matter that he saved her life, in that moment he'd caused her pain. She'd never mentioned it, and had since treated him as a loved one. Like a little girl she'd held his hand as they sat waiting in the lab between tests over the past few days. At first he was taken aback by her soft touch, but he also felt an affection growing between them. Love? Not the same as he had with Ike. More like the connection with a sibling. Perhaps if he hadn't grown up in a home wrecked by alcohol and poverty, he'd share the same type of feelings with his own brothers and sisters.

Bill figured his bond with Natara was further strengthened by the fact that they were members of a unique tribe. Along with Ike, they were the only people in the world infused with the miracle phage. Natara's lack of a penis and sperm meant she was unable to be a distributor. That left Ike as the only one able to spread the phage, and he'd refused. Bill knew it was bizarre to ask a partner to go out and fuck as many men as possible, but what choice did he have? He'd never heard Ike so angry, and even worse – disappointed. Bill had called every day since the blow-up over the phone, and so far Ike had refused to answer or return a single call. Bill left several pleading voicemail messages and e-mails, but to no avail. He had to get back to San Francisco soon and mend things in person.

The boat pulled up to the Hôtel de Ville stop, the site of Paris' ornate City Hall. Bill scolded himself – what a hypocrite he was! He'd practically ordered Ike to go out and infect as many strangers as possible, but here he had the opportunity to do the same and he wasn't up to the task either. Of course, there was no way to know if any of the men on the boat were HIV positive, and therefore likely to benefit. What if they were mostly monogamous? Such a waste that would be. He knew there was a gay bathhouse not too far from there. Maybe at a place like that he'd have a better chance of passing the phage onto someone who needed it. That would be just random luck. And, God forbid, what if they practiced *safe sex?* There was no way he could explain the miracle of the phage to a bunch of queens in a steam room and expect them to sign up to be soldiers in this war.

Bill felt a headache beginning to emerge. Infecting the world with the phage would be more complicated than he'd thought.

He got up from his seat, headed to the back across the gangplank and off the boat. He climbed the stone stairs and walked over to the closest street where he could hail a taxi.

He needed his tribe.

~

The taxi sat in dead-stop traffic two blocks from Quif's apartment. The driver threw up his hands in disgust. He said something in French Bill didn't understand, although from the gesture it was clear it was a profanity. He handed the driver enough Euros for the fare and got out to walk the rest of the way.

The sidewalks were in a frenzy, with people running and looking alarmed. A toddler screamed. His mother yanked him up by the arms and clutched the boy to her chest as she dashed down the sidewalk. Others were also running toward Bill, their faces panicked. Parisians were notorious for their cool disdain of nearly every circumstance. What could possibly cause them to be so upset?

As he turned the corner, he saw the source of their distress. He smelled it before he looked up and understood. It appeared as if an entire building was engulfed in flames. It was up the street, very close to Quif's apartment, although he couldn't be sure from so far away. He immediately thought of Natara. After all the poor woman had been through, she surely didn't need to be surrounded by chaos. She should be resting.

The wail of sirens hurt Bill's ears.

He walked in the direction of the fire. The closer he got the more he began to realize the blaze was within feet of Quif's flat. It could be her building!

He felt the sharp pain of an elbow in his rib. In his distraction, he'd walked right into an elderly man.

"Detournez! Rentrez!" the man shouted.

"I, uh, don't understand," Bill said. *"Parlez-vous anglais?"*

The man scrunched his face. "You…*allez* ze wrong way! Les flics…eh…the police. They order us…*évacuez!*"

"Do you know what building it is?" Bill said each word slowly, as if this might bridge the language gap.

The elderly man's eyes widened. "Explosion! Le gaz!" The man pushed past Bill and hurried away.

A gas explosion? *My new sister.* He had to find Natara and make sure she was okay. He ran upstream into the mob of evacuees coming toward him. As he got closer to the fire, the smoke became thick, irritating his eyes and making it difficult to breathe. He still couldn't see which building was on fire. Did the explosion destroy it? *Natara can't be hurt – she just can't be.* He hadn't saved her life just to see it lost to something like this. Please, he prayed, Natara must be safe. He had to find her.

He took the sleeve of his shirt and held it over his mouth, hoping to filter out some of the smoke. It was still too much. He choked on the fumes, coughing so hard he was forced to stop running.

"Bill Soileau."

It was a woman's voice coming from the street. Natara?

He walked toward the voice. Through the smoke emerged a sleek black sedan at the curb. The car door was open and the engine was running. Bill leaned down to look inside. He immediately recognized the face. It didn't make any sense.

"You? Aren't you…"

"Bill Soileau. You need to get in the car. We need to get you as far away from here as possible. You are not safe."

Bill knew the woman, although they'd never met before. Everyone knew her. She was possibly the most famous woman on the planet. What was *she* doing here? And how did she know his name?

"Uh…I don't understand. Aren't you Milana?" Bill struggled to talk, his lungs still crippled by smoke. "How do you know my name?"

"It's not safe for you to be on the street. Get in the car and I'll explain everything," Milana said.

It *is* her, Bill thought. The voice was as unmistakable as the face.

What did she mean he wasn't safe? *How does she know my name?* It was all too strange. Bill backed away from the car.

"I can't," Bill said. "I need to find my friend. I'm worried about her. She lives near here."

"You're looking for Natara Melikian," Milana said as she got out of the car and took Bill by the arm. "I'm afraid you're too late."

"What do you mean too late? You know Natara? Tell me what's going on!" Bill inhaled more smoke and started to choke again. Milana patted his back.

"We need to get you into the car and out of this smoke," she said.

"I'm not going anywhere without Natara!"

Milana's famous cobalt eyes locked onto Bill's. "Natara Melikian is dead. This was no gas explosion. The fire was set. Do you understand? Natara is dead and you will be too if you don't come with me. Now!"

Milana pulled Bill over to the car and pushed him into the backseat. Bill was numb. *Natara dead? The fire was set?* Who would want to kill her? And they wanted to kill him, too? Quif had told him about the murders and bombing of the Armenian oilrig. Now the killers were after him? *Natara! My new sister!* His lungs continued to struggle against the soot he'd inhaled. He couldn't stop coughing.

His arm hurt from where Milana had grabbed him. He rubbed the sore muscle. For such a petite woman, Bill marveled at her strength. Through his choking he turned to stare and size her up. The determined look on her face, the way she held herself – this was a woman you messed with at your peril.

Milana shouted to the driver, *"Toussus-le-Noble!* Hurry!"

21

Quif couldn't speak. She could barely breathe. The two men in the dark pinstripe suits had shoved a handkerchief into her mouth before securing her lips shut with a large piece of duct tape. Just as with Benoit, her wrists were bound to the arms of a chair.

Benoit. She couldn't get the gruesome scene at Pasteur out of her mind. Those viridescent eyes now dimmed forever. She wanted to believe he didn't suffer at the hands of his captors, but as a doctor she knew too much from seeing the wound. Benoit's death must have been agony, with him aware of what was happening while they slit his throat, gurgling and choking on his own blood until the final moment they cut through his spinal cord.

Quif felt sickened by the thought. She swallowed hard to keep from vomiting. If she threw up now she'd asphyxiate. *Control,* she told herself. *Stop thinking about Benoit.*

Her eyes darted around the room, looking for any evidence that might reveal where she was. It was too dark to make out many details. The height of the ceilings made it seem like some sort of warehouse. The men had pressed her face to the floor of the car so she couldn't see where they went once they'd left Pasteur. At first, Quif tried to keep track of the route by concluding which streets they had turned on, but she quickly became disoriented.

The glass panes in the tall windows looked as if they'd been painted black. She couldn't see out. How many days had passed? It was possible she wasn't in Paris any longer – they'd driven for so long. The palms of her hands were still sore from where she'd fallen in the broken glass. But they appeared to be healing. There were no sign the wounds had become infected.

She closed her eyes and silently begged. Not for her own survival, or even for the future of the precious phage. *Natara.* If the people who kidnapped her and murdered Benoit had accessed all the data at Pasteur, then they knew about Bill Soileau and Natara. Patient Zero and Subject One. Every detail about them was contained in the draft of the report. In any other research project, participants would only be identified with codes. She hadn't bothered with that protocol of secrecy since she planned to have Natara and Bill at the CODIS meeting to introduce them. Now, by using their names in the report, she might have signed their death sentences.

She should have let Bill go out and spread the phage, instead of insisting she get the blessing of the medical community. It was true that Pasteur had the resources and infrastructure to manage a vast distribution of the cure. Was the really why she insisted on waiting? Or was it a desire for that big moment of triumph, the ovation from her peers that she was denied the first time she brought them the phage. Yes, it was her vanity, her pride that had killed so many. If only she had listed to Bill and allowed him to do it his way with rampant, unsafe sex. Her hubris couldn't allow a man such as Bill to be right about such things. She was the doctor, not him. Her arrogance and need for redemption had made her blind to the most obvious answer.

Forced to breathe only through her nose, Quif noticed a chemical smell coming from somewhere in the room. It was familiar. A pesticide? That was it. It smelled like cockroach spray.

Who's behind all this?

Someone wanted to stop the world from knowing about the phage. But why? Who could possibly be against something that could cure so many people? Were the Soviets responsible for the gruesome experiments that led to the phage trying to cover their tracks? If so, why wait until now to try to hide their deeds? They had nearly twenty years to burn down that lab and eliminate the cured villagers. Yet they only acted now. It didn't make any sense.

There had to be a connection to someone who was at the original CODIS meeting. They all knew the potential of the phage. She tried to recall the faces of those who were there. There was that pop star Milana. And looming over everyone with his seat as a guest on the board was the Reverend Willie Warrant. She hated how the Reverend tried to force his beliefs on others in the room. And then there was Cardinal Umberto Uccelli, so resplendent in his ornate garb.

Two so-called holy men made it a point to be at Pasteur that day. She thought it strange, but perhaps it was more than just coincidence. They didn't know ahead of time she would discuss the phage. No one knew. They were there to meet about AIDS in Africa, to see how their money would be spent to fight the disease. More importantly, each man wanted to be sure their money was *not* spent on programs that conflicted with their moral codes, like condoms or safe sex instruction.

Sex. Maybe that's what this was all about. Morality. If they'd found out the phage was a cure that could be passed only through sex, would they kill to stop that from happening?

It's something she'd never considered. The discovery of the phage and its spread around the world wouldn't just end disease – it would also shake the foundations of most religions. The tenets that made sex a sin outside of marriage would no longer make sense. Promiscuity would save the planet. The Roman Catholic Church might not survive such an idea. People would suddenly be forced to conclude the entire religion was built on lies. If God existed, then God was ultimately responsible for the phage. One of The Church's mortal sins would overnight be transformed into a savior. Sex would be born again. To accept the phage was to accept life.

To stand against the phage and its cure spread through non-monogamous sex would be the same as advocating for the deaths of millions. To be against the phage would be to favor genocide. For Rome's theologians, the phage represented devastating evidence against their beliefs.

Zealots had killed for less in the past. The phage challenged the survival of The Church. Would Rome send henchmen to stop the phage and kill everyone who ever knew anything about it?

Would the Reverend Willie Warrant?

Damn the phage! Please don't hurt my beloved Natara.

If the kidnappers read the report they'll know Natara couldn't pass the cure onto anyone else. If the phage has to end, let it end with her still alive. She was useless as a carrier, since sperm was the only way to infect others.

Spare my sister.

If someone has to die, kill Bill Soileau instead.

Quif hated herself for thinking it. But if the kidnappers wanted to stop the phage, they had to get rid of Bill.

Not Natara. Take Bill. Just don't take my Natara.

A door from somewhere behind Quif opened, allowing a burst of light into the room. She stiffened.

The two young men in dark pinstripe suits stood before her. One held a small square metal container, the type used to store petrol. The other ripped the tape off Quif's mouth and pulled out the handkerchief. Quif ignored the sting on her skin and inhaled deeply. The air felt so comforting, although the fumes of the roach spray were more pungent now. Was it coming from the can?

"My sister," Quif gasped. "I beg of you. Do not hurt her. She is innocent in all this. I will do whatever you want. Please, please, please — do not harm my sister."

One of the men looked at the other and grinned.

"Doctor, do you know what this is?" The man rapped his fingers on the side of the metal canister.

Quif shook her head.

"It's a powerful new accelerant. Unusually effective at burning human flesh right down to the bone."

"Of course, you've seen it work before," the other man said. "Remember that cave in Armenia?"

The burning pile of bodies. Remnants of the belongings of the villagers had somehow survived the flames, but the flesh had been incinerated. It was grotesque and she remembered thinking how strange it was, but until now she'd never considered that the fire had been designed to burn that way.

"Remarkable stuff, really. Leaves very little of the living behind. Not even the tiniest germ. Am I right?" The man looked to his partner.

"Absolutely. I'd say the frog cops are going to have a tough time scraping up enough to identify the remains of...what did you say your sister's name was?"

Natara!

"Blowing up the entire building so it looked like a gas explosion was a nice touch, too," the other man smirked.

Natara!

Quif closed her eyes. She saw Natara as a baby the day she came home from the hospital – Quif's earliest memory of anything. Then came a flash of the day their mother died, and they embraced on their grandmother's bed until they cried each other to sleep. A glorious afternoon of sightseeing on the boat to Alcatraz in San Francisco. Laughing from too much champagne the day of Quif's graduation from medical school. The night she held Natara's hand when they'd learned she was HIV positive. The vision of Natara in the kitchen when she'd been reborn. Gone. Natara was gone. She'd failed to protect her baby sist—"

Quif felt her hair pulled violently from behind, forcing her to open to her eyes and stare up. *Pain!*

"Only one thing prevents me from pouring this over your head and lighting a match," one of the men said, holding the metal canister up to Quif's face.

The other man leaned over and whispered in Quif's ear.

"Where is Bill Soileau?"

22

Bill Soileau held the railing firmly as he stepped up the stairs. He still didn't have his bearings. He had yet to adjust to the constant motion, even though they'd been on board for several hours. Milana said a person never really knew if he had sea legs until a trip like this one.

It wasn't the water. He'd been on plenty of boats, although none was quite like this. They'd boarded the *Seabourn Pride* at Fortaleza. It had taken the better part of a day for the jet to reach Brazil. After taking off from the private Toussus-le-Noble airfield outside Paris, they refueled in Miami before traveling further south. Bill wasn't allowed off the plane in Florida, even for a few moments for fresh air.

"You are too valuable," Milana said. "We can't risk anything happening to you."

At the time, Bill considered using the emergency exit to escape and make a run for it. He wasn't handcuffed. Milana wasn't armed with anything more than her considerable charm. Then it hit him. If he fled, where would he go? If everything Milana had told him was true, he was the most hunted man in the world.

When he emerged from the stairs onto the deck a light drizzle hung in the air. Out of nowhere, a figure raced in his direction. Bill shut his eyes, wondering for an instant if this was the moment he'd be killed.

"Sir?"

Bill opened his eyes to find a handsome young member of the crew, looking no older than eighteen, adorned in a perfectly pressed white uniform. He held a large black umbrella over Bill's head.

"When you ran over, I…"

"Didn't want you to get wet, sir," the man beamed, displaying preternaturally white teeth. "Rain like this is quite common here on the Amazon. What is your pleasure today?"

"My pleasure? I…I don't know what you mean," Bill said. Pleasure was the last thing on his mind.

"If I can make a suggestion? The Sky Bar is open up top, with a canopy to protect you from the drizzle."

"What if I just want to stand outside for a while?"

"A splendid idea!" The young man looked genuinely thrilled. "Few rivers are more exciting than the Amazon. May I escort you over to the port side railing? The sightseeing is most spectacular from there."

They walked to the left side of the ship for Bill to take in the view. The young man remained, staring humbly down at his feet. He held the umbrella over Bill's head, leaving himself exposed to the rain.

"Uh, do you think it would be possible for me to hold the umbrella myself?" Bill asked. "I really just want some time alone…if that's okay."

"Of course, sir! I wouldn't want to intrude," the young man said with more enthusiasm. He gently placed the umbrella handle in Bill's hand and blissfully went back inside.

So this is how the rich live, Bill thought. They pay people to act as if their joy comes from serving their masters' needs, no matter how grand or minuscule. Milana had told him the Seabourn ships were the best in the world - huge yachts, *not* cruise ships. With a maximum of two hundred passengers, they catered only to the top layer of society's elite.

Bill knew he'd entered a new realm when he got to his cabin – a suite nicer than any hotel he'd ever visited. Mahogany walls, crystal glassware, plush bedding and robes – the finest finishing touches, like a Mont Blanc pen on the Coach leather desk pad. "They only have suites here," Milana explained when she'd settled Bill in and showed him the clothes she had the crew purchase and place in the closet for him. Her rooms were next door – the Owner's Suite.

Bill collapsed onto the bed, but agonizing thoughts refused to let him sleep. He was overwhelmed with visions of the brutal slaughter of innocents, people he'd been in the company of just a day earlier. He'd talked to them, touched them, heard them speak, smelled their breath. Now they breathed no more. It was too horrific to comprehend.

On the flight, Milana told him what she knew. Natara and Benoit were both dead, murdered. Quif was missing, also probably dead. Since the first meeting of a board at Pasteur called CODIS, when the phage was first mentioned, the work of the Institut had been carefully monitored by Milana, and apparently others. Her team of private investigators said they'd found evidence of phones tapped and computers hacked. Milana wept when she said she wished she had intervened sooner. If she had, perhaps the others would still be alive. She knew someone would do anything to destroy the phage – the massacre in Armenia proved that – but by the time her people discovered that others were also tracking the work being done in the lab, it was too late. Her men found Benoit's corpse in the morning. When they rushed to rescue Natara it was clear she'd been killed as well. They'd waited near the fire figuring Bill would eventually return to the apartment and it would be their best chance to grab him before anyone else did.

Who was after him? Who killed Natara and Benoit? Who wanted to destroy the phage? Bill asked the same questions twenty different ways on the long flight. Milana claimed she didn't know.

Bill couldn't tell if the tears Milana shed when she spoke were real or not. He was too stunned to cry.

"What about Ike?" Maybe Ike wasn't just refusing his phone calls. Had the killers found him, too? How could they? Ike hadn't been part of the tests at the lab. There was no record of him at Pasteur. Bill had never even told Quif Ike's last name.

"Ike?" Milana asked, suddenly alert through her sniffles. "Is that someone I should know?"

"Uh, no, it's not important," Bill lied. At least Ike was safe.

Now at the railing overlooking the Amazon, Bill stared out at the muddy waters racing by the ship. He'd never seen a river like this one. It was so inhospitable, filled with dirt and debris. It was immense, like the size of a lake back home. Far off he could see where the jungle crept up to the side of the River. No homes. No people. They really were in the middle of nowhere, cut off from civilization. Maybe Milana was right. No one would find them here. As the carrier of the phage, he had a target on his back. At least now he was a moving target, hiding in one of the most remote corners of the planet.

He needed Ike. To be held by him, to cry on his shoulder. Or at least to hear his voice on the phone. An e-mail – anything. Where was he?

Despite Milana's protests, Bill had called from the jet – and again on the boat – to reach "a friend" in San Francisco. No answer at work or home, just voicemail. Bill left messages saying he was okay and things were taking longer "uh, in Paris" than he expected. Ike shouldn't worry. Bill pleaded with Ike to at least send an e-mail so he'd know he still wasn't angry about their last phone conversation. "I love you," Bill whispered into the recording. "Please don't leave me hanging like this. At least let me know you've received my messages. I'll explain everything once I get home."

Ike must still be livid. If he knew all that was really going on he'd be more understanding. How could he not be?

A huge tree shot past the ship, tossed down the river as if it were a mere toothpick. Bill remembered hearing how the Amazon was the most powerful river on earth, but it wasn't possible to fathom what that meant until seeing it. There was violence in the brackish waters, a turbulence that looked like it could break a man in half. On the far side of the river he saw pools where the water was a different color – a mysterious black. Those areas were like pockets of stillness, immune to the waves and mud. How was this possible? Can one river really be divided into two such distinct ways? One part vicious and deadly, coexisting with another part so perfectly tranquil. Evil and good, all within the same space. Maybe it was foolish to assign morality to such things. Even a river is complex. Its rage transports life to these lands. And those serene dark pools? Bill wasn't sure what lurked below the placid surface.

"There you are," Milana said. She placed her hand on Bill's shoulder, startling him. He hadn't heard her approach. A different young member of the crew stood behind her, sheltering her with another big black umbrella. "Couldn't sleep?"

"No," Bill said. At most, Milana could have napped only a few hours, but she looked beautiful and rested, dressed in a blue designer tracksuit. He noted how the color matched her eyes and complemented her loose blonde locks.

"Come downstairs," she said. "There are some people I want you to meet."

"People?"

"Just some friends. Not everyone I'd like is here, but then again I didn't exactly have a lot of notice to set this up."

After all the secrecy Milana claimed, her demands that he not tell anyone where he was, it turned out that she arranged for *her friends* to meet them on the ship. Bill was furious. Who else knows he's here?

"Oh, don't worry. These are all people we can trust. You're going to love them," Milana said as she headed back inside.

It was hard to imagine accommodations more posh than his own, but when they entered Milana's suite, Bill was floored. The space had eight windows that offered a breathtaking panoramic view, plus its own private veranda. The room was more than twice the size of Bill's suite.

"Hello."

Bill heard a woman's voice. When he turned, he faced a dramatically posh living room. Was that a real Picasso? Sitting below the painting on a couch and chairs were four older women. On the coffee table in front of them were a plate of toast points and a large crystal bowl of caviar nested in ice.

"Decadent, isn't it?" one of the women said. "Beluga for breakfast. Well, you only live once, right girls?"

The other women nodded or giggled.

"Bill, I want you to meet my friends. Molly, Suzanne, Binky and Nan," said Milana. "I hope you don't mind if we just stick to first names. I think that will be best, all things considered."

"What do you mean?" Bill asked. Was it some subtle class insult to use only first names? It was clear the women were all wealthy. They wore impractical, expensive clothes for the middle of the jungle – one had on what appeared to be a cashmere turtleneck, another a Burberry blazer. Like many of the rich wives he'd met in the oil business, they had perfectly coiffed hair and wore very little jewelry. Only the large stones on their ring fingers confirmed their status. The youngest looking woman in the group had clearly undergone some sort of facelift. Even so, Bill figured she was at least in her fifties.

"Don't be like that, Bill," Milana said. "Say hello to the girls."

Bill gave the women a cool smile.

"These are the early birds. They really hustled to get here so quickly. Well, the early bird gets the worm!" Milana laughed and the women tittered. "More will join us when we arrive in Manaus in a few days."

"Why are you flying in your friends?" Bill leaned over and whispered to Milana. "I thought we were in hiding. The yacht in the middle of nowhere is one thing, but bringing in your friends to turn it into a party…I don't get it."

"I'm not throwing a party," Milana said loudly, sounding insulted.

"Well, darling, in a way it is like a Botox party I once attended," said Nan, her accent steeped in Larchmont Lockjaw.

"True," Milana said with a contemplative look.

"Is someone going to explain to me what's going on?" Bill felt anger and frustration begin to rise inside. These women acted as if this was all some fun game. People were dead! Murdered! This wasn't a sorority pledge drive.

"Can I go first?" Molly raised her hand.

Milana nodded.

"Breast cancer," Molly said matter-of-factly. "Diagnosed four years ago. First a lumpectomy. When that didn't work, a radical mastectomy followed by chemo and radiation. They claim they got it this time, but, well, you never know…"

"Endometriosis," said Suzanne.

"Bursitis," deadpanned Binky.

"Erythema," lockjawed Nan.

The other women gasped.

"What's that?" asked Bill.

"Red skin," said Nan. "You wouldn't believe how much make-up I need to wear to disguise it."

"You poor thing," Molly said as she patted Nan's knee. "That's tragic. I had no idea."

"What does any of this have to do with me?" Bill asked.

The women snickered.

"I just thought…" Milana paused. "Look, as long as we have you in this floating little safe house, I thought that perhaps we could make the most of the time. Put you to work."

"What?" Bill looked at the group of women.

"You know, I have a feeling he's a pretty good screw," said Suzanne to the other women. "Pardon my French."

"No, no need to apologize," chimed in Binky, sizing up Bill. "He is a very masculine, rugged man. I'm a bit astonished he's queer. He's more manly than my husband!"

The three other women chortled at the joke.

"Look, if you think I'm going to…" Bill said to Milana. "You're out of your mind!"

"Why not?" Milana's charming expression turned stern. This was suddenly the woman Bill faced at the scene of the fire – the one who tossed him in the back of the sedan like he was a misbehaving child. "Listen to me, Bill. There are a lot of people out there who want you dead. I'm offering you protection. In exchange for that, all I ask is that you spread around a little bit of that magical seed of yours. Got it? You're gonna fuck me, and you're gonna fuck every one of these women. And when we get to Manaus, you'll have a whole new batch to service."

"But…I can't." How could he explain it to her? Didn't she understand he was gay?

"You fucked that corpse Natara Melikian," Milana sneered. "Then you can certainly fuck me."

"It's not as simple as that." Bill thought of that awful night – the look of in Natara's eyes, and the agonizing memories it brought up about what happened in New Orleans. He didn't want to go through that again. He couldn't.

"It's wrong!" Bill yelled.

"What's wrong about it?" Milana fired back.

"Well, uh, for one thing…" Bill stumbled. "We only *know* the phage works to kill HIV. That's all it's been proven to do. We don't know it will cure cancer or anything else. It's a dangerous experiment."

"I read the reports on those villagers in Armenia. *The healthiest people on the planet*, according to your Dr. Quif." Milana took a deep breath. She reached over and gently placed her hand on Bill's shoulder. "Don't you see? It's not just AIDS. You might just have the cure for…everything. I thought you wanted to pass that along to whoever needs it. That's all I'm asking you to do."

Bill looked at the women. Milana was right, of course. If the phage was a cure, then it would be wrong to withhold it from anyone. He also knew the phage needed to get out to the world – so many lives depended on it. Perhaps these women could benefit from the phage, but it was wasting precious time. They would not be able to pass the cure on to anyone else. When it came to his mission to get the phage to those who were truly sick, these women were all dead ends.

If anything, Bill knew he should be spreading the virus to men. He'd asked Ike to, and that went nowhere. Worse, the request might have screwed up their relationship forever. Bill only wanted to make love to Ike. He had no drive to fuck others. For a moment he wished the old Bill was still around, the one who'd fuck five guys a day – at least they'd be capable of passing the virus along to others.

Maybe there were guys on the ship he could infect when Milana wasn't hovering. Bill thought of the young blond man who held the umbrella over his head on the deck. But how would he explain it? He'd have to charm the guy into bed, then get him to agree to bottom, *and* to allow Bill to climax inside him without a condom. Of course he could say it was all part of a master plan to spread a miracle cure… Ridiculous! He'd sound like a lunatic. They'd lock him up in the brig, if a ship like this had one.

Besides, he didn't get a vibe from the deck kid or any of the other guys he'd seen on the ship that they'd be down for it. None of them gave off that telltale scent that told Bill when a guy wanted to fuck. Instead, it smelled like something else. The *Seabourn Pride* stank of straight.

23

It didn't matter that the gag was out of her mouth, Quif couldn't breathe. The shock knocked the air out of her. *Natara. My beautiful sister. What have they done to you?* Natara's face appeared in her mind. Quif had last seen her before leaving – how many days ago was it now? – for the early train. She had nudged the bedroom door open just enough to see her sister sleeping. The horrors of AIDS finally gone, Natara had looked so peaceful and content. The memory began blurring.

"She's hyperventilating," one of the dark-suited men said.

The other rapped his fingers on the can of accelerant.

Quif choked and coughed uncontrollably. Natara consumed by the flames of that chemical – the one in the can, the one that also destroyed the bodies of the Armenian villagers. She'd seen how it annihilated human flesh. Did they kill Natara first? Or did they burn her alive? *Oh, Natara!* Who could ever do such a thing? These weren't human beings. Now the same fate awaited her. The can of fuel. Fire. Burning flesh.

One of the young men bent over and put his face up to Quif's. "You'd better stop coughing and start talking. Where is Bill Soileau?"

Quif struggled to pull her hands free, but the tape was too tight around her wrists. She was bound to the chair, unable to create even a little wiggle room. If they were going to kill her, then she wouldn't go down without putting up a fight. But how? She was trapped.

A cell phone rang.

The young man holding the can pulled a phone out of his inside jacket pocket and held it up to his ear. The other stared at Quif, his glare void of any sympathy.

The man listened on the phone for a few moments, never speaking a word. Then he clicked the receiver off and turned to the other man. "Brazil."

The man smiled wide. "Well, doctor. It looks like your usefulness just ended."

24

Bill Soileau had never felt such oppressive heat, even growing up in the deep South. It was hotter and more humid in Manaus than New Orleans in August.

The tour guide said it wasn't always this way. When the city was founded, the climate was pleasantly tropical. Enormous trees provided shade, making it a lush retreat for the rubber barons. As their riches grew, so did their city, culminating in the building of the glorious gold-domed Opera House – a feat of architecture and engineering unsurpassed in such a remote outpost. But with the expansion, trees were replaced by pavement. The beautiful stone sidewalks and plazas grabbed the sun's intense equatorial heat, and tossed it back upon residents like little ovens under their feet. The temperature of the city these days was at least thirty degrees higher than it would have been had mankind never arrived.

Bill hoped the Opera House would be air-conditioned. Seabourn's excursion planner said it was the only site worth seeing in Manaus. As the city kept growing, and the heat became worse, the rich fled. The rubber business collapsed as the plants were stolen and cultivated elsewhere. Now it was just another dirt-poor South American dive known mostly as the last place for a decent shit and shower before heading on to the remotest parts of the Amazon.

Inside was cooler, but not air-conditioned. Tourists escaped the direct scalding of the sun by walking the gilded aisles of the theater, noting the rich red velvet seats. They could take photos, but not sit.

The sweat might ruin the fabric.

Bill had to get off the ship, even if it meant enduring a few hours of awful heat. The yacht had become his prison. He received the same pampering as any other guest, but he was doing time. Hard time. While the crew flitted around him, begging to serve him in some way, he couldn't help but think of himself as one of them. Worse really, since they were being paid. He was slave labor. He had to do what Milana ordered, or possibly pay with his life.

He'd fucked the women, as commanded. He'd actually looked forward to being with Milana. Even if he wasn't attracted to women, she was sexy – an icon in the gay world. He'd be ashamed to admit it, but there was something arousing about having sex with a celebrity.

And yet when it happened, it wasn't anything like he expected. In her music, videos, movies and Page 6 headlines, Milana was always portrayed as an insatiable vixen, but she turned out to be quite frigid and awkward in bed. The sexual persona she thrust in public was only a marketing ruse.

"Ow…ow…ow," she said when she'd sat on top of Bill. He'd been judicious about using plenty of lubricant, and he'd agreed to just lie back and allow her to lower herself at her own pace, since she said that would make it easier for her.

"I'm sorry. Am I doing it wrong?" Bill asked, knowing he wasn't really doing much beyond providing a perch.

"Ow." Milana winced. "It's just a little bigger than what I'm used to."

Bill had he'd seen plenty of others and knew he wasn't freakishly large. He was surprised that someone with Milana's infamous experience would find it hard to take.

"Ow." Milana took a deep breath. "Truth be told, it's been a very long time."

"What?"

"Ow. I've never been all that keen on sex. Well, at least not having it. Ow."

Bill found himself trying to make it enjoyable for her, using different rhythms and depths. He pressed to create friction in the area he understood was a woman's pleasure point. He noticed Milana perspiring, though from the clenching of her teeth it looked like she was simply bearing the intrusion. When he climaxed, he performed an exaggeratedly loud moan, hoping the sound of his enjoyment might inspire a reaction from Milana. Instead, she was clearly glad the ordeal was over. She ended the session with all the officiousness of signing a real estate transaction and quickly managed Bill out the door with a firm handshake. She'd never even removed the top of her tracksuit.

The other women were simple in and out deals. They were all willing and wet and he found himself able to shut his eyes and pretend he was inside a man.

Until it came to Nan.

She had insisted the whole arrangement be conceived as a scene from some sort of romance novel. She wore skimpy lingerie, which only highlighted her bony, emaciated figure. Bill had read how rich Manhattan socialites starved themselves so they could remain size twos their entire lives.

Jazz played softly in the background as she poured them each a glass of chilled Dom Pérignon.

"Tell me all about you," Nan said, swirling a strand of her unnaturally dyed brown hair with her finger like a schoolgirl.

"Uh…" Bill took a large gulp of the champagne. He just wanted to get this over with. Why couldn't Nan be like the other women? Was she as starved for affection as she was for food?

"I understand you're a Southerner," Nan lockjawed. "I do so appreciate the manners of your people. It's a lost art, if you ask me."

"These days I actually live in—"

"You know what I love most about Southern gentlemen?" Nan placed her glass on the coffee table. "They know how to treat a lady."

"I suppose that's what people say about—"

Nan lunged at Bill, pressing her mouth against his. Her kiss was dry and her tongue darted in his mouth in rapid-fire taps that lacked any passion or purpose. Kissing was as foreign to Nan as a hamburger and fries.

It got worse from there. Nan tried to use "dirty talk" to liven things up. "You are going to take that big rawwwwd and teach me a lesson I lest not soon forget," Nan said awkwardly. Then she insisted on "getting things started with a little fellatio." She took the tip of Bill into her mouth with a wincing look on her face, as if she was being force fed dog crap. She started gagging dry heaves before the head got beyond her lower lip. Bill was completely flaccid and figured if things continued Nan's way he'd never be able to get an erection. He grabbed her by the arm, pushed her face down on the bed, spit in his hand to lube up, and plunged into Nan's ass. The tightness made him finish quickly. He pulled out and wiped off with the linen towel that had been wrapped around the bottle of champagne.

Nan turned over and stretched out on her bed. "That was glorious! Now, please, come over here and cuddle with your *lover.*"

The thought of that moment still made Bill shiver, even two days later standing in boiling Manaus. He needed a break – to be somewhere other than that ship. He had snuck off that morning without Milana's permission, mingling with other passengers who opted for the Opera House excursion. Milana was too distracted to keep track of Bill, since she was busy saying goodbye to the four ladies and preparing for another group of friends to arrive.

Would there be others like Nan? Bill wasn't sure how much more he could take.

The tour left the theater and headed for the plaza for a view of the dome from under the shade of a few leafy trees. As she spoke, the guide made eye contact and lifted an eyebrow at Bill. She was young and attractive, her dark hair pulled back by a silver clip. Women! Was he putting out some strange vibe that suddenly drew women to him? Like the pheromones he caught from men?

He pushed aside the thoughts of women by trying to bring back memories of Ike. It would be morning in San Francisco. He imagined Ike making coffee in his very particular way, with exactly three scoops and half a carafe of ice-cold tap water. It had become their ritual for Bill to hug an impatient Ike from behind and nuzzle his neck as they waited for "Darth Vader," the nickname they'd given to the coffee maker because it sounded like loud breathing, to finish brewing.

Across the courtyard Bill spotted a sign that said *Telefone.*

Bill left the group and headed to the shop. Inside he paid the elderly clerk a few American dollars.

"Número seis," the old man said as he pointed to the back.

Bill walked down the sweltering corridor. On each side were numbered booths with phones in them. He opened room six and lifted the receiver to dial Ike's cell phone number. The call went right to voicemail.

Bill dialed again, this time to Ike's office at Project Inform. It wasn't unusual for Ike to go into the office early, especially when Bill was out of town. Ike had always said he didn't like to linger in an empty bed.

Instead of voicemail this time, the receptionist picked up.

"Project Inform," the young woman said. Bill vaguely remembered her from visiting. He thought her name was Cherry, or Sherry. Something like that.

"Oh, hey," Bill said. "I thought I had dialed Ike's number directly. Sorry about that."

"Who is this?" The woman's tone was suddenly serious.

"Cherry, right?"

"It's Teri," the woman said. "Who is this?"

"Teri. Sorry about that. It's Bill. I'm calling from overseas. I've been trying to reach Ike. Is he there?"

"Bill?"

"Yeah, Bill. Ike's boyfriend. I think we met before."

"Bill?"

"Yeah."

"Bill?"

"Teri, is Ike there? I need to talk to Ike."

"Hold on," Teri said, her voice sounding panicked.

Bill kept the receiver to his ear. The booth was suffocating and the sweat dripped from the side of his face onto the phone.

"You still there?" Teri came back on the line.

"Yes." Bill grew impatient. "Teri, I'm calling from overseas. I don't know how much time I have left on this call. I'm at one of those phone places where you pay and they connect you. There's no way to call back. Can you tell Ike to hurry up and get on the line? It's important I talk to him."

"Bill," Teri sighed. "I'm the only one here. I was hoping someone else was around, but no one else has come into the office yet. I can't do this."

"Do what?"

"Bill, I can't. Call back later. Ask for Jimmy or Denise. Anyone else. Just not me."

"Teri, I don't understand. Didn't you hear me? I'm overseas. I don't know when I'm going to get another chance to call. What's going on? Where's Ike?"

"Bill, I can't."

Bill thought he could hear Teri crying.

"What is it? Does it have to do with Ike? Teri, I need you to tell me!" Bill's voice cracked. His body felt the pain before it registered with his brain. Teri didn't have to say anything more. Just from what little she said, Bill already knew what had happened. Ike was dead. Just like all the others. Why hadn't he seen this coming?

"Ike...Ike..." Teri bawled.

"Ike is dead, isn't he?" Bill calmed his voice. "You've got to tell me the truth, Teri. I need to know. Tell me what happened."

"A fire." She choked the words out. "His whole building went up. Ike was the only one who didn't get out. They don't know how it started. Ike...it was so intense...they could barely..."

Bill took the drenched receiver in both hands and bowed his head onto it. *Ike is dead.* The only man he ever loved. Gone. A fire. Like the one in Paris. They'd killed Ike to kill the phage. Just like they did with Natara. *Ike. My love...*

The receiver was muffled against his forehead, but he could still hear Teri crying on the other end. "I am so sorry. Bill – I am so sorry. You shouldn't find out this way. I'm only an intern..."

Bill placed the phone back on its cradle. *Ike. You can't be dead.* He put his face in his hands. His sobs echoed in the small booth. The sound of his weeping brought louder wails. *Ike!*

Bill heard the door to the booth open behind him. *Go away!* He'd make as much noise as he wanted.

"Bill Soileau?" It was a man's voice.

Bill turned to look. It was two men. Not locals, but white.

"Who the hell are you?" Bill cried. "Leave me alone!"

177

"I'm sorry," one of the men said as he took out a syringe.

The other man grabbed Bill and pinned him against the wall, his forearm wedged under Bill's chin. He struggled to free himself. "No. No!"

"May God forgive us," one of the men said.

A jab of pain hit Bill's neck.

"What the...? Let go of meeeee—"

The men's faces abruptly vanished into darkness.

25

Quif closed her eyes. She heard the cap on the metal canister turn.

This was it. They'd held her captive for days. No food. No water. Not even a chance to use the bathroom. Just waiting. For what? Until they finally captured Bill Soileau?

She wished she'd never heard of the phage. She thought back to the first time she walked into that creepy, old Soviet lab. If she had never opened that door, everyone would still be alive.

Now it was her turn to die. Just like Natara, Benoit, the Armenian villagers, and soon Bill Soileau, if they hadn't murdered him already.

Maybe her death would be the most brutal of all. If so, she deserved it. Her obsession with the phage had cost so many lives. The price for her myopia was too high, and now the world would never receive the miracle. She tried to pray to God in her final moments. She struggled to conjure up an image of the Holy Spirit. She couldn't. How could there be a God who allowed such things to happen? Natara had never hurt anyone, and yet she was forced to suffer for years, only to be reborn and slaughtered. There is no God. Just evil.

Tears streamed down her face and she clenched her eyes tight. If she was to be burned alive, she didn't want to see the moment when the match was lit. She wanted to make her consciousness flee her body. Was it possible to do that if she concentrated hard enough?

She felt liquid pour onto her scalp and run down her face. The fumes were so strong! She tried to hold her breath, but the intense chemical vapors penetrated her sinuses. She choked. When she opened her mouth the fuel got on her tongue. She gagged. Her body wrenched as if vomiting, but nothing came up. There was no food in her stomach.

Do not open your eyes! She pleaded with her body to comply. The accelerant would surely burn her cornea, even before any match was lit to consume her in flames. Her hands struggled to free themselves from the restraints. The tape was still too tight. She wailed. She was terrified of the fire still to come, and yet she wanted this moment to end. She'd rather welcome death, than continue to suffer like this.

She heard an explosion.

Was this it? Had they lit her on fire?

She tightened to prepare her body for agony.

Another explosion. Then two more.

But no pain.

Maybe she was on fire and the accelerant worked so quickly it singed her nerve endings before she could feel anything. Or maybe what medical science thought it knew about fatal burns was wrong. She was inside that horror now, and all she felt was the suffocation of the chemical's fumes.

If she opened her eyes, she could see what was happening – to see if the flames were really consuming her flesh so quickly that she felt no pain.

No. For the first time in her life, she did not want to know. This was the end. She just had to accept that. For once in her life, she would tame her curiosity. She needed to let go. To end her struggle.

"She's alive!" A man's voice yelled from behind her.

He spoke English, but it didn't sound like either of the two young men. Who was it? Was he talking about her?

"Doctor – do not open your eyes!" Now the voice stood in front of her. "Do you understand me? Keep your eyes and mouth closed!"

It *was* a man's voice. And he was talking to *her*. She wasn't dead! Perhaps she wasn't even burning.

"Fill that bucket with water!" The man shouted.

A shock of intense cold splashed down on Quif's head.

"Don't move! Eyes and mouth shut!" The voice yelled.

Then another dousing. And another. The fumes washed away. It was water! Wonderful, beautiful, miraculous water. Bucket after bucket poured over her head.

She felt cloth on her face, vigorously wiping her eyes, nose and mouth.

"You can open your eyes now," the voice said.

Tentatively Quif opened her lids, expecting her eyes to sting. Nothing. There was no pain. She looked down at her body. She wasn't burned. She was whole!

On floor in front of her were the two young men in the dark suits. They stared up to the ceiling with what remained of their expressions. Both had been shot in the face. The explosions. They must have been gunshots.

"We'll have you out of that chair in a moment," the man said.

Quif turned to finally see who had rescued her. Clean-shaven, short hair and gray suit – the uniform of a flic of some sort. An American?

"*Merci,*" Quif said. "*Merci...de tout mon coeur merci.*"

The man squatted down and took a knife from the holster on his belt. He cut the tape that bound Quif's wrists to the chair. "I'm afraid this isn't over yet, doctor."

26

Bill Soileau studied the room. Plainly furnished. A crucifix above a simple pine bed. The walls a stark white, matching the bedspread. No windows. No paintings. No other furniture. Who lived like this? Was he in prison?

Standing in front of the only door were two large men. They stared at Bill, their faces blank. He'd tried to talk to them several times since he woke up, but they remained completely silent. Where was he? Why had he been kidnapped? How long had he been knocked out? Bill rushed for the door, but one of the brutes gently pushed him back. The giant's hands were meaty and huge. The men didn't need to say anything – it was clear their job was to make sure Bill never got to the other side of that door.

Bill sat on the edge of the bed. His head throbbed. He wondered what drug they'd given him. He couldn't be sure if he was even still in Brazil. His sleep had been so deep, the last thing he remembered was...

Ike.

The phone call in Manaus. Gone. Murdered. The fire was no accident. Just like Natara, Ike was incinerated. *Ike.* He placed his hand on the mattress and the feelings came rushing back. Of lazy Saturdays spent lounging in bed with Ike. Bill had never been in bed with a man before, just to sleep. If Bill woke up first, he'd lay there and stare at Ike, wondering what he might be dreaming. He'd reach over and lightly run his fingers in Ike's mussed morning hair, amazed he could feel so much joy simply by being in someone's presence. Carefully he'd move his body up against Ike's back, spooning so their bare skin became one. He'd never had that before with a man. With others, it was all about climaxing and leaving. With Ike, the climax was in the staying.

Ike.

Did you suffer? Of course, you did. How could you not? I caused you pain. I caused your death. My love killed you. I'm sorry. I'm sorry. I'm sorry. Forgive me, Ike. Can you ever forgive me?

Bill's eyes welled up. He didn't care that the two men at the door stared at him. How dare they intrude on his grief. He hated the men. They were part of this. Part of this awful conspiracy that killed Ike. For all he knew, these men committed the murder themselves. Were those hands the ones that set the fire? The same hands that killed Natara? Bill's sadness began to change form into a purpose: rage. He was overwhelmed with an uncontrollable desire to hurt the men. To kill them.

He looked around the room. There was nothing that could be turned into a weapon. He could try to break a leg off the bed, but they'd be able to subdue him before he got very far. With their body weight alone, they could easily pin him to the floor. However futile his attack might be, he wondered if he should try anyway. If they killed him in the fight, he'd be better off. He didn't want to live anymore. He'd lost everything that ever meant anything to him. He still had the phage, but a world that took the only man he ever loved didn't deserve the miracle cure.

Bill looked up to the crucifix over the bed. He stared at the face of Jesus, so serene despite the blood dripping from the crown of thorns and nails through his flesh. *Fuck you! All you've ever done is torment me! Why did you even put me on this earth?* The crucifix. Maybe that was his weapon. He could take the cross off the wall and attack the men with it. The end with Jesus' feet was small enough to pierce an eye to blind one of the thugs, and then maybe he'd have a chance to get past—

A loud knock came from the other side of the door.

One of the guards opened the door and signaled for Bill to get up to leave. Bill looked up to the crucifix again. Was this his final moment to strike back?

No. If he attacked and failed it would all end here. As he stared at the bloodied figure of Christ, it suddenly hit him. All the others infected with the phage had been brutally murdered – on the spot. No mercy. No hesitation.

Yet he'd been kept alive. Why? They could have killed him back at the phone booth. Instead, they drugged him and kidnapped him. For some reason, he was spared an immediate death. Did they want the phage? Or did they just want to make sure that the only person left on earth with the cure was gone – to witness his death with their own eyes.

If they really wanted the phage, then they were out of luck. He knew the only way it could be passed to anyone else. If that's what they wanted, they would not get it. He would never give it to them.

Who were they? What type of fiends wanted to prevent people from being cured of disease? It was incomprehensible that someone would believe that the world was better off filled with people dying agonizing deaths.

He was overcome with the urge to know who believed that suffering was more important than life. The only way he would see this true face of evil was to get up and walk out that door. Somewhere on the other side was the answer to who killed Ike, Natara and soon…himself.

Bill stood up and went with the men.

They walked down a long, dark corridor. Again, there were no windows. It was impossible to know if it was night or day. The walls were stone, reminding him of the tunnels that led into the Parisian Catacombs. These hallways had that same feel to them, a musty smell, as if they too represented a place of death. Or was he just sensing his own end?

After several turns, they stood in front of a large door. This one was more modern and reinforced, as if for security. One of the guards opened the entrance. On the other side was another corridor, but this section was wider and illuminated by candles. The guard gestured for Bill to walk into the ethereal glow.

Bill stepped through. The security door slammed behind him and he could hear it lock tight.

To the left was an alcove rounded out of the tunnel. On the floor was a white marble slab, raised higher at the far end. Chiseled into the rock and finished in gold were large bold letters that read, "JOANNES PAULUS PP.II."

On the wall above the crypt was a stone relief depicting the baby Jesus in Mary's lap.

The Pope? The tomb of John Paul II? Bill was in Rome. The Church – the same church he was raised in as child – they were the ones behind all this. They were the ones who killed Ike. The Catholics murdered Natara. They were the ones who wanted the phage destroyed.

A door at the other end of the hallway opened. An old man in a scarlet robe walked in, followed by two different large men in dark suits.

"I'll be fine," the Cardinal said and dismissed the men with a gesture.

"Maybe you shouldn't be so quick to send away your bodyguards," Bill said. He could feel his anger rising. He wanted to rush the Cardinal and strangle him with his crimson garb.

"Why is that, my son?" The Cardinal asked. "Do you intend to do me some harm?"

"Do you some harm?" Bill seethed. "After all you've done! I had no idea you people were so…evil!"

"That's an interesting word to choose," the Cardinal said. His voice was oddly congenial, almost friendly. He slowly approached Bill and stood overlooking the Pope's tomb. He made the sign of the cross and closed his eyes for a moment in prayer. "'Man always travels along precipices. His truest obligation is to keep his balance.' John Paul said that. The Holy Father knew we are all sinners. His was a message of redemption. That's why the people loved him so much. He'll be made a Saint, you know. It's fitting."

"You won't!" Bill scowled.

"Ah, yes," the Cardinal smiled. "You are right about that. My sins are considered far worse than most. At least by the Church. Although I suspect God does not judge me as harshly as my fellow man."

"You think God supports all you've done? You will rot in hell!" Bill raged. Was this Cardinal looking for forgiveness from Bill before his execution? Absolution from the condemned. Is that what all this is about?

"I think we're getting off on the wrong foot," the Cardinal said amiably. "I'm Cardinal Umberto Uccelli. I'm a special envoy for the Vatican. I suppose by now you've figured out that's where you are."

"Why am I here?" Bill asked. If they were going to kill him, why hadn't they just done it in Brazil?

"We knew that showing you this place would prove beyond any doubt who we are. Besides, ever since your trip to the Catacombs, we figured a flair for the dramatic appealed to you," the Cardinal said, gesturing to the Pope's final resting place.

"The Catacombs? You knew about that?"

"We've been keeping an eye on Dr. Melikian, and then you, ever since we learned of the miracle. We've taken extraordinary measures since the doctor's first presentation on the cure at Pasteur. The phage represents a huge challenge for The Church."

Challenge! Bill fumed. Did life have such little meaning to these zealots that they could dismiss the murder of innocent people as simply a challenge? It was such a strange word to use to justify such heinous behavior.

"I know all about your extraordinary measures," Bill said bitterly. Ike's face flashed in his thoughts. He imagined flames consuming Natara. And whatever happened to Quif? They'd probably killed her, too. "You can never justify what you did. Never!"

"I don't believe it was all that wrong," the Cardinal explained cheerfully. "It was invasive, I grant you. But you're here now. And safe. That's what really matters."

"Safe!" Bill yelled. "You're a *murderer!* You killed Ike! My love! Yes, you hear that, you fucking homophobe! I *loved* Ike – and you killed him! Just like you burned Natara to death – and butchered Benoit!"

"Wha—" The Cardinal's face changed from banal pleasance to numb.

"You killed them! Why? The same reason you deny condoms to people who need to protect themselves from AIDS in Africa. You think your beliefs serve a higher moral purpose. They don't! You are no different than the extremists who fly planes into skyscrapers, or blow up Planned Parenthood clinics, or beat people to death because they're gay. You're all the same! You extinguish the lives of other human beings because you think you're doing God's work. You're not! God didn't order the murders of Ike, Natara and Benoit and everyone else you've slaughtered to try to destroy the phage. God didn't do any of that. You did! God says THOU SHALT NOT KILL!"

Bill wanted to pummel the old man, to bash his head into the marble stone of the dead Pope's memorial. That's what he deserved. Let him answer to God for his crimes.

"You misjudge me. I...I am a sinner," the Cardinal stammered. "I admit that. But I did not kill your friends. The Church had nothing to do with that."

"Nothing to do with it! I'm here in the tomb of the Pope!"

"But..."

"You kidnapped me! Why didn't you just kill me in Brazil? Don't tell me you lost the nerve – the church has been killing people for centuries! It's all just one more body thrown in the flames with you! Damn you all!"

"See where you are, my child," the Cardinal said calmly, despite Bill's rage. He took his aged hands, grasped Bill by the shoulders, and turned him toward the tomb of the Pope. "You are in the holiest of Holy places. Would we really bring you here if we intended to do you harm?"

"You killed them. All of them." Bill said, though the old man's gentle touch had a strange calming effect. "At least now as you kill me, you can admit to the truth."

"Oh God be blessed, we are not going to kill you."

Bill tried to make sense of what he was hearing. He stared at the memorial stone, then up to the image of the baby Christ on the wall. This was wrong. If they were going to kill him, it wouldn't be here. Not this place. In that, at least, the Cardinal was probably telling the truth.

"We brought you here to rescue you. To keep you safe. Your life is most precious," the Cardinal said. "That clever woman smuggled you to Brazil. When we learned what she had done, we knew that others would also soon find you. Others who absolutely want you dead."

"You didn't murder Ike?"

"No, my son."

"And Natara? And Benoit?"

"We mourn the deaths of those innocent souls. If we had learned sooner they were in such mortal danger we would have intervened," the Cardinal said. "I know you think The Church has committed great sins for the sake of its moral authority on Earth. But we are not killers. Let no man destroy what God hath created."

"And Quif? Have you kidnapped her, too?"

"Ah, yes, Dr. Melikian. She was kidnapped. I understand she's safe now."

Quif. She was safe. At least he had that much left in the world. But if the church wasn't behind all this, Bill wondered, then who was? "I...I don't understand. Who's doing all this? Who killed Ike?"

The tears began to rush from Bill, held back for too long. He couldn't stop them now. Just saying Ike's name aloud made all the emotions surface. He cradled his face in his hands.

"You can let go now. Let it all out," the Cardinal said as he grasped Bill's hand. "God gave us tears thus we could weep for those we love. You are a lucky man to feel for someone so much. Sorrow is a gift from God. It teaches us to be grateful for those who come in and out of our lives, especially those we love."

Gift? Bill was supposed to be thankful for what happened? This old celibate fool knew nothing of love. What Bill felt for Ike was the type of love the church condemned. He didn't need to hear this hypocrisy. He had to get out of this tomb and find the only person he knew in the world who didn't judge him. She was still alive.

"Where is Quif?" Bill shook off the Cardinal's touch. "I want to see her. Now!"

"I don't know where she is," the Cardinal said. He sounded disappointed.

"What do you mean you don't know?" Bill shouted. "You just said you rescued her!"

"I said she was rescued. But she's not with us. We weren't the ones who saved her."

"If not you, then who?" Bill was tiring of the Cardinal's cryptic meanderings.

"She's with your government. I'm told the Americans have the situation fully in control now. You'll be able to see her soon."

"My government?" It didn't make sense. With the moralist right-wingers running the country now, they'd be the last people to want the phage to survive. Was Quif in even greater danger? "Why am I here with you? Tell me what's going on!"

The Cardinal looked at Bill. His expression changed from benevolence to one more somber.

"You said earlier you believed the Church was guilty of murder for the way it's handled the plague in Africa. That to deny people the means to protect themselves and prevent the spread of AIDS due to notions of moral superiority was the same as committing genocide." The Cardinal took a deep breath and was silent for a few moments. "There are those of us in the Church who agree with you. Yes, there are many who hold onto the idea that what we're seeing is God's Will, and we must maintain our tenets and let it all unfold as the Heavenly Father sees fit. That's the Church's official position."

The Cardinal gestured to the tomb. "That was the Holy Father's stance. As much as I continue to love him, on this we disagreed. I mean to say – why can't one argue that life-saving treatments and the knowledge to create them are also God's Will? We take that position when a dying woman is hooked up to ventilators and kept alive only by machines. At that moment, man's ingenuity is a divine blessing. And yet a condom is a mortal sin. You make a powerful argument about hypocrisy."

Bill looked at the Cardinal. He hadn't noticed it before. There was pain in the old man's face.

"As I said before, we are all sinners. Every one of us. Some of us in the Church believe God is challenging us anew with issues like AIDS, and now the phage. There are those of us who believe the Church is failing God's challenge. We advocate another way. We desire to travel another path."

"Why am I here?" Bill struggled to follow what the Cardinal was saying. "You kidnapped me in Brazil. You could have left me there. Or handed me over to the Americans to be safe with Quif. You didn't bring me to Rome just to listen to philosophical arguments."

A knowing grin began to emerge on the Cardinal's face. "You are right, my son. You are here for a reason. After we're finished, you'll be returned to the United States. Just beyond the Vatican gates a small army of CIA agents in armored cars wait for you. They'll make sure you are safe and reunited with Dr. Melikian. Of course, they won't wait forever. We'll need to act quickly."

"What do you want from me?"

"We want your miracle. The gift that God chose you to bear. That burden. We're willing to share that with you – to make sure it's passed to those who truly need it. We are all given crosses to bear in life. This is one you no longer need carry alone."

"But Cardinal…" Bill couldn't believe what he was hearing. The Cardinal *wanted* Bill to pass the phage to others. And the Church was going to help him do it? "I'm not sure you fully grasp exactly how this is done. I mean, I'm a little embarrassed to even discuss it with you. You're a Cardinal, for God's sake!"

"Yes, I am a soldier for God," the Cardinal said as he grabbed the corner of his crimson robe. "This is merely my uniform. But under all this I can assure you I am still a man. Merely a man. And a sinner…just like you."

"Like me?" Absurd, Bill dismissed. "You don't know what you're saying. It's not possible that you're a sinner like me. No one could be as big a sinner as me, at least not as far as the church is concerned."

"I assure you, I am."

"Cardinal, uh, with all due respect, you don't get it. I'm gay. I got infected with HIV from sex. The condemned. You're not like me. There's no way you can be."

The Cardinal removed his scarlet shawl, carefully folded it, and placed it on the ground. He began unbuttoning his long white undergarment robe.

"*Let him kiss me with the kisses of his mouth: for thy love is better than wine,*" the Cardinal chanted. "*Because of the savour of thy good ointments thy name is as ointment poured forth—*"

"Stop!" Bill panicked. Was this headed where he thought it was going?

"*He brought me to the banqueting house, and his banner over me was love,*" the Cardinal continued singing. *"Stay me with flagons, comfort me with apples: for I am sick of love. His left hand is under my head, and his right hand doth embrace me."*

Here on the tomb of the dead Pope? This old Cardinal expected him to– "No! I can't do this."

The Cardinal placed his aged hand on Bill's cheek. His thumb caressed across Bill's lips. "It's time for you to do God's work. Yes, I'm a sinner. Yes – just like you. When it first happened to me, I prayed to understand why God had chosen such a path for me. As an adolescent, when I first realized I was not like other boys, I agonized and wondered why. Later when I found out I was infected, I was incredulous. As I ascended the ranks of the Church, I have to admit I feared perhaps my fate was to die in some horrific way that it might be a message from God to my brothers. It was a date with destiny I did not welcome, yet I made peace with it. I never lost my faith that it was all part of His plan for me. I needed to be patient. When I heard of the phage, and then learned of you, I knew my time had finally arrived. I am asked to spread His message of love in a way no one else has been tested to do."

Bill studied the old man's expression. In the cracked forehead, serenity. The gray eyes, happiness. There was no doubt the Cardinal believed what he said.

"From the Gospel of Mark, there is The Parable of The Sower," the Cardinal said as he removed his undergarment cloak and let it fall to the floor. He stood in a plain white T-shirt and light blue boxers. Under all the garb, he was just as he said, merely a man, his body revealing all its years in sagging, spotted flesh. And yet there was an undeniable strength in the old man, his words carrying a power and purpose that defied his elderly frame.

"Behold, there went out a sower to sow." The Cardinal reached out his hands as if speaking from a pulpit. "And it came to pass, as he sowed, some fell by the wayside, and the fowls of the air came and devoured it up.

"And some fell on stony ground, where it had not much earth, and immediately it sprang up, because it had no depth of earth. But when the sun was up, it was scorched, and because it had no root, it withered away.

"And some fell among thorns, and the thorns grew up, and choked it, and it yielded no fruit.

"And other fell on good ground, and did yield fruit that sprang up and increased, and brought forth, some thirty, and some sixty, and some a hundred."

A musky scent came from the Cardinal, the same smell Bill had inhaled hundreds of times. The fumes of pheromones, the effusion of want.

"Bill Soileau, you are The Sower. I am the good ground. And just like you, I am to be…God's vessel."

27

Quif faced the computer screen, careful not to turn her head. In her peripheral vision she could see the soldier across the room near the door.

She clicked on the little electronic window she'd hidden in the bottom left corner of the screen, enlarging it to only a few inches wide. She silently slid her chair and shifted her body to make sure that portion of the screen was blocked from the soldier's view. Her fingers trembled as she typed in her account and password. Would this finally be her escape to freedom?

It was Benoit who helped her create a profile page on Facebook – an amusing diversion one night as they waited for samples to finish spinning in the centrifuge. *Benoit.* Sometimes he could be such a boy. Now one of his adolescent moments could free her from this sterile jail.

Her captors had successfully prevented her from accessing her e-mail accounts, or creating new ones. She could get on the internet, and any research she desired was at her command. But it was all one way. There was no communication with anyone outside of CIA headquarters.

The Americans saved her from being burned alive, and now she was their slave. The clean-shaven man in the gray suit who rescued her was actually an agent assigned to the bio-terrorism team. He said she'd been under surveillance since the explosion at the Armenian refinery. He claimed the CIA had nothing to do with that bombing, or the murders of the villagers. Quif didn't know what to believe anymore. He wouldn't even tell her his name.

Maybe being held hostage was a set-up – a psychological game they played to try to break her will and manipulate her into doing their bidding. For a moment, Quif's pulse raced at the sudden thought that it was all just an elaborate ruse. Perhaps Natara was still alive! Then the images of the bodies of the two thugs flashed in her memory. The bullets had ripped open their heads. No, those weren't theatrics for her benefit. She'd done enough autopsies to recognize real brain matter.

That day at the warehouse her rescuers had placed her on a stretcher and wheeled her into an ambulance. During the ride, the agent assured her everything would be fine. The vehicle pulled up a short ramp and a door clunked close behind them, submerging the ambulance into complete darkness. She heard a burst of sound. Jet engines. Then the unmistakable rush of hurtling down a tarmac.

A silent medical technician expertly treated the cuts in her hand during the flight. She was allowed to watch from a window as the plane landed at an airbase outside Washington, DC. The agent had told her she was being taken to Langley, Virginia. They would be able to protect her there. After all she'd been through, being ensconced in CIA Headquarters sounded reasonable.

Until they told her what they wanted her to do.

Bastards.

Quif returned her attention to the screen. Facebook was a kids' thing. Benoit called it a *social network* – its own little online universe. The CIA would never think to find her here. She'd send messages asking for help, a plea to contact the chairman at Pasteur. He would have the connections to find her, wouldn't he? Unless, he was part of the conspiracy too.

The door swung open.

"Dr. Melikian, why do you persist in acting like a child? Do you really think we don't know about Facebook?" It was the agent. "My teenage daughter uses it. And you can forget about posting a personal ad on Craigslist, or adding a comment on a New York Times story. None of that will work either."

Quif spun her chair and stood up. "You cannot treat me as a

prisoner! I am a citizen of France! I demand to see my ambassador!"

"If you were a prisoner, doctor, you'd be in Guantanamo," the man patronized. "You're an *esteemed* visiting researcher."

"I have told you already many times," Quif said, trying to compose herself. "You ask for a thing that is not possible. I do not have the phage. It is not something I can make for you."

"Yes, so you've said." The man sighed. "We believe you."

Quif shut her eyes. Finally. They believed her. Now they would have to let her go.

"Quif?"

That voice. Not the agent's. Another man. She opened her eyes. It couldn't be true. He couldn't be alive.

"Bill Soileau?"

He walked over and took her in his arms, pulling close. She breathed in his scent, triggering the memory of that day in the kitchen with Natara. The day Bill brought her sister back to life. Quif felt her eyes tear over, followed by a sudden rush of shame. Only days earlier she'd wished him dead to save Natara...

"How?" Her voice cracked.

"There will be plenty of time for you two to catch up later," the agent interrupted. "I suggest you get to work right away. I'm sending in a technician to collect phage samples from Mr. Soileau. In fifteen minutes you'll meet with the other members of the team and we'll begin mapping out a plan to figure out how to harness the power of this virus."

"I agree," Bill said as he released Quif from their embrace. "There's no time to waste. I just need some volunteers. Preferably men who have no qualms about passing it on to as many others as possible. I can probably do three in the next hour. The transformation is nearly instant. If they can do two others each, and so on, we can probably have fifty guys good to go by tomorrow morning. They could head over to Walter Reed – there must be people there who can immediately benefit."

Any traces of pleasantness disappeared from the agent's face. "That is never going to happen."

"What?" Quif snapped. "This is how the phage is passed. It is the only way! You said you spied on us. Then you know this is so."

"Yes, doctor, I read your research. I've studied your data. I have no doubt you're telling us the truth. The only way to pass this cure is through semen during sex." The agent looked over to Bill, sizing him up with a repugnant stare. "But no one is going to Walter Reed, or anywhere near our soldiers. They'd rather be dead than turned into a bunch of faggots."

"You are insane!" Quif yelled. "This is the cure for millions. You would rather condemn them to death?"

"You should put your passion into your work, doctor, and leave the politics to us." The agent strained a smile. "Our job is to protect the American way of life. You two can still save the world. You just have to figure out a way to turn this..." The agent gestured to Bill. "...disease...into a pill."

"That could take years!" Even with the world's best scientific minds, Quif knew it was possible they'd never be able to synthesize the phage into a mass produced medication. The Soviets had done it, but without their notes it was impossible to know how long it took them to create the phage – and they'd killed countless human beings for their breakthrough. Even if they could somehow figure out how to reverse engineer a pure phage serum from Bill's semen, clinical trials would take many more years. "You are wasting time. The villagers lived for nearly two decades without side effects. That is longer than any clinical trial needed for approval."

"The villagers are all dead, doctor," the agent deadpanned. "And your field samples are destroyed. You have no proof of anything, do you?"

Quif walked over to the agent, narrowing in on his wicked mouth. With all the might of her tiny frame she slapped his face. Then again. And again. The agent did nothing to stop her, unflinching, seemingly unfazed by the assault – his stance a clear message of complete control. The rage built in Quif as the images of Natara, Benoit and the doomed villagers filled her head. "I knew it! You killed them! Murderer! They hurt no one – and you killed them!"

She felt her wrists grabbed and twisted behind her back. The soldier pulled her hands up toward her shoulder blades, making Quif cry out in pain.

"You have it wrong, doctor." The agent rubbed his cheek with his fingertips. "We didn't kill the Armenians."

"Why should we believe you?" Bill finally spoke. "Only something like the CIA would have the reach and resources to do this. Bombs. Murders. Kidnappings. What you did to Ike…"

The agent shook his head, apparently trying to dismiss the sting of the slaps. Quif noticed a deep scarlet mark next to his mouth where her fingernail must have clipped him.

"You are right about one thing," the agent said as he sat on the edge of a desk. "Only something *like the CIA* could do this."

"What are you saying? Another government?" Quif struggled against the guard.

The agent nodded his head and Quif was released. "Well, in a way, it is a government. It's certainly as big as one. It's larger and more powerful than most countries."

"You'd better start explaining what's going on," Bill demanded. "Cuz there's only one way to get the phage out of me, and you're not getting any samples unless we hear the truth. Now."

"I'm sure we could figure out a way to collect your semen without your cooperation, although I suspect it would be much less pleasant than the usual manner," the agent said. "But if knowing the truth will motivate you, then why not? You two aren't going anywhere anytime soon."

The agent gestured for them to sit down. Bill pulled over a chair. Quif gave the agent a look of contempt and stood her ground.

"Well, boys and girls, this is a tale that starts with a little history lesson. That would be *American* history, doctor, so listen up.

"The last thing President Eisenhower did when he was in office was warn the American public about the dangers of the Military Industrial Complex," the agent lectured, his words soaked in condescension. "You see, he was worried that the business of war, the profits of the defense industry, threatened the sovereignty of the United States. He was right about what was coming, but he didn't foresee the whole picture. It wasn't just the business of war that put democracy in peril. It was also the business of life.

"Let's call it the Pharma Industrial Complex. Pharmaceutical manufacturers and the health insurance companies. Collectively, they control wealth and power that eclipses the war machine. Warmongering dictators can be deposed, and presidents can be impeached, but people are *never* going to give up their medicines. In the past forty years, we've become a world dependent on pills. There are drugs for everything now. In some cases, we seem to be creating illnesses in order to manufacture drugs to treat them."

"What does this have to do with anything?" Quif interrupted.

"Your myopic crusade to find this cure has blinded you, doctor, and made you incredibly naive about how the world really works. Do you have any idea how much money is involved? What would your miracle phage do if it really did cure all the cases of HIV in the world? All the cancer?"

Quif thought back to the day she made her presentation to the CODIS board at Pasteur, when she first alerted them to the existence of the phage. The drug companies were there. They'd silently absorbed all she said, no doubt realizing immediately that her discovery meant their doom. She'd been so focused on the benefits of the phage, she'd only calculated that some would oppose it for moral reasons. Money. In the end, people were killed for greed.

"Drug makers stand to lose everything with the phage. And not just the pharmaceutical firms – so are health insurers." The agent pointed to Bill. "Your life means death to trillions of dollars in business. Trillions. This is why they've tried to kill you and anyone associated with the phage. Your loved ones are dead, the villagers were murdered, there's a crater the size of Texas in Armenia and a city block in Paris has been burned to the ground – all because of money.

"Even with the backing of the French government, your Pasteur colleagues could not track down the Soviet butchers who did the original experiments that created the phage. The drug companies found the Soviets. They're all gone. Dead."

"But the refinery explosion," Quif said, remembering the incredible destruction. "You want us to believe that these businesses possess weapons that most governments do not have?"

"*Mademoiselle,* insurance companies are like big investment machines. Who do you think owns controlling shares in the defense contractors? They all sit on each other's boards of directors. Just like your phage is a disease that kills other diseases, the enormous wealth of the Pharma Industrial Complex has consumed the Military Industrial Complex."

"And your answer to all of this is to keep us locked up here at CIA headquarters?" Bill asked. "Why aren't you going after these people? They're murderers! They should be in jail… not us."

"Normally we tend to look the other way when it comes to American business interests. The market tends to be the best judge and jury of these things. But when companies get too big for their britches and start killing people wholesale, well, that's when my bosses take notice. It's all about power. No one is allowed to run a conspiracy this big unless they get our permission first. Leaving us out is like saying that we don't matter. And we can't have that. So don't you worry about the bad guys, okay? We'll take care of justice. In the meantime, this is the safest place for you two to be. You don't want to be out there. They *will* find you, and they *will* kill you. So you might as well make the best of it and get to work on a pill. Heck, look at it this way – figure out the phage, make the cure, and it will destroy them…or at least their stockholders."

The agent stood up and walked toward the door.

"Wait!" Quif said. "Your plan still does not make sense. Put the phage out in the world. Do not wait for a pill. We do not need to synthesize it. We know it works."

She needed an argument, something even an American could understand. She spotted a first aid kit on the wall next to the door. "Did you know that aspirin was used by your American Indians? They discovered it by chewing the bark of the birch tree. And later it was turned in a drug, one of the most popular in history. It worked. It made headaches and pain go away. Yet for centuries, no one knew *how* it worked. It was not until 1982 when three researchers finally figured it out – and they won the Nobel Prize! So you see? We do not need to know how a cure works before giving it to the sick. We must cure the dying. That is our first priority."

The agent sneered. "Doctor, there's a big difference between taking an aspirin and getting fucked up the ass. Maybe our boy here will explain it to you."

The agent walked out the door, then popped his head back inside and said to Bill, "Speaking of being fucked, we've also got a very angry pop star and four middle aged women in protective custody. One is asking for you, keeps calling you her *lover*. Any message you want me to give her?"

Quif heard the agent laughing as the door slammed shut. "What is that about?"

"Uh," Bill said, appearing stuck for words. He motioned over to the computer. "Does that work?"

"*Oui*," Quif said, struggling to remember the English slang for *sens unique*. "But it is one direction. In, no out."

Bill sat down at the keyboard and began typing. Quif looked over his shoulder as he scrolled through the websites of newspapers. *The New York Times. The London Evening Standard. The Herald-Tribune.*

"What are you looking for?" she asked.

Bill went to the news section of Google and typed in several words too quickly for her to take note of them all. The results provided a link to a story on *Le Monde*.

"I'm afraid my French is a little rusty," Bill said. "What does this article say?"

Quif scanned the article. It was unusual for a crime report to make the front page. A mugging in the Marais. The flics said it was a robbery turned violent, and the victim had his throat cut. An executive in his mid-fifties, the CEO of—

"One of the top drug companies in Europe. The boss. He is dead on the streets of Paris," Quif explained.

"You think maybe they're telling us the truth," Bill asked. "A powerful drug company executive suddenly dead. He said the CIA was working on justice. This sounds like something they'd do."

Quif didn't doubt the CIA capable of such a thing. And if they'd decided to settle matters by killing off those responsible, then it was a very bad sign. It meant there would be no arrests. No trials. Nothing that could ever make knowledge of the phage public. That would allow the Americans to keep them imprisoned indefinitely.

"Click back," she said to Bill.

Her eyes scanned the other headlines on *Le Monde*'s main page. Had other drug company executives already been killed or disappeared? Bill got out of the chair and she sat down to take control of the mouse. Nothing else in the local news. She clicked on the international, health and business sections, but she found no other bulletins involving drug or insurance companies. When she went back to the main page she spotted a curious headline in the features box.

Dateline: Johannesburg.

She opened the story and began reading. With each word a rush consumed her, inciting short, shallow breaths. She felt her eyes well up.

"What is it?" Bill asked. "What does the article say?"

Quif wiped her eye with the back of her hand. "We are free."

28

Bill Soileau stared at the gray limestone. Ike's name was chiseled into the rock, followed by the phrase *He Gave His Life So That Others Could Live*.

Bill picked the epitaph, knowing some tourists might misinterpret it as a religious phrase referring to Jesus. Far more who visited the site would know exactly what it meant. The story wasn't secret anymore. The whole world knew of Ike's sacrifice.

Bill looked at the trees in that sad patch of forest. Ike's tombstone sat between two large birches at the western end of a stretch of lawn called The Meadow. Ike was the only person allowed buried at the National AIDS Memorial Grove in Golden Gate Park. There were many stones engraved with names scattered throughout the grounds, but they didn't mark graves. They were memorials to note some of the fallen by name. The disease snuffed out so many bright lights in San Francisco in the course of nearly three decades. Here in The City, AIDS was the holocaust.

Ike was its last victim.

Bill expected a fight to make this Ike's final resting place. After all, it was public property. He was shocked when the usually contentious Board of Supervisors approved it without debate. No one denied Bill anything he wanted these days.

But what he really wanted was gone forever.

Ike.

It had been three months since he learned of Ike's death, and the tears still flowed. Maybe he still wasn't ready to see this place – to face what had happened. As he sobbed, he felt small fingers grasp his.

"He was a good man, *oui?*" Quif said.

"Better than me," Bill wept.

Quif squeezed Bill's hand. As they stood silently for a few minutes, he began to feel her body shaking through the connection of their fingers.

"I think of Natara everyday," Quif whimpered. "And Benoit."

Bill looked around the forest. When he arrived, he went straight to Ike's grave. He hadn't noticed all the other people walking around the grove. Now he could see he was among many somber faces. The day was overcast, as it often was in this part of The City. Peeling cypress trees hovered overhead, hunched over as if they too were weeping. Wandering mothers, fathers, brothers, sisters and loved ones paused to hug one another. They too mourned their losses. The plague was over, but the victims were still in this place.

"They live on," Quif sniffled and composed herself. "In millions of people, they live on."

In his grief, Bill also felt an undercurrent of bitterness. Ike, Natara and Benoit didn't have to die for those millions to live. The phage was the miracle cure they'd always thought it would be. At what price? If not for Ike, countless souls would still suffer from disease and death.

The drug companies had tried to destroy the phage and anyone connected with it, and the CIA plotted to keep the cure from the public. But in the end, it was Ike who defeated them all. Despite his outrage to Bill over the phone, conversations that had been under surveillance, Ike had done what no one expected.

With the help of Mark Hazodo.

"Ike hunted me down at my office," Mark later told Bill. "He said he'd been trying to reach you. I said I didn't know where you were. He wouldn't tell me what it was all about over the phone – said it wasn't safe. So I had him come over to my loft. He wasn't in the door two minutes before he started telling me about the phage. I thought he was nuts, I gotta be honest. Then he said you told him to go out and fuck as many guys as possible. I remember thinking, yeah! My man Bill Soileau is back to being his old fellow degenerate self!"

"Did he say why he changed his mind?" Bill had asked.

"That's the funny thing. He kept talking about some sort of rush, a tingling sensation he felt that went through his whole body the first time you guys hooked up. He said he used to think it was love, but something you said last time you spoke on the phone convinced him it was more than that. He kept saying over and over that he believed you now. He wondered if you could ever forgive him for doubting you. He said a lot of shit like that."

Forgive him? Bill looked down to the ground, remembering Mark's words. Ike would still be alive if he'd never met Bill. Yet he went to his death worried that he was the one who'd done harm. Bill spotted an older couple standing near the edge of the grove, embraced in each other's arms. The woman cried. Had they lost a son to the pandemic? Bill wondered if anyone could ever get past such grief. Could he?

Mark had admitted to Bill that he never believed Ike about the phage. It didn't matter – the idea of a bareback party was enough to pique his interest. Within an hour he arranged for another orgy, gathering the same guys from the roulette sex party. But it wasn't the arousing scene he wanted. "Ike acted like he was a school nurse giving vaccinations," Mark complained. "There was no passion. Instead, Ike lectured the meth heads about the phage, how it was a cure, and that they needed to discreetly spread it to as many as possible." That was the last time Mark saw Ike. The following morning he heard about the fire and Ike's death – it was all over the news.

Later that same day Mark began receiving calls from the guys at the party. Soon he became a believer himself. He saw men transformed from meth zombies back to real human beings. The guys from the orgy became fervent apostles, setting up a secretive system to make sure everyone they knew who was HIV positive got the cure. Those who received the phage took a pledge: they had to cure at least two others, and make all recipients promise to do the same. In just one weekend, Mark guessed that HIV was pretty much wiped out in the entire city of San Francisco.

From there a bunch of do-gooders, as Mark called them, chartered a plane and headed to South Africa. Mark said he couldn't imagine how they talked their way into the pants of the infected there, but somehow they did.

Dateline: Johannesburg.

Bill remembered the article Quif had found online at *Le Monde*. It was a report about a miracle cure of AIDS sweeping across South Africa. A tribal shaman had told the reporter that "white angels came down from the heavens" with the cure. When pressed to describe how the cure worked, the shaman said cryptically it was passed "by love." The angels, he went on to say, spoke in a language he recognized as English, but they continuously used a word he'd concluded was their spell for magic. "Fah-boo-luss."

Dr. Greene? Bill enjoyed the thought, but figured it wasn't possible.

Other news reports surfaced from the ghettos of Brazil and Manila of the "miracle" happening there, but instead of angels the cure was being attributed to Catholic missionaries. Cardinal Uccelli turned out to be the Lord's vessel he always wanted to be, although in true church style, that part of the miracle story never became public. It was a secret shared only by the Cardinal and Bill.

Soon the scientific world stepped in, and Pasteur identified the phage. The chairman held a press conference and held up a photograph of Quif, giving her credit for the discovery and begging for any news of her whereabouts.

"Someone with a higher pay grade than mine wants you released," groused the agent as he delivered them to a black van for transport. Before they drove away, the agent stared down Bill. "I will never take your fucking cure."

"Ah, then as you Americans like to say," Quif quipped, "It is one last asshole we will deal with not."

But the agent would have the last laugh, substituting one form of imprisonment for another. The van took Quif and Bill to an alley next to a downtown Washington hotel. The driver opened a door and ushered them inside. They found themselves on a stage in an ornate auditorium filled with news cameras and reporters. The chairman from Pasteur stood at a podium. "And here they are," he said. Cameras clicked with blinding flash. What seemed like a hundred questions were all asked at once.

They'd been on the run around the globe ever since, pushed,

promoted and managed by Pasteur, to get the message out about the phage. From Thailand to Chechnya to Buenos Aires, they told the story of the miracle. Instead of being pursued by killers, they now found themselves hunted by the media. A cure for AIDS and possibly most other diseases made them instant heroes, discoverers of the biggest scientific marvel since man first walked on the moon. The once dying begged to touch them in Calcutta. Healed tribes worshipped them as gods in Botswana. Countless magazine covers, television newscasts and millions of inches of coverage in newspapers and on the internet were devoted to their world tour. Quif appeared to relish the attention. She said it helped distract her from her grief. Bill found the whirl of reporters overwhelming. He'd gone from guarding his privacy to having every moment of his life now front-page news.

Even his mother had heard about it and called. Bill wondered if now she'd finally be interested in him, or at least say that he'd turned out to be a good son. Instead, she asked if there was going to be any money in any of this. When he said he wasn't sure, she sighed on the other end of the line and said, "Well, I always told the girls I thought you was a sissy. Guess there's no hiding *that* anymore."

After three months, the firestorm of attention finally started to subside. Pasteur thought the world well informed enough to allow Quif and Bill a break. After a stop in Pyongyang, the two headed to San Francisco. No fanfare. Bill's homecoming would be too personal, and painful. Quif offered to stay a few days, noting how she and Natara had such fond memories there. "Besides, I am not eager to return to Paris and face the tombs of the people I led to their deaths."

Now standing in front of Ike's grave, Bill knew he had to start to come to terms with what he'd lost. He'd never get Ike back, and he had no interest in anyone else. The days when he could bed any man who caught his eye were over. He craved the one thing he'd had only with Ike. *Love.* During the years when he'd slept with countless men, he never once desired their affection. He spurned it. Now love was all he wanted. Yet it was gone. Was it enough to know he *could* actually love someone? He wondered if the phage had somehow healed part of him that was so broken for so many years. Did it really have that power? No virus could do that. But the phage was a miracle – wasn't it? Everyone said so. Maybe the HIV was never really Bill's terminal illness. Perhaps the phage had cured his true sickness.

Radio static broke the silence of the woods and pulled Bill from his thoughts.

Walkie-talkies. Bill turned around and gazed up the hill overlooking the grove. At the top of a curved stone staircase stood a man in a grey suit with dark glasses. He wore an earpiece. Bill was swept up in a moment of déjà vu.

"Mr. Soileau," the man said. "It's time for us to go."

Bill turned to face Quif. This would be the first time they'd been apart in months. They'd take their separate paths from now on.

"I don't know why they won't let you come with me," Bill said.

"Ah, it is their way," Quif wiped her eye with a handkerchief. "It would be the same in France."

As they hugged to say goodbye, Bill held the petite doctor hard against his chest. He didn't know when he might see her again. He breathed in the smell of her thick black hair. The scent was familiar. It brought back a vivid memory. *Natara.*

29

The helicopter from Andrews Air Force Base touched down on the pad. Bill was told it was a standard military chopper, the type that landed several times a day at Camp David. It would be seen as routine – nothing to arouse suspicion. After all, the White House aide said several times, "You weren't officially ever here."

Bill and the aide, a redheaded woman in her thirties who constantly wrote into a leather notepad, were shuttled by a sailor driving a golf cart from the helicopter pad across the wooded grounds over to a low-rise cabin. Bill noted how unimpressive it was. Nothing more spectacular than he'd seen on a hundred different lots near Lake Tahoe. Just one story tall, it was little more than a ranch house with weathered wood exterior. The pool beside the house was grand, a large eight-shaped in-ground surrounded by an expansive stone patio. Despite dozens of inviting Adirondack chairs and beautiful weather, no one was around.

"This is the Aspen Lodge," the aide said, then paused and shot Bill a serious look. "Not that you can ever tell anyone that you've been here."

The cart pulled up to the front door. Two marines stood at attention. One opened the door for them.

The foyer was simply decorated. Bill had expected a presidential retreat to be somehow palatial, but this looked about the same as any other lodge. Wood paneled walls, basic pine floors, and no artwork. Why not a bronze bust of JFK? Or maybe a Gilbert Stuart painting? On a small table sat a wooden duck decoy, the only touch of decor that hinted at the interests of the person inside.

They stood for a few moments and a side door opened. Bill caught his breath. The man who emerged wore blue jeans and a green plaid shirt, but the slicked back snow-white mane made him instantly recognizable.

The Reverend Willie Warrant.

The Reverend stopped and stared. His eyes took a full account of Bill, starting at his feet until they reached his face. The Reverend's expression became stern, his brows furrowed, and he locked his intense glare on Bill.

Bill flinched. What was *he* doing here?

The Reverend continued to glower at Bill. It might have only been a few moments, but it felt like an eternity. Bill had never felt such intensity. It was as if a laser pointed into his eyes. A laser powered by hate.

Finally, the Reverend relented. Without saying a word, he walked past Bill and out the front door.

"Oh, don't you mind that there Willie. He's a good ol' boy, when it comes right down to it."

The president stood in the doorway.

He held out his hand. Bill reached forward to shake, feeling suddenly self-conscious that his grip might not be firm and masculine enough. He noted how the president was taller in person, his smile less goofy than on TV, genuine, even charming. In thinking about this moment, Bill had intended to keep a stiff formality. After all, this president had never done anything for people like Bill. Quite the opposite. Bill planned to be aloof, but now that he was standing in the man's presence, it was different. This was the most powerful person on the planet. And he was smiling...*at me.* Bill felt his planned tension disappear. He was disarmed.

"Uh, Mr. President, I'm...uh...so." Bill lost his train of thought.

"Come on in," the president said. "Set yourself down on the couch."

The door shut behind Bill. The aide that had accompanied him the whole trip had evaporated. Now he was completely alone with the President of the United States. At Camp David.

"Can I get you something to drink?"

"Sir?" Bill fumbled. The president was offering him something to drink – as if he was just a regular host and Bill was just an ordinary guest at some normal summer home. Was this really happening?

"I gotta keep to the diet soda myself, but Camp David has a fully stocked bar," the president grinned.

"Uh, no thanks," Bill said, still tongue-tied. "I'm fine."

The president sat down across from Bill in a brown leather chair. He had on jeans and boots, and Bill noted how the president kept his legs wide apart like a cowboy, completely relaxed and confident.

"You know, I should be pretty mad at you," the president said.

"Me?"

"Well, heck yeah," the president laughed. "I was supposed to be the one to save the world. Darn it if you didn't go ahead an' do it."

"I…uh…"

"Hell, I'm just giving you shit, Bill. It's okay that I call you Bill, isn't it?"

"Sure."

"What I really mean to say, of course, is thanks. You needed to hear it from the man at the top. Thank you."

Bill looked around the room. He shook his head a little. A thank you from the President of the United States. Only no one would ever know, except the two of them.

"I know what you're thinking," the president said, his voice taking on a note of sympathy. "What the heck is a thank you worth when it's done in secret? I understand. But I really mean it. Thank you. Your country thanks you."

"You're welcome." Bill believed the president. There was no reason to be ungracious. After all, the president didn't have to bring him here and thank him in person. Even if it was in secret, this was still the president. It was still an honor.

"I know you've gone through hell. People trying to kill you." The president's face became serious. "Your friends being killed and all."

"Thank you for saying that, Mr. President." Bill thought of Ike. It wasn't possible for the president, especially with his public stand against gay people, to understand the love they shared. Bill wasn't the hero to be thanked. Ike was.

"I mean it. You had the fate of the world on your shoulders. I know what that's like. To sacrifice. To heed the call of duty…"

Sacrifice? Did the president bring him here to listen to a political speech? After all he'd been through, Bill didn't need any words of wisdom about the price he'd paid so that the phage could survive. Bill struggled to keep the civility on his face. Calm down, he told himself. There was no point getting into an argument with the President of the United States. Just accept the honor of this visit and leave. It will all be over in a few minutes. He could bear it.

"I didn't just ask you to come here to Camp David to express my appreciation," the president said. "You've been called for a higher purpose in life. There's no denying that. Even Reverend Willie said that about you. God works in mysterious ways and all. Now, you see, I need to ask you to do your duty one more time. Bill, your country needs you."

"Me?" Bill sat forward on the couch. "With all due respect, Mr. President, I can't imagine what else I could possibly do?"

The president leaned back in his chair. "They tell me this phage of yours don't just heal the sick. It's also some sort of inoculation. That right?"

"That's what they tell me," Bill said. "Based on what they found in some villagers in Armenia. They also apparently got the original phage."

"I heard about them. And now you are the only one left who got the source right from the tap, so to speak."

"I guess."

"Which means you've got the most powerful version of the phage."

"I don't know about that. I think once the virus is passed—"

"And I'm the President of the United States. Supposed to be the most powerful man in the world. Only makes sense that I get the most powerful version of this inoculation. Right from the tap, so to speak."

That's why he was here? This wasn't about thanking him for helping discover and spread the miracle phage. This was about the president getting the virus for himself. For *his* protection. The president really didn't care about Bill, or Ike, or anyone else who had sacrificed.

He wanted what he believed was the purest form of the phage – for himself.

"I...I think," Bill tried, but a building fury made it difficult to speak. "I think I understand what you're asking me to do, Mr. President. I...I can't do it."

"What do you mean you can't do it?" The president's face became serious again. "This is for your country, Billy Boy. I can call you Billy Boy, right?"

"Well, I..."

"Billy Boy, this thing here is bigger than you as an individual. I'm ordering you as your commander in chief to do your duty. This is America. We're a nation built on the notion of sacrifice for the greater good."

"Sacrifice!" Bill burst. He couldn't hold it in any longer, even if it was the president. He'd already lost everything that mattered, and now he was being asked to give what remained of his flesh to this...*bigot*. "I've already made my sacrifice for the sake of this! You have no idea what I've lost!"

"Calm down," the president whispered. "I don't want the secret service bustin' in here at the wrong moment."

"Why should I calm down? You lure me here with the idea that you want to thank me, but what you really what is for me to fu—"

"Don't be disrespectful. I'm the president."

"The president of what?" Bill was incredulous. "Gay bashing? You've spent your entire political career demonizing and scapegoating people like me. If it weren't for the phage, I'd never count with you and your bullies. With the help of Willie Warrant you used gay hate to get yourself elected! And now you want something from me? I won't do it."

Bill again thought of Ike. The love they shared was exactly what this president condemned. It was part of this White House's official agenda to relegate gay people to second-class citizenship, the only president in modern times to take a step backward on any issue involving civil rights. Bill hoped Ike was somehow able to hear all this right now, to see how Bill still fought for their love, even if they could no longer be together.

"Look here, Billy Boy," the president sighed. "I'm a practical man. In politics, we make deals with the devil all the time. I'm not saying you're right or wrong about Reverend Willie. What I am saying is…well…what do you want?"

"What do I want?"

"Yup. Name your price."

Bill thought for a moment. The only thing he wanted was Ike back, and even the president couldn't do that. *Ike.* If Ike was here, what would he say?

"I want," Bill paused. "I want you to stop spreading hate about gay people."

The president looked confused. "I don't spread hate."

"A constitutional amendment against gay people? You'd never get away with that if it was against Jews or black people. What did you think it was? Love?"

"That's jest politics. I need bubba's vote, else I can't get elected." The president threw up his hands. "Heck, that's the appeal my side has."

"Well, unless bubba learns to understand the appeal *my side has*, then he's not going to get the phage. There's only one way to get the cure. Death from AIDS or cancer is more appealing than giving up hate?"

The president nodded. "That's a good point."

"Promise you will kill the constitutional amendment. It was never right to try to pit one group of Americans against the other. You need to stop it before it goes any further."

"Done."

Had Bill heard correctly? He could have sworn he just heard the president concede. "Excuse me?"

"I'll do it," the president said. "Hell, we only came up with that thing to scrape up redneck votes. It was never gonna pass. In fact, I'm thinking this whole phage thing jest might make people change their minds about you gays. You're all regular Florence Hendersons now."

Bill was pretty sure the president meant to say Florence Nightingale.

"Picking on the gays. Heck, smart politics says that dog won't hunt anymore." The president scratched his chin. "Tell you what. I can't publicly retract what I said. A president's gotta keep his word. But I won't say anything more about it. The amendment will die a slow, quiet death. And I'll tell Reverend Willie to cool it, too. Deal?"

"For real?" Bill was astonished. He'd just made two of the world's most vocal bigots back down on their hate campaigns against gays. Maybe they had no choice. The president was right – the phage had changed everything. Immoral was moral. Sin was savior. Sex no longer meant death. Sex meant life, as it had in the beginning.

The president stood up and opened an adjacent door. On the other side was a bedroom. All the curtains were drawn. Like the rest of the cabin, it was plainly furnished. Up against the far wall was a king size bed with rustic wooden posts and a floral comforter, the corners neatly turned down.

"I've always been a little curious about this. Will it hurt?" the president asked.

Bill thought for a moment. He could *make* it hurt plenty for all he'd been through. Seeing the bed made Bill think once more of Ike. If Ike was in this situation, he wouldn't be brutal. Ike was naturally kind, in a way Bill wanted to be. As much as it would feel great to fuck the president hard to pay back for all the pain he'd caused gay people, Bill thought better of it. There was a different way to do this. A path with passion and affection. He'd seduced many straight men in the past. It was his expertise – perhaps even his destiny. He could be gentle and employ all his years of training until the president *loved it*.

"No," Bill Soileau smiled. "I promise it won't hurt."

ACKNOWLEDGMENTS

I wrote the last chapter of *The Sower* several years ago. I'd just learned that the leader of the free world had decided he wanted to pass a special law, a constitutional amendment no less, to specifically target a minority group for discrimination. A group that included me.

This provoked a "what if?" idea. A magazine article about former Soviet bloc countries experimenting with phage as a cure for infections was also fresh in my mind. As if possessed, I wrote the last chapter in longhand, start to finish. I put those pages into a box and they sat on my desk, untouched, for years.

I rarely thought about them. Then one day it hit me. The rest of the story emerged in a swoosh. I found myself furiously pounding away at my keyboard until tens of thousands of fresh words somehow neatly connected with my old pages of scrawl. During all those years I spent not thinking about this book, somewhere in the back of my mind the novel was being written.

That was just the start of the journey. I'm so fortunate to be part of a literary community that doesn't flinch (well, okay, sometimes they do, but not often) when I take them to strange places. Instead, they push me to do my best work.

I'm especially thankful to the members of the Writers' Bloc writing group in San Francisco: Sean Beaudoin, Melodie Bowsher, David Gleeson, Ken Grosserode, Arlene Heitner, Jeff Kirschner, and James Warner.

The San Francisco Writers Workshop, a free weekly critique group that's been running continuously since 1946, also helped with this book. Thanks to workshop leader Tamim Ansary, and members Ransom Stephens, Erika Mailman, and many others.

I have an office at the Sanchez Annex Writers Grotto, a converted crack house that's now a creative community of writers. There's such a wonderful energy there. It's my safe haven. Thanks to founder Doug Wilkins and my fellow inmates.

Other authors who read this book in its early stages and gave me terrific feedback and support include Michael Chorost, Kate Douglas, Raj Patel, Joe Quirk, and David Henry Sterry.

Part of my process for fine-tuning a novel involves reaching out beyond the world of writers to (radical thought here) actual book *readers*. I'm grateful to those who gave *The Sower* a test spin, kicked the tires, and then shared their thoughts. They include: Ryan Barrett, Steve Garrity, Karin Hastik, Heather Johnson, Rose Lamoureux, Sam Ray, Kimberly Uttermann, and Jan Vaeth.

Added thanks to Cara Black and Joshua Citrak for helping with the final preps for publication.

This novel was first released as a digital edition (with an astonishing amount of media attention) to launch e-book selling on Scribd.com. Many thanks to Tammy Nam, Kathleen Fitzgerald, Michelle Laird, Kathleen Miller, James Yu, Jason Bentley, Ed McManus, Timoni Grone, Tikhon Bernstam, Jared Friedman, Trip Adler, and the rest of the team at Scribd for making *The Sower* a part of this exciting new venture.

And a heartfelt thanks to Julie Supan. Silicon Valley is filled with circuits, but she is the loveliest connector.

This first edition of *The Sower* as a printed book is by Numina Press. I'm so thankful to Yanina Gotsulsky for embracing this novel and making it part of her fast growing imprint. She sees the future of publishing, and I am fortunate to be in her flock.

Bookseller Praveen Madan of The Booksmith in San Francisco has been an invaluable coach and supporter in the transition from digital to paper. I'm grateful for his encouragement and vision, and to the many independent booksellers throughout the Bay Area who have supported my work and are behind this book.

I need to single out two people for special appreciation. Shana Mahaffey is always by my side through the daily machinations of being a writer, and Jon Stuber is indispensable as co-editor of SoMaLit.com.

Thanks to my family and friends for cheering me on.

And to my one true love, Jerry, who does dinners and movies too.

Kemble Scott is the author of the bestselling novel *SoMa*, finalist for the national Lambda Literary Award for debut fiction.

He's the editor of the literary e-zine SoMaLit.com, and was the first author to launch a novel using YouTube. An alumnus of the Columbia University Graduate School of Journalism, Kemble has three Emmy Awards for his work in television news. He lives in San Francisco.

Kemble is a frequent public speaker and enjoys meeting with groups and book clubs. If you'd like to arrange an appearance, or have a comment to share, contact him at:

kemblescott@gmail.com
www.kemblescott.com

You can also find Kemble on Facebook, Twitter, Shelfari, Goodreads, Redroom.com, and LitMinds.org.

Printed in the United States
154427LV00004B/2/P

9 780975 361559